MW00803196

By LYN GALA

DESERT WORLD
Desert World Allegiances
Desert World Rebirth
Desert World Immigrant

Published by DSP PUBLICATIONS
www.dsppublications.com

desert world
world
IMMIGRANT

LYN GALA

DSP PUBLICATIONS

Published by
DSP PUBLICATIONS

5032 Capital Circle SW, Suite 2, PMB# 279, Tallahassee, FL 32305-7886 USA
www.dsppublications.com

This is a work of fiction. Names, characters, places, and incidents either are the product of author imagination or are used fictitiously, and any resemblance to actual persons, living or dead, business establishments, events, or locales is entirely coincidental.

Desert World Immigrant
© 2015 Lyn Gala.

Cover Art
© 2015 Maria Fanning.
Cover content is for illustrative purposes only and any person depicted on the cover is a model.

All rights reserved. This book is licensed to the original purchaser only. Duplication or distribution via any means is illegal and a violation of international copyright law, subject to criminal prosecution and upon conviction, fines, and/or imprisonment. Any eBook format cannot be legally loaned or given to others. No part of this book may be reproduced or transmitted in any form or by any means, electronic or mechanical, including photocopying, recording, or by any information storage and retrieval system, without the written permission of the Publisher, except where permitted by law. To request permission and all other inquiries, contact DSP Publications, 5032 Capital Circle SW, Suite 2, PMB# 279, Tallahassee, FL 32305-7886, USA, or www.dsppublications.com.

ISBN: 978-1-63476-159-8
Digital ISBN: 978-1-63476-160-4
Library of Congress Control Number: 2015901360
First Edition September 2015

Printed in the United States of America
∞
This paper meets the requirements of
ANSI/NISO Z39.48-1992 (Permanence of Paper).

chapter
o n e

VERLY HELD the edge of his seat, feeling the machine struggle through the air. The seat vibrated and the vehicle rolled a little left and then banked to the right before evening out for all of two and a half seconds and then repeating the cycle. Verly understood the irony of a pilot bothered by the bucking of a shuttle as it fought its way through air, but normally he was the one in control. He trusted his own flying more than Lieutenant Gilson's.

"How's it going?" he asked.

"Not much longer, sir." Gilson managed to sound almost respectful, but Verly had seen the sneer when Gilson had first heard his name.

Sometimes Verly wondered how he would handle an entire planet of people who didn't recognize his name, assuming he could call Livre a planet. Today, the Planetary Alliance would never allow colonization or even mining in such a fragile environment. The planet had huge mountain ranges that interrupted deep deserts and an underground water supply too contaminated with poisons for human consumption. That led to a relatively limited range of flora and fauna.

Back before the civil war and before ships could carry people to countless systems, humans had put boots down on planets that could barely sustain them. They terraformed and carved out niches in places where no human should go. Most of those colonies had failed, but against all odds Livre was still here. And now Verly was going to make this one small planet his home—his refuge from the past and the mistakes that still haunted him. Step one had been learning all about this new home of his.

Honestly, Verly had studied the ecosystem out of a desire to avoid ending up a meal for some carnivorous plant or rodent, which Livre seemed to specialize in. He'd fought in space for most of his life... fought the dirty war of terrorism and bombs that had followed the official end of the Alliance War. So dying with his foot in some pipe trap while rat-sized mammals ate him... that was not an option.

Of course, thirst posed as much of a danger as the plant life or the local predators. Naturally occurring pure water was too rare for human survival, but huge tankers had once landed on Livre carrying water to begin the terraforming. That had been before Verly's birth. He hadn't even heard of Livre before its two rather eccentric ambassadors had negotiated an interesting treaty that put Livre off-limits to all but preapproved applicants on official business.

Verly had one of those rare visas.

As a planet, Livre left a lot to be desired. He wouldn't find cities or long rails for aircars or shuttle launches. He wouldn't live in sealed buildings or even walk manicured natural spaces with carefully controlled ecosystems. This was a border world like Verly had never seen before, and he wasn't sure what he could expect to find.

Dust.

People as odd as Ambassadors Gazer and Polli.

Citizens who didn't look at him oddly the moment they recognized his name.

The shuttle did an odd little hop as it passed through a column of hot air. "Final descent before landing," Gilson said, and then the engines shifted into a lower gear, the bottom jets firing to keep the shuttle from dropping too fast as it slowed.

White sand interrupted with streaks of yellowed land, and red and brown rocks rose up under them. The lack of actual landmarks was disorienting for someone who'd grown up in a jungle of buildings where the skyline always told you if you were north or south of the river—east or west of a main landing. And the sky back home on Diamond was always streaked with the trails of planes and shuttles. Here the cloudless blue stretched out to the edge of the world.

Eventually, he could see a line of ragged mountains in the distance—young rocks pushing up from below the surface with all their sharp edges pointed to the sky.

"Are we going over those?" Verly asked. He didn't bother defining "those" because any pilot worth half a credit would have an eye on those mountains. Those were the sorts of formations that could chew through every safety feature and turn a shuttle into a steaming pile of junk if it got too close.

"Yes, sir. We're staying well above them and landing in the dunes on the far side. Most of the settlements are on the west side."

"Great."

Verly kept his eyes on the land as the shuttle screamed through the heavy air of the low atmosphere. The shuttle bucked like a great beast, and then it finally scraped its belly along the ground, landing gear useless in the fine white sand. Enormous clouds of dust rose up. The shuttle slid across the face of Livre, slipping to the right until it finally settled.

"Any idea how long until the dust settles?" Verly studied the glow of the sun through the sandstorm.

"No idea, sir." Gilson didn't sound very interested in having any sort of conversation because he started reading off shutdown procedures. Pilots never had to read out loud, not after their first dozen flights, but Verly let the man retreat into his administrivia. It took at least thirty or forty uncomfortable minutes before the sand slowly settled and Verly got his first look at his new home from the ground. If things went well, he'd be here for years. If they went poorly, his commanding officers would lose his paperwork and leave him here a whole lot longer.

"This is shuttle Zulu requesting permission to disembark," Gilson said.

"Sure, come on out," the radio answered. The Planetary Alliance was not a fan of informal procedures, so that voice coming through the official PA radio sounded very odd. At least Verly had the advantage of having worked with Ambassador Gazer, so he'd been prepared for less than orthodox people. Gilson looked over at Verly as if seeking some reassurance. Turning his seat around, Verly busied himself with his personal belongings while Gilson cracked the side door open.

The smell of heat hit Verly like a storm front. He hadn't even realized heat had an odor until this moment, but he sneezed several times.

"That's an interesting scent," Gilson said quietly, but then he cleared his throat. "Sir, after you," he offered stiffly.

Verly gave a nod and hiked his bag's strap over his shoulder as he strode down the metal planking to his new planet. His first impression was that it was bare, and then he started sneezing again, and Verly didn't have a cloth. He was in danger of making a snotty mess out of himself. That would make for a great first impression. Wiping his face, he tried sniffing, and that made his eyes water as the heat seemed to invade his head.

"Here," a gruff voice offered, and a man shoved a cloth toward him. "Rula had the same reaction. It makes me wonder what sort of air you have up there."

"Thanks." Verly took the cloth and blew his nose before checking out his savior. His first impression startled him so much that he took a step back. The man was a warped mirror image of Ambassador Polli. He was an inch or so taller—tall enough that he nearly reached Verly's own six five—and he carried a lot more muscle, but the two men shared the same prominent nose, dark eyes, and dusky skin. Honestly, they were both exotic and beautiful the way a sharp-edged weapon was. He had angles that were simply interesting to look at.

"You got more stuff?" the man asked with a disgusted look at the shuttle. Usually the disgust was focused more on Verly.

"Nope. This is it." Verly held out his hand. "Verly Black."

This sharp-edged man with his wide chest and shoulders eyed Verly for a second, and Verly drew himself up to his full height. They were a matched pair, although Verly didn't have as much muscle. Piloting didn't provide much of a workout.

The guy finally took Verly's hand. "Naite Polli."

"Ambassador Polli's brother?" Verly guessed.

Naite gave a snort and turned toward a cluster of low buildings so far away that you could have landed a shuttle before hitting them. "At least you didn't bring armfuls of shit," Naite commented before he started striding across the sand.

Clearly Naite was as unconventional as his brother. That was fine with Verly. Leaving the shuttle and the surly pilot behind, Verly blew his nose and set off across the blowing sand. He made it less than half the distance before he had to slow down. His eyes watered, and his cheeks ached from squinting, but still the sunlight seemed to reflect off every speck of white sand. Worse, his lungs ached from the heat, and the sand dragged at his feet.

Stopping, Verly closed his eyes and tried to shut out the stabbing sun for a second as he caught his breath. He'd been on a dozen alien worlds, but none of them had felt alien. Every world had trees and rivers and square buildings rising toward the heavens. Some worlds required more effort to get those pieces all in place, but the Planetary Alliance had a firm policy of not allowing any planet to suffer from a lack of terraforming. But Livre was truly alien.

Verly opened his eyes when Naite returned. The man stood a foot away, arms crossed over his chest.

"Are you planning on throwing up?"

"No, I can safely say I'm not," Verly said. The frown on Naite's face made it pretty clear that he questioned the veracity of that statement. "The sun is much brighter and the air much hotter and drier than I'm used to. I need a second to catch my breath."

"Well, hurry up so we can get out of the heat. We're fools for standing out here."

If Verly had the energy, he would have danced for joy. If the heat made Naite miserable, that meant they were headed someplace cooler. That thought gave Verly the strength to wave Naite toward the building. "I'm good."

One dark eyebrow twitched, but Naite headed for the building. The low squared sides still showed the tool marks from the drop ship's claw. This was the first settlement. Verly had once visited the first settlement on Diamond. Most schoolchildren walked in the steps of the colonists as a memorial to those first humans who had braved Diamond's vicious swamps and poisonous wildlife. However, this place was still used.

Naite clambered down a ladder with more grace than Verly had expected from such a large man.

"Are Ambassadors Gazer and Polli here?" Verly asked as Naite pulled a heavy blast door open. The stamped metal suggested it'd been salvaged from some colony ship. This place was like stepping into a historical reenactment.

Naite gestured for Verly to head into the slightly less hot interior of the building, which he was only too happy to do. Waiting until after he'd pulled the door shut leaving them in an artificial twilight, Naite answered, "Shan and Temar are over at Blue Hope trying to talk some sense into some folks who don't have any to start with."

"Well, I'm sure Ambassadors—"

"Don't call them that," Naite cut him off as he headed across a narrow room.

"Call them what?"

Naite stopped and eyed Verly. If they'd met in a bar, Verly would have assumed Naite wanted to have some very hard and very fast sex. If Naite had been a superior officer, Verly would have assumed that look meant an upcoming demotion. Naite had this odd combination of sexual heat and personal aggression—of carnal looks and suppressed anger. Maybe it was Verly's self-destructive streak showing up, but he wondered whether Naite bedded men. "Don't call them ambassador anything. They're just plain Shan and Temar," Naite said firmly, and Verly was in danger of losing track of the conversation.

"I don't want to be disrespectful," Verly said carefully.

Naite snorted. "And I don't want you giving those two an overinflated sense of their own importance."

That surprised Verly. The Planetary Alliance was full of difficult people who all knew that their beliefs were the only correct beliefs for anyone to hold. The ambassadors had navigated political waters that would have sunk lesser men, and they'd done that after giving the breakaway worlds a run for their money. As far as Verly was concerned, those two could have some fairly large heads without overinflating anything. They deserved a few bragging rights.

However, Naite's expression made it clear that Verly did not have permission to argue. "Okay," Verly said slowly. "So, they're talking to this other city?"

With a small nod of approval, Naite turned and headed through a door into another identically sized room, only someone lived in this one. "Hopefully Temar's doing the actual talking," Naite said. "Shan's version of persuading people usually involves large amounts of guilt and God, two subjects that plenty of people have a rather uncomfortable relationship with."

Verly had misunderstood Livre's political scene. He hadn't expected the leaders to inspire such resentment. Usually Verly saw that on much more developed planets, not small worlds with scattered settlements that had to work just to survive. "I suppose I don't have a very clear impression of Am... Shan. He was injured most of the time I knew him."

Naite stopped near another door and studied Verly. "Huh. That's right. You're the one who saved him, are you?"

Verly gave Naite his widest smile. When he was sixteen, he'd spent an embarrassing amount of time learning how to give potential partners a crooked, devilish smile, in part to make up for his rather austere expression with a square jaw and prominent chin. His masculine features were even more noticeable with his fair skin. He had a manly face, a face the military had once chosen to put on the front of an advertisement for pilot training. But he'd intentionally developed a boyish smile.

"The official reports say that I'm the one who put him in danger. Luckily, Temar gave a direct order, so very little of that blame fell on me, or I might have been dropped back another rank."

"It's hard to see Temar giving orders." Naite opened the door, and the brutal heat of the planet once again pushed against Verly's skin.

"Actually," Verly said as he squinted, "Temar threatened to bring me to Livre and let the sandcats strip the flesh from my screaming body if I double-crossed him or didn't follow orders."

Naite's mouth fell open. "He what?"

"That's not a threat a man forgets soon," Verly pointed out. "I get the feeling Temar is very attached to your brother and a little overprotective."

"Obviously more than I knew. He really said that?"

Verly nodded. When Naite's angry exterior dropped, he looked even more like Shan, although Verly wasn't fool enough to say it. Naite didn't seem like a big fan of his brother.

"Well, you're lucky it wasn't the other way around with Shan making the plans and Temar in danger. Shan's plans are downright suicidal. So, since those two are off doing whatever they're doing, you're stuck with me. Shan suggested that I show you around, but I have work, so I figure I can show you the working end of a dig-stick. Unless, that is, you have some problem with putting in a day's work." Naite crossed his arms again, clearly waiting for Verly to make a protest.

"No problem at all, at least not as long as you keep in mind that I have no idea what a dig-stick is."

"It's a stick. You dig with it."

Verly smiled. "I had gotten that far in my analysis of the term. I don't know what to do with one, and you don't have to suggest that I dig."

Naite grunted and closed the door to the silent base behind him before setting out for a newer and much less level building. This one was made of native twigs. A cargo hauler of some sort waited in the shade.

Climbing up into the driver's seat, Naite waited as Verly got up into the passenger side. The vehicle had two ovals of plastic right in front of the driver and passenger seats, but they didn't feel like enough protection. Verly felt a little like he was perched on top of some teenager's version of a bootleg motorized vehicle. Naite started it, and the machine yanked itself into motion with an uneven lurch. Verly grabbed at the nearest stable point as he tried not to fall. He grabbed Naite's arm.

Naite looked down with a barely veiled humor. The edge of his mouth twitched. "Problem?"

"Old machines and worse, old machines that I'm not driving."

"Do you even know how to drive a hauler?"

"Nope. But pilots are all the same. We don't do well if we're not steering."

Naite gave him a long look. "I generally prefer to steer," Naite said, and his voice had an edge that almost sounded like an invitation. Almost. It'd been so long since anyone had invited Verly for a quick tumble that he wasn't sure whether he could trust his judgment. Perhaps he only wanted that invitation so much that he imagined Naite's interest.

"You need a sand veil," Naite said, his voice suddenly businesslike as he pulled a white cloth out of his pocket. It resembled burn gauze with heavier strips of white fabric on either side, trailing off into long tails. "You tie it around your face to make sure you don't breathe in too much dust. If you do, you can get sand pneumonia."

"Charming." Verly took the veil and started tying it around his mouth and nose. Naite tied his own sand veil around his face, the white of his fabric already gray with dust.

"That's never going to stay." Naite half stood and leaned over to roughly tug the veil into place. Reaching around, he tied it around the back of Verly's head, and that left him so close Verly could smell his musk. The scent reminded Verly of barracks and men pressed close together, of dirty little moments stolen between drills and hand jobs in corners. Verly's cock was already aching with need, but Naite finished arranging the veil and then sat back down.

"We'll get to the valley in an hour or so," he offered as he put the hauler into gear and made the machine lurch forward again. Either it had been far too long since Verly had gotten laid, or this trip to Livre might prove more interesting than Verly had expected. Maybe both.

chapter two

THE VALLEY impressed Verly more than he could say. The settlers had carved out the rock sides and fitted the top of the valley with a thin mesh that softened the sunlight. The entire valley was protected from the mountainous sand dunes by a blast door tall enough for a missile launcher to drive through. Some enormous machine had set the sides of the huge gate into metal struts that went into the hard rock and were covered with metal salvaged from a ship.

"I didn't think colonies brought heavy machinery with the first few waves."

"What?" Naite shouted over the rumble of the metal doors sliding open.

"The doors. That must have been some serious machinery to get this in place."

Naite gave him an odd look. "You would have failed Anderson's history class."

Verly waited for more of an explanation, but Naite got out of the hauler and grabbed a flat-edged tool that he used to start shoving away the wispy drift of sand that pushed in when they entered. Verly got out to help, especially since the blast doors were closing fast. "I got it," Naite said shortly. He scooped up the last of the sand and shoved it through the crack before the huge doors closed with a heavy thunk. Naite headed back toward the hauler and pulled the sand veil off his face. He had a dark complexion, but the dust of the desert had settled over his hair and eyes so he looked like he'd been dusted with white.

"The doors came from about a hundred colonists tying ropes to the top and pulling them up while welders dangling from rope harnesses welded the frame into place. If something needs doing, we find a way to do it."

"So it seems," Verly said, ignoring Naite's attitude. "So, you're one of the council members?" Verly opened his mouth as he tried to pop his ears. The blasting heat of the desert invaded his head.

"Where'd you hear that?" Naite froze in the middle of climbing into the hauler. The cold suspicion surprised Verly. The defensive posture of Naite's body surprised him even more. Shan and Temar never moved like soldiers. They stood with their backs to unsecured doors; they walked past strangers without a second look. But Naite's coiled muscle and his careful balance with one hand holding the hauler's bar—that was pure soldier.

Even Verly fell back into those habits—that hypervigilance that left him watching the world and expecting enemies. In Verly's case, that came from PA training and his own ugly history. But on a world without war and armies and counterterrorism training—on a world without the sort of conflicts that had marred Verly's life—he wondered where that razor edge of emotion came from.

"The corps provided a dossier with what information they had," Verly said carefully. He could almost taste the suspicion on the air, and he reached up to pull off his own sand veil so Naite could better see him. "And Shan mentioned in passing that his brother was a council member."

"Idiot," Naite announced. He got in the hauler, but the atmosphere had turned cool.

"So, I assume that means you are a council member even if you choose not to discuss it." Verly summarized the conversation as Naite guided the hauler down the wide road toward the open valley with its green fields and filtered sun.

"Yep. I am."

Verly leaned back, intentionally putting his own arms back and presenting the metaphorical bared throat. Maybe he was wrong. Maybe Naite was an asshole. But then the second Verly went out of his way to pose less of a threat, Naite's fingers eased off the wheel of the hauler they'd been clutching. Oh, this was interesting. "Clearly politics is more honest around here than back home."

"Meaning?" Naite growled the word, and he had a voice rough enough to make a man's cock sit up and take notice.

"Meaning you don't look like the sort to reach a political office by paying a fortune for it and then spending a second fortune to spread lies about your competitors."

Naite did a double take as if that caught him off guard. "That sounds fairly stupid."

"That has always been my assessment of politics, yes. So I take it that it's different around here."

"Why?"

Verly angled his body away and looked out over the neat rows of plants that covered the floor of the valley. "Why what?" he asked, ignoring the way his skin itched at putting a near stranger at his back. But then something told Verly that Naite Polli was the sort of man to stab someone in the front.

Naite pulled the hauler up in the shade of the first building they came to. "Why are you asking? Are you looking to fill in all the holes in that dossier you got from your people?"

Now Verly did a double take. "You think I'm a spy?"

"I know you're a spy. I'm just not sure how direct you're planning on being. If you're playing a game here, I suggest you put your cards on the table because I am known for being a very poor loser."

"I can believe that," Verly agreed. "But I'm trying to figure out why you think I'm a spy. I've been on this planet for less than a day, and I haven't done anything except nearly choke to death on sand. If I were a spy, it wouldn't be the best start."

"And I'm not a man who accepts that sort of bullshit nonanswer." Turning off the hauler, Naite angled his body toward Verly. The fact was Verly could defend himself from a farmer, even one as well muscled as Naite. He was simply more interested in figuring out where this had started to go wrong.

Putting his hands up in surrender, Verly offered up another charming smile. "It may sound like bullshit, but I am not a spy. I am asking for your logic in making that assumption only so I can tell you where we have misunderstood each other."

Verly slowly lowered his hands. It took a long time for Naite to answer, but Verly could appreciate that some people weighed their words more carefully than others. He could also appreciate that Naite had not mentioned any of his suspicions until after Verly was separated from the shuttle and on totally unfamiliar territory. A little rub of fear made Verly's heart beat faster because one wrong word and he would be discovering what the Livre penal system looked like from the inside.

"You aren't the first to immigrate."

"Okay. Honestly, you need to put the dots a little closer together."

For a second, Naite pressed his lips together in an angry line. "They've already admitted that their primary mission is spying."

Verly closed his eyes. Shit. "I know I'm the first person here from the Planetary Alliance, so you have to be talking about people from the breakaway worlds. We are not from the same government, and we do not have the same missions. I can promise you that I am not here to spy."

"I didn't say they were spying. I said they were sent here to spy."

Verly processed that bit of startling information. Turning rebel spies was an art, one that PA officers spent years learning. However, if Naite was telling the truth—and Verly suspected he was—Ambassadors Polli and Gazer had visited an Alliance of Free Planets ship for a few days and had managed to turn one of the AFP spies. The more Verly got to know these people, the more he suspected he didn't know anything.

"I'm impressed," Verly said slowly, not sure how to handle this. He wasn't the most diplomatic of men. He'd once risen to the rank of base subcommander on the back of his bravery and damn good piloting skills; however, talking his way out of trouble had never been his forte.

"And if you think I'm going to believe that somehow your people are so much more moral than Rula's—that you've never even thought of spying—you're stupid too."

Verly ran a hand over his face. "I'm not going to claim to have some moral high ground here, but I'm not a spy."

Naite crossed his arms, and the truly sick thing was that Verly still felt those sparks of interest, even when Naite clearly wanted to throw him in the brig and forget to send food.

"The breakaway planets are touchier... more concerned about security. The Planetary Alliance is more likely to...." Verly stopped, not sure how to phrase this without ending up in the brig. And honestly, the PA wouldn't be sending any rescue.

With a sigh, Verly decided to go for brutal honesty. "The PA thinks you're an unimportant hick planet that happens to have some optic-quality glass and raw materials they can cheat you out of. You aren't important enough to risk a spy because that position requires very specific and very expensive training. What you got instead is a has-been officer who normally patrols the farthest corner of PA space, and I do mean that literally. That's why I was close when the ambassadors got in trouble on that AFP cruiser."

Naite took a step back, but his body language relaxed some. "Then why send you?"

Verly shrugged. The truth was complicated, but he could offer up one small corner of it without lying. "Because I'm not important. I'm a failed officer who tends to annoy my commanders, and Ambassador Gazer... excuse me... Temar invited me to come. Now, I won't lie. If this planet turns out to have some strategic value or if they decide they can't trick you out of your resources, I have no doubt they'll ask me some very pointed questions about which of your politicians could be corrupted or blackmailed. Right now, I don't think anyone is interested in asking me anything."

Most civilians would have taken that as a threat... as proof that Verly was dangerous because he might become a weapon later. Most soldiers would have taken that as a rare bit of honesty because they had already figured the rest out. Verly didn't know how Naite would react.

For long minutes, he didn't. He moved to the rear of the hauler and spent some time moving a woven twig basket from the vehicle to the cargo area, but he didn't react.

"Grab something, and let's get it inside before we cook our brains and do them more damage than either of us can afford," Naite finally said as he picked up another basket.

Verly let out a breath in an explosive sigh. He'd avoided the brig again. He'd found a new talent, that's for sure. After getting out, he grabbed a wooden crate filled with PA sample boxes used to collect plant varieties. When he followed Naite into the building, he was pleased to find the inside of the barn fairly cool. A deep shaft in the center of the wide room sank down forever into the ground. Fans overhead stirred the air, and there was a scent of something acidic.

Verly moved closer to the rail around that uneven hole, and the scent was definitely coming from there.

"Native water. Don't fall in." Naite walked over to the side of the barn where four large pens held forty or fifty chickens. Leaning over, he ran his hands over a number of animals' backs before he stood and faced Verly again. "Our people aren't as easily manipulated as you seem to think."

"I don't think you can be manipulated at all. I'm talking about my commanding officers back home."

"So, you don't think we should trade with the PA?"

This was feeling like an interrogation. And again, Verly had to give Naite credit for doing it well. The threats were all veiled—the presence of that deep well, the isolation, the silence. It all made for a very uncomfortable situation.

"I think they'll offer good money for optic-quality glass."

Naite gave one nod, and Verly figured Naite also heard that Verly wasn't endorsing his side. If report of this got back home, Verly was going to end up in military prison without a doubt, but if he wanted a new life, he had to make new choices.

"And what about the AFP?"

Verly sucked in a breath. "I don't think you want to ask me about them."

"Why?"

Verly shrugged. "I may not have the most objective opinion when it comes to the breakaway planets." Between the open war and then the dirty war of terrorism that followed, Verly had a deep hatred of all things AFP, but he also understood that some of that anger was irrational. His own side wasn't innocent. Of course, his own side wasn't on the crazy side of religious either.

Naite started crossing the barn, his eyes scanning the room—the crates of grain and the stacks of tools that Verly didn't recognize—the piles of heavy cloth and ropes. This was uncomfortable, but Verly held his ground. He did, however, start to question his own assessment that he could take any mere farmer. Naite didn't move like any farmer Verly knew. He moved like a predator or a soldier. Danger lay in the loose roll of Naite's shoulders and the way his arms were poised to come up into a defensive pose. Verly had no doubt Naite was prepared to defend himself.

"Tell me anyway," Naite said, his voice low and rough. And again, Verly felt that entirely inappropriate frisson of interest.

"They're assholes," Verly said. He suspected Naite would appreciate honesty more than diplomacy. He must have guessed right because Naite stopped and straightened up. All his defensive posturing vanished, and a smile pulled at the very corner of his mouth.

"Okay," Naite said slowly, the tone of his words infinitely more casual. "Why do you say that?" Naite leaned against the rail that went around the deep well.

"Because they are." A stool sat between two crates, and Verly headed over and sat, hooking his heel on one of the support rungs. "They arrest anyone who doesn't agree with their crazy policies, and I can't count all the crazy policies they have. Gay people are sick and should be tortured out of being gay or just killed. Children are great raw material for assassins and spies, so they put them in training camps. They restrict women and won't give them full rights. They control all writing and music, and if you're caught sharing unapproved files of any sort, you face large jail sentences or public whippings. When I say they're crazy, I mean it. They're nuts." Verly didn't add that he was more than a little worried that AFP representatives had gotten here first.

Naite slowly nodded. "And the PA? Are your people perfect?"

Verly scratched his neck. "I could be accused of betraying my vow as a soldier if I get into specific military policies, but I will say I think the PA tends to assume anyone who disagrees with their policies is deluded and ignorant. Now, ninety percent of the time, I agree with that. If you think that loving someone of the same sex is evil and deserves torture, I think you're deluded, ignorant, and evil. It's true the PA also sees people like the Alitura movement as being a little nuts, and while the PA would never imprison them for their beliefs, they would make it difficult for citizens to raise their children with that set of beliefs."

"Alitura movement?" Naite slurred the unfamiliar word.

"Naturalist movement. They want to get away from all science and technology. They believe that a pure environment makes for a pure body and soul. They're an alternative religion."

Leaning back against the rail and resting his hands on either side, Naite took a little time to think about that. "So, you wouldn't call them evil?"

"The PA? No. I wouldn't even call the majority of the breakaway population evil. I think they have some evil leaders."

"And if there were AFP people here?"

Verly shrugged. "I'm assuming there are."

"Natalie, that work for you?" Naite called. Verly tensed at the evidence they had an audience, and there were very few reasons for keeping an observer hidden during interrogation. None of them boded well for Verly. He stood and scanned the room until he spotted a woman standing up from behind one of the enormous storage crates on the far side. She was curvaceous and beautiful with delicate features and long brown hair that curled around her shoulders. And she moved like a predator. The odds suddenly shifted, and the sweat started to gather along Verly's spine.

"I still think allowing him here is a mistake," she said coldly as she looked Verly up and down with such hatred that Verly felt like taking a shower when she was done. Verly had been a soldier most of his adult life, but every nerve sang at him, screamed at him. This was a dangerous woman.

"Well, I guess it's a good thing that it's not your call, then." Naite shifted so he faced off against her. For a second, she held his gaze, and then she dipped her head, agreeing that he had the final say. What the hell was going on? Few women rose high in the AFP, but this one, this one was not used to taking orders.

"Verly Black, pilot, meet Natalie Aral, protocol officer."

If this woman was a protocol officer, Verly was eating his uniform. He raised an eyebrow at her, and surprisingly, she gave him a smile. "Or something," she said wryly, practically admitting her job had less to do with protocol than other activities, and Verly had one or two suspicions about what those might have been. She certainly didn't look like a comp tech.

"If you two are ready to stop glaring at each other, let me make something very clear." Naite stepped between them. "Shan is an idiot who didn't understand that inviting both of you could cause some trouble, and I will be the one cleaning up any messes you might make. If either of you bring your dumbass war down here, I will end the war in ways that are very unpleasant for you personally. Clear?"

"Yes, sir," Natalie Aral said, dipping her head in agreement.

"I can live with that," Verly agreed. The last thing he wanted was to bring this war down here, but if Aral knew his name, she'd be trying to use certain historical facts against him in the near future. She might try blackmail or try to ruin his name with these people, but she'd do something. And if Verly's response earned him Naite's wrath, he'd have to deal with that as it came.

"Now that we're all clear," Naite told Verly, "let's get you settled in the house. Temar's sister Cyla runs the house, but I run the farm. You have two hours to get settled, and then I'm showing you the working end of a dig-stick. Make sure Cyla shows you the water restrictions we live by, because we've got strict rules about rationing."

"Understood," Verly agreed. He knew the PA had sent two tankers of water as a gesture of goodwill, but on a planet this size with five settlements and three agriculture valleys all competing, that wouldn't go far. Rationing was only reasonable.

Naite gave another of those grunts that meant he wasn't happy, but without commenting further, he headed out of the barn. The hair on Verly's neck stood up at the thought of turning his back on Aral, but he had to trust these people to keep the peace because he didn't have the weapons to defend himself. Up to this point, the Livre restrictions on weapons seemed normal. Most worlds did limit them. But right now, Verly would give anything for a good stun blaster.

chapter
three

NAITE PUSHED his hat back and wiped the sweat from his brow before scanning the field. None of his workers had finished their rows yet, but they were all making respectable time. Aila Freewind had almost reached the end, and she looked up at him for a second. He jerked his head toward the far side of the field, and she gave him a quick nod. She'd check those rows when she finished.

Naite moved a couple of rows down and started walking the length of the field, checking the work his people had done. He offered Roman a slap on the shoulder as he passed. The man was improving. In the past, he'd left wisps of weed roots in the ground and doubled all their work, but his holes were clean.

When Naite reached Verly's row, he found a different story. The man made no sense. His row was a God-awful mess. Naite could forgive him a certain ineptitude in the fields, but the man's strange behavior set Naite's teeth on edge. He didn't act like Natalie and Rula had when they'd first appeared. Those two women had been defensive and secretive.

Verly seemed open enough... honest enough. His light brown hair and blue eyes gave him an exotic look, and already Naite could see the fair skin on his arms pinking up. However, he had something going on with him. Naite had always been good at reading people. From an early age, he'd learned that recognizing the subtle differences in his father's moods was a crucial survival skill.

"You're leaving weeds behind," Naite said when he reached Verly's last hole. Reaching down, he plucked out the white threads of root and tucked them into his recycle bag.

Verly gave him a crooked smile... one Naite couldn't quite place. Maybe it was an invitation to a quick fuck. Other times, this boyish charm felt like nothing more than a façade, and that made Naite nervous. "I'm not that good at this," he admitted. Naite eyed Verly's row and silently agreed. "Now give me a ship, and I can pilot her."

"Too bad we don't fly any ships around here," Naite said, crossing his arms. He understood why Natalie and Rula were here. Their own government would imprison them for being in love with each other, and why a government should give a shit about two women having sex Naite did not understand. On Livre, most people had same-sex relationships. With no contraceptives available, avoiding opposite-sex relationships was the best way to avoid pregnancy. But apparently Natalie and Rula both faced arrest and possibly torture for having sex with each other.

Their defection to Livre made sense. Verly made no sense. He was a pilot who had grounded himself on a dry, sandy colony. He was a soldier from an Alliance that offered its own people a certain level of freedom. He had no reason to be here. And still he was offering up his most boyish smile. On the far side of the field, Aila was grinning at him, gesturing with a go-on motion. That woman had sex on the brain.

Naite stepped over the line of small bean plants into Dano's row. "Follow me," Naite said. Dano gave him a small thumbs-up. Naite rolled his eyes. Okay, so he'd slept his way through half the population as a young man. He wasn't a young man, and he didn't have anything to prove. Naite certainly wasn't fucking anyone he didn't trust.

Naite headed toward the house, but at the last second detoured toward the unskilled workers' quarters. He didn't need drama, and Temar's sister was drama. Now up to this point Naite had appreciated how Natalie and Rula had both brought a calming influence to the Gazer house, but ever since they'd learned of the arrival of a PA pilot, they'd been about as likely to start drama as to calm it down. Naite would have to grab some supplies in the bunkhouse.

The unskilled workers had their own hierarchy. In the bunkhouse, the bunks nearest the door were stacked three high. Each bed had a sizeable shelf at the head of it, and tall shelves next to each set of beds offered the workers more storage, but these were for workers drifting through or working a quick harvest. The more permanent workers had their bunks several rows back. These were two high and significantly larger with thin partitions offering privacy on one side and brightly colored fabrics and quilts hung over the front.

Naite took Verly past the sleeping quarters and into the main room. This was larger than any room in the house. Several handmade couches and chairs littered the room. A couple of handheld vid machines sat on a bench against one wall and the tables had a combination of jigsaw puzzles and cards and various other games. Naite weaved his way through to the kitchen.

"I feel like I'm back in the barracks for training. So, how long do people live here?" Verly asked. He took off his hat, set it on the counter, and sat on one of the stools that lined it.

"Most people pick a farm they like and settle. I'll be here for a few years for sure, and after that I'll have to decide if I want to settle here long-term or pick another place." Naite liked the farm well enough, but most farms had children running around and older folks telling their tall tales and doing the light cooking and cleaning. However, since Temar had inherited the farm from that old asshole Ben Gratu, most of the workers hadn't been the family sorts. Hopefully that would change. Unless Naite missed his guess, Aila Freewind had been taking time with Yelta Carlson, and usually a woman only bedded down with a man when she was interested in children or marriage. Naite hadn't heard any marriage talk.

Verly was looking around with a confused expression. "You mean these are permanent quarters?"

Naite pulled the aloe out of a cupboard. "Yep. Why, not good enough for you?"

Verly opened his mouth and then shut it again. Naite hated feeling like the man was editing himself.

"It's hard to trust you when you keep not saying what you're thinking," Naite pointed out. After untying the string that held the oilcloth to the top of the jar, he scooped out some aloe using a flat stick. "Give me your arm."

"What?" Verly pulled back in alarm. Naite rolled his eyes.

"Your arm. You're sunburned, and it'll get worse before it gets better. This will soothe it."

"Oh." Verly slowly leaned forward on his stool and offered his arm. Naite held the man's wrist in one hand and slowly slid the flat of the stick down the arm, leaving a thin layer of aloe behind. "I guess I really am burned. I'm used to being able to go get a derm spray, but I suppose you don't have any of that around."

"Nope." Naite quickly and efficiently finished coating Verly's left arm and reached for his right. The second his fingers closed around Verly's wrist, he could feel the man tense up. Yep, having his weapon hand out of commission made the man twitchier than a chick in a sandrat nest. Well maybe if he was nervous he'd be more willing to spit out a little truth.

"Why'd you come here, anyway?" Naite came right out and asked. It was the one thing Temar had told him not to ask, but Naite wasn't used to taking orders.

"New world, new adventures," Verly said with that same boyish smile.

"Try again," Naite suggested. Verly's arm tensed even more, but Naite kept on applying the medicine.

"Has anyone ever pointed out that you have trust issues large enough to swallow small galaxies?" Verly asked. Redirection and attack. Oh yeah, he was hiding something.

Naite looked right into Verly's blue eyes. "Yes."

And here came that confusion—that moment of mental shift as Verly tried to regain his balance after hearing something he hadn't expected. Either the Planetary Alliance didn't grow men like Naite, or Verly had some very strange assumptions rattling in his head. After that half second of shock, the rakish grin made its reappearance. "Okay then, just making sure you knew. It's like having psychological toilet paper hanging off your ass, and what kind of friend would I be if I didn't point that out?"

Friend. Interesting choice of words. Naite finished tending Verly's arm and dropped the stick into the jar without letting go of Verly's wrist. Looking Verly right in the eye, he asked again, "Why did you come here?"

For a second, Verly weighed his options, and Naite could respect that in a person. Then Verly leaned forward. "Why is a farmer and a council member so battle fatigued?" Verly asked him.

Naite frowned. "What?" That didn't make any sense.

"You watch every movement, you keep an eye on exits, you keep your body poised for violence." Verly glanced down at where Naite still held his arm. "You only start conversations like this when you have me at a tactical disadvantage severe enough that I know I can't reasonably expect to win the fight."

Naite let go of Verly's wrist, but Verly didn't move. He sat on the stool, his right arm stretched across the counter. "Are you a soldier?"

That made Naite snort. "I've never touched a gun in my life," Naite answered. "I'm an unskilled worker, and on a planet where workers are either trained in a skill—mechanics, medicine, computers, blacksmiths—or unskilled workers who do the grunt work, that's not exactly impressive."

"But you're a council member."

"Council always includes a skilled worker, an artisan, a landowner, a child-raiser, a priest, and an unskilled worker. They have to have one of us on there."

Verly tilted his head to the side. "And they chose you, which is not surprising. You have a certain presence, and you move like a soldier—like a dangerous man."

This was moving into uncomfortable territory. "If I'm that dangerous, you can tell me why you get all twitchy every time you start thinking that I'm trying to back you into a corner." Naite couldn't very well deny that he'd been trying to manipulate Verly a little... push a few buttons and see if some fear didn't inspire the truth.

"Dangerous men may be exciting, but I'll admit that I sometimes get uncomfortable around them. I was tortured and raped for three months by some rebels who thought I knew supply lines." He sounded more matter-of-fact than particularly upset by that bit of history.

Naite sucked in a breath. He'd expected a lot of potential answers, but not this one, and he hadn't expected to believe Verly no matter what he said. After long talks and some brutal honesty, he'd come to trust Rula, and she was convinced the PA had sent a spy. However, Naite suspected they had sent a reject officer the way Verly suggested. The flash of pain in Verly's eyes, the way he sat up a little straighter as if refusing to accept that the rape had made him less of a man... that was too specific of a reaction. Either someone had carefully coached Verly, or the man was telling the truth. "That sucks," Naite observed without much emotion. He hated it when others smothered him with emotion, and he'd be damned if he'd do it to someone else.

"Sucks hairy monkey balls," Verly agreed wryly. Slowly he pulled his hand back and leaned against the counter in a more comfortable pose.

"Monkeys?"

Verly held up his hands to indicate size. "Small mammals that swing through the trees."

"Yeah, we learned about those in school." Naite rolled his eyes at the way Verly assumed that living on a desert meant he didn't know anything else. "Seemed sort of pointless to study them since the chance of me ever seeing one is about zero, but I did see vids of them in school. I guess I was more surprised at the phrase."

Verly laughed. "You know, I suppose it is stupid. So, what would you say here?" The boyish smile returned, but this time Naite didn't feel like the smile was some carefully deployed tactic designed to make Naite start thinking with his dick.

"You mean something offensive enough to make sanctimonious little brothers blush?" Naite considered for a minute. "I suppose we'd say 'sandcat prick on a stick.'"

Verly whistled. "That's vivid."

"Sucking monkey balls isn't?"

"No, it is." Verly shrugged. "I guess I've heard that one so often I don't think about what it means. So, a sandcat prick?" he asked after a minute.

"We dissect the cats in biology."

Verly nodded knowingly as he made the connection. "And the boys cut off the pricks and stick them on the end of a stick." He huffed with amusement.

"Yep. Nasty looking things, sandcats. Long and spiny and about as ugly as anything else on the planet."

"Sandcat prick on a stick. I'll remember that one."

"So, why are you here?" Naite asked for a third time. He was not a man to repeat himself, but he had the feeling Verly's story was interesting enough to invest the time.

Verly stretched his neck first one way and then the other. "Have you ever done something, or had something done to you, that others won't forget, won't stop trying to bring up?"

Naite's guts turned to stone. He couldn't even count how many of those mistakes he carried around in his belly with him. Sometimes he felt like the ghost of his father stalked him, and one day he'd open the wrong door and find the old man standing there stinking of pipe juice with his unkempt hair and lewd expression.

"Yeah, you know," Verly said softly even though Naite hadn't said anything. Most people called Naite stoic—sometimes they even accused him of not having feelings because he didn't go around showing them. That made it even more surprising to have a stranger read him so easily. And the pain in Verly's face was too familiar, etched too deeply in his features to be anything other than the truth.

"If you could leave everyone behind and start on a world where no one knew your past, would you?" Verly asked.

Naite stopped and gave the question serious thought. Verly had earned that much. "I wouldn't leave my home behind," he finally answered. As much as he sometimes wished the whole valley didn't know the sordid story of his father, he hadn't left for Blue Hope or Zhang. This was home, and he wouldn't rip out his own roots because of some misguided hope he'd find more fertile ground elsewhere. Fact was, he considered Verly a bit of a fool for doing exactly that. However, if that was his motive, Naite could understand it. He didn't agree with it, but he understood it.

"I guess that's the difference," Verly said. "You have a home, but Diamond was never anything more than the planet where I was born." He looked down at his aloe-slicked arms. "So, what do I have to do with this medicine?"

"Don't wash it off," Naite ordered before he walked out. He didn't do emotions. He didn't discuss them with Father Div, he certainly hadn't discussed them with Shan when his brother had been the priest for a few years, and he wouldn't discuss them with a near stranger.

chapter
four

"NAITE!" CYLA called from the porch of the house, and Naite cringed. The workday was over, and he should be able to find himself a comfortable chair, play some cards or read a book while doing a little people watching.

Instead Cyla waved wildly as if he couldn't hear her screeching. Worse, Verly watched with unpainted interest. Great. Naite felt raw, like he'd shown too much of himself, and he wasn't used to that. He'd be happy when Temar and Shan got back and found some landowner willing to take in soldier-boy and let him discover a few facts of Livre life, like if you kept digging after blisters formed, you'd make a raw mess out of your hands.

Realizing he couldn't get out of a conversation without making a scene, Naite headed for the porch. "Cyla," he offered dryly.

"How's the new immigrant?" Cyla looked past Naite to where Verly stood. She wasn't winning points for subtlety, but then she never had.

"Near to worthless in a field."

"Temar is not going to like that you worked him all day."

Naite crossed his arms and waited for Cyla to say something that was worth responding to.

She moved a step closer, and her voice fell to a whisper. "What in the name of both moons are you doing? You're taking him to the day room alone? You're working him in the fields?"

That still wasn't worth responding to. Cyla, like Temar, had one of those rare fair faces with watery eyes and light hair. It meant that the blush of anger that spread from her reddened chest up into her face was even more evident. The last thing anyone needed was another Cyla meltdown. Naite was trying to make this place welcoming, trying to get the best workers to move here. Ben Gratu had run a cold and loveless place, and most unskilled workers wanted to find a farm that was a family with people they could trust. And no one willingly joined a family with a shrewish cousin who shrieked.

"I took him to the room to tend his sunburn."

"Which he had because you worked him all day."

Naite clenched his teeth for a second. "It seems like I asked Rula and Natalie to contribute to this farm without you...." Naite stopped before he accused her of throwing a fit like a child. Everyone else wanted to pat her on the head and talk about how she grew up without a mother and how she had a father who had sent the best parts of himself to the grave with his late wife. He'd drunk himself to death. But that was a pile of chicken crap. His own father had been worse, and Naite wasn't running around waving his arms to get everyone to pay attention to him.

"They said he couldn't be trusted." Maybe Cyla thought she was whispering, but her voice had a sharp edge that carried.

"This is not the time to discuss it." Naite turned to leave, but Cyla jumped down from the porch and grabbed his arm.

"Don't treat me like I'm some sort of child."

"Then don't act like one," Naite shouted back, putting his face right in hers. He was larger, but she pushed up onto her toes and shook a finger at him like an old grandmother.

"I'm not the one thinking with my dick and chasing some spy around and taking him into private corners."

"Seeing as how you don't have a dick, that's a given." Naite's own temper was rising. He'd never hit anyone half his body weight, but he did have some fantasies. If Cyla would only grow another six inches and put on a hundred pounds of muscle, he would not mind planting a fist in her face. Until that happened, he had to keep the battle to words, though. And she had a definite advantage. Naite had been a rather indifferent language student and time working the fields hadn't improved that.

"What are you thinking? Did you even listen to Rula and Natalie, or are you ignoring them the way you ignore me?"

"I didn't ignore anyone. I heard what they had to say. Natalie and I made it clear to Verly Black that he wouldn't be able to walk all over us." It went against Naite's nature to threaten a pure stranger the way he had, but he'd listened to their warnings. Rula in particular was a plain-speaking woman, and he had a lot of respect for her lack of game playing.

"Oh yeah, you listened so well that you're fucking him?" Cyla spit the words out, and part of Naite understood that her anger was all about her. She had her own issues, and striking out at the world was easier than checking in a mirror. He got it. He did. He didn't give a shit because she had no business talking to anyone like that.

"At least someone wants to share a fuck with me," he said, eying her coldly. She went deathly pale. "Are we done here?"

Cyla backed up onto the first step of the porch, and Naite took that as a yes. When he glanced up toward the door, Natalie stood there, her long hair loose around her shoulders and her eyes taking in the scene. If Temar or Shan had witnessed that, Naite would expect another lecture about respecting Cyla's tender little feelings, like she was some newborn rabbit that couldn't bear the breeze against her skin. However, when Naite caught Natalie's gaze, she rolled her eyes and gave him a small nod the way one parent might offer another when a child was particularly difficult to deal with.

Turning, Naite headed for the bunkhouse, but two steps in that direction, he realized his path would take him steps from Verly Black. The man leaned against a fence and waited. Maybe people from other planets didn't have any manners because a decent man would have walked away to offer at least the illusion of privacy.

"So, she thinks we're having sex?" Verly asked when Naite got close, and there was far too much delight in his voice. Worse, Rich appeared in the door to the bunkhouse, his own amused gaze going from Verly to Naite. What in the name of a dry hell was wrong with all these people who had sex on the brain?

"So, any taboos about sex here?" Verly asked.

Naite stopped and glared, but Verly kept offering that boyish grin. The light from the twin moons gave his face new shadows that made the grin look almost like a sneer, though. That fit Naite's mood better than any sweetness. "You want it, you ask, that's about it." He crossed his arms and waited to see how far Verly would take this little game.

"No taboos about who I ask?"

"If you ask someone who doesn't want to have sex, they'll tell you clear enough. You keep pushing after that, and a council complaint can send you off to another farm or even another valley to work. You press it to the point of raping someone, and they'll confiscate your

shoes and turn you loose on the desert for the sandcats to eat alive."
Naite figured that was not only true but very likely to kill the mood.

"Well that's vivid."

"That's justice for a rapist."

"I'm not disagreeing. I guess I'm used to worlds where they try
to...." Verly looked around as though he'd find some word sitting in
the distant fields.

"Let rapists get away?" Naite asked dryly. He expected Verly to
defend his way of life. He wanted that because he wanted a fight with
someone large enough and stable enough that Naite could unbridle his
anger.

"Yeah, I guess they do," Verly agreed in an amiable voice, "and
they call it civilization."

"Sandcat prick on a stick. That's not civilization. That's
cowardice." Naite moved to a spot against the fence several feet down.
"If something needs doing, you do it. If a man needs killing, then you
should have the balls to see it done. You have a problem with that?"
The anger turned Naite's voice into a growl.

Verly chuckled. "Naite, I was a soldier. I don't have a problem
with that at all. I'm just not used to civilians who don't have a problem
with that."

"Well, I'm unique. Don't think most people on Livre feel the same."
Sometimes it drove Naite crazy how many people would talk about the
right thing and then never do the dirty work that needed doing.

"And yet they execute rapists around here," Verly observed.
"They must—"

"They turn them out on the desert and pretend their hands are
clean. If they don't have to pull the trigger or tie a hangman's noose, it
isn't them doing the killing." Old frustrations and resentments rose up
to sit next to his new anger. He wasn't fit company for the common
room tonight. He wasn't fit company for anyone human, and if he had
even a speck of kindness in him, he'd leave before he said something
truly cruel to this Verly with his own buried wounds. He didn't.

"Pulling the trigger isn't as easy as it seems." Verly shifted so he
rested both forearms against the rail.

"That's the definition of cowardice, plain and simple. If you can
take a man's life, you can look him in the eye. And playing all these
word games, pushing the ugly off into the corner and closing the door

so you don't have to look—it doesn't make you better. It makes you a fucking hypocrite." The slow embers of Naite's anger had been fed too much oxygen tonight.

"I agree. So, do you want to have sex?"

Naite blinked and took a step back. It wasn't often that people surprised him. They disappointed him all the time, but he wasn't generally shocked out of his words. "Your timing sucks," Naite said slowly because now that Verly had asked, Naite's cock was getting insistent about just how much it did want to have sex. Hard sex. Angry sex. And while Naite had enjoyed that in the past, the drama after wasn't worth it.

Verly played stupid. "Why, are you involved?"

"Hell no. But I'm not in the mood tonight."

Verly looked down at Naite's crotch. "If that's what you define as not in the mood, then I am very impressed at how large you must be when you're interested."

The humor struck the wrong chord with Naite, and he lunged forward, barely restraining himself from grabbing Verly's shirt. "What, you want a hard fuck against some rock? You want me shoving my dick into you without giving you time, without stopping when you cry out? Do you want to be pushed face-first into the ground?"

For a long time, Verly studied Naite's face, his gaze sliding over him, and Naite knew what he saw. Naite's body was coiled with anger, with frustration. Fisting his hands at his side, Naite struggled to maintain iron control over himself when he wanted to fuck someone or fight someone. When he got in this mood, he'd spend his night walking the edges of the fields and letting the moonlight soothe his rough edges before he did either of those things.

"I really want exactly that," Verly said. Before Naite could react, Verly reached up and fisted Naite's shirt, pulling him close and bruising Naite's lips with a brutal kiss. Naite reacted without thought, grabbing Verly's ear and yanking his head to the side. Verly cursed, but Naite ignored him and sunk his teeth into the vulnerable arch of Verly's pale neck hard enough to leave indentations in the tender skin. Verly leaned closer, his hands reaching between Naite's legs, and Naite pushed away, using his greater strength to force some space between them.

"Not here. I'm not into an audience." With no more of an invitation than that, Naite walked away, his cock aching in ways that

Naite remembered from his younger years. The hot need, the all-consuming fire of lust had been drained away by a dozen years, by two dozen hard fucks between corn stalks, by a million poor choices. Now, though… now it all returned, and there was nothing Naite wanted more than to push himself into Verly's writhing body.

If Verly had two active brain cells capable of making a good choice, he wouldn't follow. He'd stay in the safety of the bunkhouse and the shadow of the house. He'd avoid Naite and all his hot fury until this mood passed, and Naite would spend the night walking the fields. That would be the smart move.

Naite led them up through a pair of boulders, listening carefully. Behind him, Verly's steps mirrored his. Ahead, there were only the cries of buteo that had settled into their nests for the night. If some other pair had claimed this spot, Naite could have blamed fate and a lack of gakka and told Verly to go back. After all, neither of them wanted a dry fuck.

However, as Naite came around the last boulder, the clearing stood empty. The cramped space was sheltered on two sides by a bend in the cliff, and tall boulders that had either fallen or been cut loose littered the ground on the other two sides. It made an open-air shelter with moonlight that highlighted every crack and lit up the flat rocks larger than bunks where once some equipment had stood, leaving small bolt-holes in the surface.

Naite wanted to grab Verly, to slam him onto the rock, but he wouldn't tear the man's clothing, especially when he'd had the good sense to limit himself to one bag. Instead, Naite ordered, "Strip," without even turning around. Maybe that would send the fool running. Instead, the rustle of clothing suggested Verly was following the insane order. Naite leaned against one of the rocks, his heart pounding, his cock aching, and his fingers itching to grab Verly so much that he didn't dare turn around and look at him because Naite would lose control.

He could feel the threads slipping through his fingers, and he blindly fumbled for the small niche where the workers kept gakka juice for exactly this sort of encounter. When he found the bottle, Naite felt some piece of himself slip away leaving behind the pure need, the hot hunger that had once consumed him.

Only then did he turn to consider Verly's strong, fair body standing naked beneath the moons of Livre.

chapter five

VERLY SHOOK his head. Someone had lasered flat surfaces on top of two huge slabs, and the other rocks had a machined quality that made Verly think of hastily built camps and using rock for cover. It also made Verly wonder why he always ended up nude in the middle of some rough encampment instead of a bed. In his defense, sometimes he ended up half-naked in the hangar of a shuttle carrier or the back of a cargo ship, but there was a definite lack of beds in his love life.

Naite stalked forward, those angles and edges coordinated into a predator's gait. For a man who claimed to be a farmer, Naite Polli didn't move like one. "Last chance to say no," he growled.

Either Naite liked to play rough, or he was genuinely on the edge of losing self-control. Verly didn't know which he wanted, but either worked. "I'm not saying anything," he pointed out. Letting his hands hang at the sides of his body, he waited. This was Naite's game.

"You're pushing when you have no fucking clue." Naite pressed his lips into a thin line and got right into Verly's personal space. They stood nose to nose, and the emotion practically vibrated through Naite's body.

"I would understand more if you explained anything to me," Verly commented. He'd shared part of his story, so a little reciprocity seemed fair.

"Right. And I would trust you because you're a trustworthy person."

"I am."

"Is that why you're a war criminal?" Naite threw the words like weapons, and Verly felt the ice-cold shock flow through him. Naite knew. Well fuck. Verly shouldn't be surprised because the AFP people knew and hated him even more than the Planetary Alliance. If it were up to them, he would have been executed for his mistake instead of being demoted several ranks and exiled to patrolling the border.

"What I did doesn't define who I am." Verly barely got the words out through his clenched jaw even though he'd practiced them dozens of times. He'd said those exact words often enough to have them carved on his fucking gravestone. "So, is this a game?" If Naite was playing psy-corp games, Verly wasn't interested, and he wasn't going to cover himself like some fucking virgin. He crossed his arms and let his very fine cock hang out there.

"You push when you shouldn't." Naite closed the gap another half inch.

"And you don't?" Verly pressed forward, and because they were so close, that put them chest to chest. The buttons of Naite's shirt dug into Verly's unprotected skin. A shiver grabbed him hard.

"What do you want from me?" Naite sounded defensive and raw now.

"Up until two minutes ago, I wanted a hard fuck. Now... now I don't know. I might want a fuck, but I'm kind of toying with the idea of punching you."

Naite raised his chin—a clear challenge that Verly practically ached to take him up on. Before Verly could decide what to do, Naite's hands came up and caught his shoulders, shoving Verly back into a rock. For half a second, Verly's fight-or-flight response kicked in and he shoved back, but the rock was tilted at an awkward angle, and before Verly could regain his footing, Naite's mouth was on his. The kiss was bruising, brutal... familiar. This was the hard touch of a soldier who'd denied himself too long, and before Verly's higher thought processes could veto it, he'd grabbed Naite's shirt and pulled him closer.

Naite's fingers pressed deep into the flesh of Verly's arms, and the heat gathered between them. Even in the cooling night air, Verly felt overheated, and sweat gathered along his spine.

Then Naite pulled back, his stark features shadowed by the twin moons so he appeared alien. By now Verly's cock stood out hard in the night air. He needed this. He needed someone to touch him, even if hate and disgust stained the encounter. He needed human contact. Verly surged forward and grabbed Naite's arms, forcing them back toward that flat stone platform.

"Are you saying no?" Verly demanded as he pinned Naite up against the edge of the platform. Naite's smile shone white and cold and vicious in the moonlight. He didn't bother answering.

Using his greater muscle mass, he forced Verly to the side and then reversed their positions so Verly was pinned. Adrenaline made the hairs on Verly's arms stand up, but then Naite's mouth was on his, Naite's tongue pressing into Verly's mouth. When Naite pushed his hand between their bodies and grabbed Verly's hard cock, Verly went up on his toes. He still had his boots on although he'd stripped off his clothes, and one boot slipped on the loose sand.

Before he could go down, Naite caught him with a knee shoved up between Verly's legs, and Verly widened his stance, inviting the inevitable. Without breaking the demanding kiss, Naite used his knee to shove Verly up toward the stone platform. Putting his arms up on the waist-high edge, Verly helped lift himself up.

Surprisingly the rock was warm and smooth under him, certainly no worse a place for a quick encounter than the shuttle wings Verly had favored in his youth. Without a word, Naite broke the kiss and started pulling his shirt off. His pants followed, but rather than take them off, he shoved them down past his thighs, and then he was grabbing for Verly again.

Strong hands pulled at his hips, sliding Verly toward the edge until his hips were almost ready to fall off the rock and his ass was fully exposed. Clearly they wouldn't be negotiating positions tonight. Even though he still wore his boots, Verly brought his legs up and braced his feet against Naite's hips.

For a second, Naite explored with his hands, pinching Verly's left nipple, running a ragged fingernail down the center of Verly's chest, palming Verly's balls. Verly threw his head back and grabbed the edges of the rock. If he tried sitting up, he'd slide off the damn platform, so until Naite moved or until he had a chance to do a lot of unmanly squirming, he was trapped. He could only endure Naite's rough exploration. Naite pulled at Verly's right nipple, the skin rising like a tent. A hard shiver ran through Verly's body before Naite released it.

Naite panted now, his dark gaze pinning Verly as firmly as those heavy hands against Verly's hips. For a second they were trapped there—Verly's fingers splayed against the rock as he tried to keep his balance, his legs wrapped around Naite's body and Naite looking down at him hungrily.

They stood silent. Motionless. The moonlight cast long, blurry shadows that cut through them as they were caught inside the moment.

Then Naite reached for a thick glass bottle off to the side. Verly watched without comment, afraid that the least word could shatter this raw need and the anger would rush in to fill the empty space.

Naite poured a small amount out into his hand, and Verly's mind went immediately to oils. Oils would be good. He didn't want a dry fuck, not when Naite's cock was so thick.

Cupping the oil in his hand, Naite reached down and started massaging the skin around Verly's ass. Even angry, Naite had a careful nature. He worked a finger in, and Verly arched his back and hissed as the oil warmed. Tingles joined the chorus of sensations demanding his attention, and Verly struggled.

"Fuck. I think I'm allergic."

"It's gakka."

"It stings."

Naite gave him a smirk. "It's supposed to." With that, Naite put the end of his cock at Verly's hole and started pressing in.

The ring of muscle strained around that huge cock, and Verly fell back against the rock as his body was forced to yield. He hadn't felt so full in years, and Verly's own cock ached with need as Naite pushed in, centimeter by slow, hard centimeter. He finally buried his whole length, and then he stood between Verly's legs, his hands braced against Verly's hips.

"Move, damn it," Verly cursed.

"Fuck you. I'll move when I want."

"You're not fucking me.... That's the problem."

Naite gave a frustrated growl, but he also moved. Flesh slapped against flesh, and Verly felt himself shoved up higher onto the rock. Halfway through Naite's next hard thrust, he tightened his legs around Naite. Naite's cock drove deep into him, filling him. The heat of the oil and the endless tingling made him want more. Need more.

Verly reached for Naite and caught a strong forearm. Naite responded by grabbing Verly's shoulders and pinning him down so that the angle of their bodies changed and now Naite's cock drove up into Verly's prostate.

"Fuck yes. Harder."

Naite's grunt and the twist of his lips suggested he didn't appreciate the advice, but he did drive himself in harder and harder. His whole body tightened, his balls drew up, and Naite felt about three times bigger as he kept plowing into Verly.

Verly cursed as his body spasmed out of control and his come splattered between them. Little white freckles stained Naite's chest, and the warm trickle of come followed the line of muscle down his stomach.

With a loud grunt, Naite finally started coming, his thrusts forcing Verly farther up the rock platform. Finally Naite settled, his softening cock still in Verly as he leaned forward. His palms rested on the rock on either side of Verly's head, and Verly was caught between wanting to run his hands up those strong arms and not wanting to poke the anger rolling just under Naite's skin.

They'd fucked. Verly knew better than most that it didn't mean much. He'd had lovers turn against him before pulling up their pants. He wanted more from Naite. The man had a quiet strength that didn't match Verly's impression of a farmer. He had a common touch that Verly didn't associate with being a council member. However, if Naite knew about his past, this might be the only contact Verly got to enjoy.

Naite caught his breath and pulled back, but Verly could still feel the stretch and the heat and the odd tingle from that gakka oil stuff Naite had used. Verly felt well fucked and happy. Sort of. He was a little uneasy about what Naite might do with the information from Verly's past.

Naite eyed him. "You okay?"

Verly raised his eyebrows. That almost sounded civil. "Physically I'm feeling great. Psychologically, I don't think 'okay' has described me in a very long time," he joked. It was true enough.

Naite looked at him, his cock softening but his expression as hard as ever. Without a word, he started pulling his pants up. Since Verly's clothes were on the other side of the small clearing and Naite still stood close enough to make getting off the rock platform awkward, Verly simply watched. His own cock had softened and settled down into its curls, and unless Verly was seeing things, Naite had checked him out. Interesting. Maybe this wasn't going to be a one-time thing. Verly wouldn't mind being the secret on the side.

"How long does that gakka oil keep tingling?" Verly asked. The warmth was pleasant enough, but if Verly had to sit through a meeting, he wouldn't want the distraction.

"A few hours. It's not oil. It's the sap of a succulent."

Verly nodded. That made sense. The native plants pulled on poisonous water supplies, so trace amounts of the poison probably found themselves into the gakka, giving it that property. If someone exported the stuff to PA sex shops, they'd make a small killing. Assuming, that is, that the drug regulators didn't have it banned.

Naite turned his back and headed to where he'd dropped his shirt. Verly took the opportunity to hop down from the rock. He sucked in some air as his overstretched muscles complained. Ignoring the odd feelings in his ass, he headed for his own clothes. "So," Verly said, "what exactly have you heard about me?"

Naite turned, and all the emotion had vanished from his face. This was going down as one of Verly's odder encounters. "Natalie said you'd committed some crime, and I told her that I didn't much care what any of you did before you landed here."

Verly froze with his hand halfway to his shirt. "You didn't ask?"

"Nope."

"Are you planning on asking me what happened?" Verly stepped into his pants.

"Nope," Naite offered, and without another word, he headed back the way they'd come.

Well, now Verly had time to think about what he wanted to say. And he needed time to let his ass recover… either that or talk Naite into allowing him to return the favor and trade positions. It had been a long time since Verly had gotten fucked that hard.

chapter
s i x

NORMALLY THE council house was full, both of people and noise. Today it was nearly silent, and the light that spilled in through the windows cast long shadows since no one had turned on the overhead lights.

Temar stared at the surface of his tea. Part of him wanted to go back to being the youngest child of a man with no real land or power of his own. It had been easier. Ever since he'd been forced to negotiate with two interplanetary alliances to try to preserve Livre's independence, he'd been forced out of the private life he'd prefer.

"Avoiding my gaze does not change reality," Lilian commented.

At one point Lilian had been a force of nature—like a sandstorm or a fire tornado. No one tried to challenge her because doing so was a quick path to humiliation. Now the disease that was killing her had caused her to wither. The white hair that had been like a mane was thin and pulled back so he could see her scalp in places.

"Avoiding reality can be as pleasurable as changing it."

She smiled at him. "For a time, yes. However, you are wise enough to know this complaint from Blue Hope can't be ignored." She pushed the paper across the table toward him.

Temar looked at it for a moment, as unwilling to touch it as he was to pick up a sandrat. They wanted the original measure of water. If every drop of the first two tankers of water both went to Blue Hope, that would only fulfill 40 percent of the original contract. And every town was desperate for water. Even if Temar agreed to this, it would only make all the other towns despise Blue Hope and him for agreeing to an idiotic bargain. "They know this is unreasonable."

"Of course they do. They are boars shaking their tusks to try to drive away a predator."

"They're going to alienate the other valleys."

"Or unite them against us," Lilian said quietly. "We are the oldest, and we have the fullest water basins."

"Because we had a water thief siphoning off our supplies. We put more effort into conserving." Temar poked the table with his finger. "If we suffered, then we have earned that water."

Lilian shook her head slowly. "Would you make that argument if two pigs came to a water hole at the same time? Would one say that his lack of water in the past earned him the right to more now?"

"People are not pigs."

"If you see them as animals fighting for their territory and their families, you will predict their behavior better than most can."

Temar thought of his own habit of seeing people through the lens of glass blowing. He searched for sources of heat and pressure, watching for breaking points and avoiding quick changes in temperature that could shatter the glass. "I tend to think of them as pieces of glass, strong but liable to shatter given the wrong pressure."

Lilian leaned back in her chair. "It says something important that the two of us, who have reputations for understanding people better than most, have to resort to analogies to interpret human behavior. I just don't know what it says."

"That we're an illogical species?"

Her smile made her face light up. "Given the madness the rest of the universe is engaged in, I believe that. The two tankers of water—we must decide what to do, or we run the risk of fracturing, with each city trying to negotiate separately."

Temar rubbed his eyes.

"Closing your eyes to the danger changes nothing."

He glared at her. "I understand that. If some towns side with the AFP and others the Planetary Alliance, we could get sucked into their civil war."

"Which would be unfortunate," Lilian agreed in the understatement of the millennium.

As far as Temar could see, there was only one solution. That's why he'd agreed to the meeting—to convince her to follow the most logical course of action. "You need to go and talk to Blue Hope. They won't listen to anyone else."

She gave him a sad look. "I can't go, Temar. If our people unite behind me, that will be the world's shortest alliance. I'm dying."

Temar shook his head. "You could have years."

"I don't have months," Lilian said sharply, "and I won't have you pretending otherwise. You will go to Blue Hope, and you will show them why they are unprepared to deal with the madness that waits up there."

"How do I do that?"

"Lie. Manipulate. Shake your tusks more furiously than they shake theirs. Be willing to take damage if it means you inflict more. Make them doubt your sanity... there are a thousand ways to take power."

"And you know them better than I do."

Lilian leaned forward. When she reached for him, Temar took her hand. She felt frail and dry. "You are so young, younger than I was when my father died and I became the heir apparent. If I could save you from this, I would. But the problem is that the others see you as a half-grown child. They truly believe that if you could outmaneuver these strangers, then they can as well. You have to go. You have to show them that you are stronger, and you have to let them see the real danger these foreigners pose. Given the general stupidity and arrogance of the two sides, I suspect they will give you the ammunition you need with very little prompting." She tightened her fingers.

"I hate this."

"I remember that feeling well. After my father died, I cursed his soul about as often as I cried for him. I had so hoped to groom Bari to take over as head of the council. His love for family would lead him to be a great caretaker and peacemaker, but that's not what is needed now. What is needed is one who can fight and hold territory."

Temar thought he was the last person capable of that task. He was small—frail when compared to most on Livre. His fair hair and slender frame were less noticeable on the ships where people weren't as solid and dark as most on Livre, but even there he stood out.

Maybe she saw his doubts. She leaned in toward him. "You blew up a ship and risked killing your lover in order to save him. You can do this."

"Should I put Livre in danger of getting blown up?"

"If that's what it takes to save her from the madness of the rest of the universe, yes." Lilian pulled her hand back. "I'm tired, Temar. Go, take care of this mess while I'm still healthy enough to enjoy the irony of someone else having to deal with all these bad-tempered boars." She pushed herself up to her feet, and Temar ached with grief as he watched her walk unsteadily to the door. Bari and one of her daughters were waiting outside, but she shooed them away and insisted on walking under her own steam to the small hauler waiting beside the council house.

Temar trailed after her and stopped at the door. Outside everything seemed normal. Children played in the dust, several vendors sat in the shade of common spaces and sold their goods, and the wind carried the scent of spiced meat. But under all that was a wariness. The kids were a little quieter, and they stayed closer to their parents. Shopkeepers watched him, not even hiding their interest in what might be going on in the council house.

Shan started walking closer. He stopped to exchange a few words with Lilian, and that ended with Shan having to dance back out of range when she used a fan to try to beat him. "I have missed your warm conversation," Shan said in a teasing voice.

"Rascal," she accused him, but like Shan, she sounded more amused than truly upset. Lilian's daughter still reacted poorly, coming around the hauler with her finger shaking in Shan's direction.

Temar tended to think the woman had too much heat on her, and it was applied too unevenly. Her mother's illness had pulled her life out of shape, and she was in danger of cracking. Using Lilian's analogy, she was an animal, rallying around a wounded member of the pack and seeing danger in every harmless movement. Both worked.

Shan backed away until he was almost to the wall of the council house, and then he turned to give Temar a pained smile. "I hate seeing her like that," he said softly.

"Me too." Temar watched as Lilian's daughter fussed over her for a time before Lilian drove her away with the same fan.

"What did she say?"

"Let's wait until we're on our way home," Temar said. He didn't want to risk being overheard. Most people in Landing hadn't yet fully embraced the idea that Lilian was dying. It was like suggesting that it would rain—physically impossible. And yes, the people of Livre lived a hard life and learned about loss early and often, but Lilian defied the odds. She had given birth to five children, all of whom lived. She had ruled the council for decades, and every member of the town could point to at least one major conflict she had defused through her combination of patience and a dangerously sharp tongue.

Shan slipped his arm around Temar without another word. Leaning into that strength, Temar allowed himself one moment of feeling utterly helpless. The universe was too large, Livre was too poor, and he was too clueless to do anything about the first two items on that list.

"A couple of the workers said the new guy is making eyes at that idiot brother of mine," Shan said, neatly changing the topic as he guided them to their own small hauler.

"Good. Naite deserves some happiness."

"Or his government is trying to get him in with a council member."

Temar gave Shan a strange look. Usually Shan was talking about fate and finding your path only when you let go of control and trusted God to reveal it. "When did you turn into the cynical one?"

"When did you turn into the romantic?"

Temar gave Shan a smile before climbing into the hauler. "When I figured out that Polli men are worth loving."

"Should I be jealous?" Shan teased, but there was no heat behind the words. He got in behind the wheel, and for a time he sat staring out at Landing. "I'm not comfortable with him taking an immediate liking to the only available member of the council."

"As opposed to Natalie who came out and told us that she was under orders to seduce one of us?" Temar asked.

"Under orders to seduce you," Shan said. "I'm the distraction there to make sure people don't see the power behind the throne."

Temar fixed his sand veil across his face. The way other people interpreted their relationship confused him. Natalie's people had twisted sexuality around until it made no sense to him. Shan insisted that other human cultures had done the same throughout history, but Temar liked to think that as a species they had evolved beyond that. Clearly he was wrong, but he liked to think it anyway.

"He could just honestly like Naite," Temar said. He pulled his sand veil up higher.

"Have you met my brother? Bad tempered, foulmouthed, arrogant, and utterly convinced that he is always right. I don't know of anyone who likes him."

"They elect him as the representative for the unskilled workers every time."

"They respect him," Shan said. "They simply don't like him." Shan finally started the hauler, and the machine lurched forward, the sand that had settled on every flat surface all sliding off. The roar of the engines made talking impossible, which might be good. Shan had a giant blind spot when it came to his brother, and Temar didn't understand it. As much as Temar didn't deal with his sister very well, he did see her clearly. He understood how much she felt a need to prove herself and that she had good motives behind all the sharp temper.

However, Shan always looked at his brother using a warped mirror. When Temar had first started courting Shan, before they'd ended up having to go up into space to deal with their homicidal cousins, Lilian had pulled him aside and told him to be wary of Shan's wounds. She'd made veiled comments about their childhood, but Temar still didn't understand it entirely. Neither Shan nor Naite ever talked about their father, so other than the common rumors of his drunken exploits, Temar didn't have a lot of evidence to work with.

When they hit the deep desert, Shan turned the engine up to full. It screamed as the hauler went up the front of a dune, but then they hit the crest, and Shan took it down to a whisper as the hauler slowly tilted and started sliding down the other side. Temar always liked this moment—the silence filled with the shush of the hauler's skids against the slipping sands.

"I don't want him hurt," Shan said. The wind pushed his voice so that sound distorted it.

"I know."

"Verly happened to conveniently settle on the one member of the council who really has issues with lovers. I mean, he either uses them up the way sandcats rip through prey, or he gets moon-eyed and stupid."

"Moon-eyed? Naite?" That was about the last word Temar would ever use to describe the man.

Shan took the hauler to the top of the next dune and slowed them until the hauler was balanced on the top. The hauler broke the sharp edge of the dune so the sand was deep on either side of the machine, but Temar could see the long sweeping curves of the dunes and the white sands for miles.

"It's been a long time," Shan said, "but Naite's been known to get stupid around people he liked. I think that's why he avoids relationships altogether. But if we've finished talking about my idiot brother, what did Lilian have to say?" He pulled his sand veil off and shook it out. Fine sand dust trailed away on the wind.

"I still can't believe she asked you to leave the room," Temar said.

Shan smiled. His sharp features made him look devilish, like he was considering some prank. "I can. If I stayed, then Lilian's daughter would have wanted to stay, and then Bari would have insisted on staying because that girl is driving her mother crazy. So, what did she say?"

Temar described the conversation, and slowly Shan's smile faded. "She doesn't have the right to ask this of you. The council hasn't even met. You can't negotiate when Landing doesn't have a position yet," Shan said.

"Has Lilian ever waited?"

"That's not a fair comparison. Lilian is nearly eighty. She can get away with it because she's a cagy old woman who knows everyone's secrets. Besides, she scares everyone."

"And I don't," Temar said. That wasn't true. He'd frightened the people of the AFP and the PA, in part because he'd taken actions they'd seen as rash and dangerous. Hell, they were rash and dangerous.

"No," Shan said softly. He reached over and ran his hand over Temar's cheek. Temar hadn't taken his veil off, so the fabric dulled the touch. "I know how strong you are, but she can't ask you to try to force people to bend, not when they see no reason to bend."

Temar pulled off his veil. "Then who will get them to bend?"

Shan pulled back. "Bari is the senior member of the council."

"And how will he deal with this when Blue Hope is angry and determined to demand more? Lilian is convinced that he won't know how to hold his own against them."

"So she sends you?"

"Do you think I can't handle it?"

"I would never assume that. You ordered that idiot who likes my brother to blow up a ship I was on at the time. If you can handle space terrorists, I'm fairly sure you can handle Blue Hope, but should you have to?"

Temar looked out at the planet. If their ancestors hadn't been cut off from the rest of the universe by a civil war, would the desert be gone by now? Would sandcats and sandrats and all the rest be exiled to some small region where the native desert would be preserved as some sort of monument? Would his people be like Verly's? They seemed very judgmental—using scorn to try to shame people into changing instead of using harsh laws the way the AFP did. Neither side had impressed Temar, and he couldn't imagine Bari trying to stand between Livre and those idiots.

"I shouldn't have to, but if I don't, I'm not sure anyone else understands the danger. Well, obviously you do, but let's be honest, you sometimes aggravate people."

"I often aggravate them," Shan said. "But I'm good at providing you a distraction so you can figure out how to work around some problem. So, do we follow Lilian's advice?"

"We could go back and tell her that we're refusing," Temar said. Just as he expected, Shan cringed.

"Right," he said. "We're going to Blue Hope." He revved the engine on the hauler, and it tilted forward.

chapter
seven

TEMAR SAT and watched Shan clench his teeth until the muscle at his jaw bulged. Ebi Raw glared right back. "You don't speak for this planet," Ebi said, his voice low and angry.

Amantha slid her hand across the table until it rested close to Ebi's.

"I'm not going to sit back while Landing repeats the same crimes as in the past," he said firmly. Amantha was the artisan on the council, and Ebi was the unskilled worker, but he wielded his power on this council like a blunt weapon. Aiden was more of a mystery. The landowner watched without adding much. At first Temar had thought he was like Lilian, someone who would speak only when the decision was ready to be made. However, he seemed distracted.

"What crimes are you talking about?" Shan asked.

"We were promised water," Ebi said, poking his finger into the wood of the table. "Every other township got establishment water. We never got our full share."

Temar had no idea that Blue Hope had held that grudge for so long.

"Landing didn't promise that water. It should have come from the terraforming company," Shan explained. At least it was an attempt at explanation even if the volume was a little loud. It was logical as far as Temar was concerned, but looking around at the Blue Hope council, he could see that they didn't accept the same logic. Kaylor was the representative of the child-rearers, and she looked as angry as Ebi. Vivian, a doctor and representative for skilled workers, appeared less emotionally involved, and Aiden looked bored.

Ebi leaned back with a smug expression. "The company run by the government that has just now sent two tanks of water, which they owe us. That's our water." Clearly Ebi and Kaylor were unmovable, and Temar suspected Amantha was nearly as resolute, although she also seemed to want to play peacemaker. Applying more heat there would only crack the piece. No, he needed to work on Vivian or Aiden.

"That's ridiculous!" Shan said, going for the obvious target. "The company is gone. This water is a peace gesture toward the whole planet."

"So our fields should die so you can take showers?" Ebi demanded, and his voice grew louder to match Shan's.

"Maybe that's their definition of fair," Kaylor said. The woman would give Cyla a run for her money in the sarcasm department.

Ebi nodded. "It seems the sort of definition that Landing would use. You people might forget debts, but we don't."

While Shan continued to fight with Ebi, Temar thought about what Lilian had said about lying. He didn't have any real way to move Vivian or Aiden, but he could lie with the best. Shan was in the middle of arguing when Temar stood. Shan stopped midword.

"We're leaving," Temar said. He noted the various expressions. Shan was confused, Ebi and Kaylor looked victorious, and Aiden relieved. That would change.

"Okay," Shan said slowly before he stood.

Temar turned to Aiden. "I am giving official notice that I plan to charge you with failure to repay debts and request not only the ten shares of seeds you owe me, but another ten as punitive for failing to repay for such a long period of time."

That made the landowner take notice. "What?" he squawked. It was a very undignified noise. "I have never borrowed from you." The added heat was enough to get him fully into the game, and now Temar had to shape his emotions carefully.

"No, but if Blue Hope maintains the legal position that debts never expire and they travel from generation to generation, then I will have back the seed that my grandfather loaned your grandfather during the blue storm of your valley's seventh year."

"I... what?" Aiden sounded panicked now, and Ebi's expression had turned furious. He saw the trap. And while it didn't affect him, he knew Aiden would now be forced to argue against the inheritance of debt.

"I have the paperwork at home," Temar said, or he could ask Lilian and Natalie how to forge it. He had faith those two would be able to come up with something that could pass as legally binding and legitimate, and both the grandfathers in question were long dead. "We will be back to place the legal charge, and I plan to ask someone from Gambles or Zhang to come out and ensure fairness."

Aiden shot to his feet. "Wait. I'm not even the one trying to make that argument. If you're angry with Ebi, be angry with him."

"This is not about anger," Temar said.

"No, just politics," Ebi said, and he made that sound like the most disgusting word in the universe. Temar knew if Naite were here, he'd agree with Ebi. It saddened Temar that he had to manipulate his own people the way he had others, but Lilian was right—someone needed to.

"This isn't politics," Temar said softly. "If we cannot work together, then I plan to do everything I can to earn the Planetary Alliance credits to buy a seat off-world. We are trapped between two governments. One sees us as mewling children that will eventually come begging them for help, a help they will offer with so many conditions that you might as well sell your children. The other kills people who have sex. Natalie and Rula came to this world because their own people would have murdered them for touching each other."

"None of those people are here," Kaylor said, but she sounded less sure of herself now.

"No," Temar said, "but if they suspect that we have politics between us, they will be down here, each trying to gain the support of different cities."

"Speculation," Ebi said. Clearly more heat was required.

Temar slapped the table, and everyone jumped. "I forced Verly Black to open fire on a ship, to blow up the ship where a terrorist was holding Shan and threatening to torture him to death. I watched as Shan was pulled out into the vacuum of space unprotected, and I prayed that Verly would get to him before he died. If he had made one mistake, if I had made one mistake with his equipment as I used a tether to pull them back in, then Shan would have frozen to death, his lungs turned to ice crystals by the absolute black of space. Don't tell me I'm speculating because I've seen these people. I've killed these people. And if you want to try to play games, then you go ahead. I will sue Aiden for every measure of grain I can. I will ask Lilian to go through Landing's paperwork in search of every debt we can find that has not been repaid. I will tell the people I care about to get off this planet before our dissent turns it into a playground for these monsters who send us water and hope we are too foolish to understand that the gift comes with teeth as sharp as a sandrat's."

Temar spun around and headed for the door. Not even Shan moved. Temar was outside and fixing his sand veil when Shan finally came running after him. "Temar?" he asked, clearly uncertain about how much of the anger was real.

"We're leaving," Temar said. They had too many eyes on them for any other answer.

Shan nodded, but his gaze darted over to where most of the council of Blue Hope stood in the door of their council house madly whispering.

"Now," Temar said firmly.

"Now it is," Shan agreed, his voice still uncertain as he followed Temar to the hauler. They got in, and Shan started it toward the edge of town without even fastening his veil. Temar firmly ignored the curious gazes that followed them out of Blue Hope. This was the newest of the settlements, started right before the company abandoned Livre. The homes were small and clustered closely together on the slope of a mountain that overlooked the desert.

Their valley was so far away that you could only catch glimpses of the distant slash in the earth where their farms were tucked between shallow valley walls. It wasn't like Landing and The Valley, which were separated by only a couple of miles. Landing was on the edge of the bedrock shelf that made the rough mountains of The Valley, and Landing had the convenience of durable streets, electrical generators, wells, and other infrastructure the first settlers had set up. Blue Hope had none of it. They did need more, but Temar worried that if he gave in they would never stop pushing.

People resented Lilian and her habit of strong-arming the other councils, and part of Temar wanted to escape bringing that same resentment down on himself, but he couldn't see another way to keep his people from self-destructing.

SHAN HAD eased the hauler down several rocky slopes before he stopped and put on his own sand veil. "How much of that was real?"

"I am going to go get paperwork to bring back here, and I am going to ask Lilian for help going through the records. Blue Hope had some rough years in the beginning, and I know a lot of people made loans they had no intention of collecting on."

"So we're going to remind them of that?" Shan asked. He fixed his veil and started the hauler back down the path.

"No, we're going to ask for repayment."

"Temar, that's not fair to these people," Shan argued. He was clearly getting ready for a full lecture, so Temar cut him off.

"And they are not being fair to us, threatening to undermine our alliances when we need each other."

"So you would slap the other cheek instead of turning it?" Shan asked.

Temar smiled. Leave it to Shan to argue for those people ten minutes after arguing against them. They reached the place where the dunes met the rocky mountain where Blue Hope sat, and the sand swirled around them until Temar couldn't even see where they were going, but Shan steered confidently enough in one direction.

"Temar?" Shan asked over the howl of the wind. "What are we doing?"

"I'm applying some heat. They need to see that if they continue, they are going to leave this world uninhabitable."

"So, you're lying?"

"Not as much as you might think," Temar said. If he couldn't do the impossible, if he couldn't unite people the way Lilian had, he might recommend they leave this world. It was home, but that's why seeing it pulled into a civil war would hurt even more.

Shan laughed. "You know, some people still question why you would choose someone twelve years older than yourself. I think those people don't know you very well because you have an old, old soul."

"I'm trying to protect my world."

"Don't carry the weight of the whole world, Temar. We can both do our best to guide the others to see the truth, but you can't hold yourself responsible for the entire world."

"You're going to say that's God's responsibility, aren't you?"

"Yes," Shan said. "But I also know that sometimes we have to give God's plan some help, although Div continues to tell me that it's my own arrogance that makes me think that."

"You are the least arrogant man I know, and I'm trusting you to tell me when I've gone too far."

Shan glanced over, and Temar half expected him to say Temar had already gone too far.

"You didn't kill anyone," Shan said softly. "You shouldn't have told them that."

Temar frowned. He'd told the council that he had killed people, although that was an overstatement. He had killed one. He had watched the body of the terrorist who had taken Shan fly out into space, and he hadn't felt one ounce of regret. "I ordered Verly to open fire on that ship. I knew that if our plan succeeded, that man would die, and I knew if it failed that you would die with him. I took his life."

"You saved mine."

"I did both," Temar said. Shan kept glancing over, but he had to keep most of his attention on the dunes. Temar figured he would wait for another time and bring this issue up again, but Temar knew what he'd done. He'd taken a life—a decision that Shan likely wouldn't have made. Shan would have tried to bring everyone back together. He would have argued and quoted the Bible and talked about moral debts. Temar had killed. Unfortunately, Temar suspected he might have to make that choice again if he wanted to keep Livre free.

chapter
eight

VERLY WOKE to the sound of voices. He had a room in the main house, so he had more privacy than the unskilled workers, but the voices were still insistent enough to rouse him. He rolled over and felt a twinge in his ass that reminded him of the night before. He enjoyed feeling stretched and worn. Pushing himself out of bed, he headed to the window and looked down onto the dusty farm. A motorbike sat near the barn, and everyone gathered around the door to the bunkhouse. For a second, Verly had a flash of paranoia that they were discussing him, but that didn't make sense. If Ambassador Gazer had any problem with Verly being down here, the man was direct enough to say it.

He dressed soldier-fast and hurried to shift the dresser he'd used to block the door. The main house was silent as Verly moved through it.

When he'd come up last night, he'd passed Rula as she sat in the kitchen, in the dark. He didn't have any trouble spotting her sort. She was one of their female corps—women who owed the state, usually because the state had spent money feeding them as orphans, and the state demanded service in return. They protected women important to the AFP, they were prison guards in women's facilities, and sometimes they ended up on PA planets with bombs strapped to their chests as they claimed to work for some fringe terrorist group.

Even knowing all that, he was more comfortable around Rula with her direct stare than he was around Natalie. That one did psy-ops work for sure, and she'd probably left a long line of dead operatives behind her. Of course, Verly didn't exactly have clean hands, even if the dirtier side of the war had never appealed to him.

Outside, the sun already shone bright enough to make him squint. The fine mesh that covered the top of the valley filtered the light, but not enough for Verly's eyes. He straightened his sleeves as he identified the people hovering in the yard. Rula and Natalie stood near the edge of the crowd, with Cyla near them. Verly had an uncharitable thought about how those women might warp Cyla, but the fact was that if they were lovers, they couldn't have any love for the AFP. And if he privately wondered whether that story was true, he wasn't fool enough to start saying it out loud. He was on thin ice here, and attacking others was a sure way of having suspicion cast on him.

He spotted the two ambassadors, Shan leaning against the bike and Temar standing halfway between Shan and Naite. A number of the workers Verly had met the day before were there, and oddly, Naite wasn't yelling at anyone about getting back to work, so something was happening.

"Good morning," Verly greeted everyone. Figuring that if he was in for a penny he should be in for a pound, he moved closer to Naite.

Naite gave him an odd look without commenting on the move, but Shan started grinning.

"Verly." Temar smiled warmly. "I'm so sorry this mess with Blue Hope took so long."

"Problems?"

"Yes, but more the normal kind of disagreements and petty annoyances that we're used to than the sort of drama you get up there." Temar nodded toward the sky.

"I don't know, we seem pretty good at drama lately," Shan pointed out. "If I were suspicious, I would start to worry about the good Lord sending us challenges."

Verly's guts knotted. Natalie and Rula frowned at Shan's words. The AFP were religious zealots—Paulists who believed in the nastier parts of the Christian Bible that had little to do with Christ. Verly could admit his own comfort level with religion dropped every time the news covered another crazy story smuggled out of one of the breakaway planets. However, Natalie and Rula didn't say anything, and Naite's eye rolling appeared more brotherly than anything else.

"I don't think God has anything to do with it," Naite said. "Now your ability to stick your nose in trouble... that might be related." He gave his brother an unfriendly look.

"You're assuming I'm not an agent of God."

Temar interrupted what looked like a fight about to break out. "I'm assuming you're enjoying your ability to annoy each other, but I'm tired."

Cyla spoke up. "If Lilian went—"

"She'd die halfway across the desert. She's too sick for that," Naite cut her off. Verly could see the instant fury in Cyla's face.

"She's not that weak."

"She pretends she's not, but she is," Naite said, ignoring all that anger, which was about the worst thing he could do. Verly had seen lots of officers like Cyla—they were so determined to prove themselves that everything became a challenge, and they took stupid risks. Hell, Verly suspected he might have been that officer.

"Lilian. Lilian Freelander, the representative for the landowners, right?" Verly asked.

"Freeland, and yes," Naite answered. "She's one woman who won't take an answer she doesn't like."

"Which is why she could convince Blue Hope to compromise." Cyla crossed her arms over her chest. Her body language dared them to disagree, but given the number of strong personalities in a very small space, Verly figured someone would.

"Unless she died halfway there," Naite said. "I need three men on watering duty on field four. Volunteers?" Naite turned away from Cyla and started looking to his workers. Verly cringed a little for Cyla. That was cold. Of course, Naite had never pretended to be good with people skills. Verly's ass was a testament to his impatience.

Shan stepped in to try to smooth the ruffled feathers. "Temar talked to them. They're reconsidering their position." And that sounded like a nonanswer to Verly. No one else noticed, or perhaps they just didn't react to the quick sidestep.

"And if they won't agree?" Natalie asked.

Verly was irrationally annoyed that Natalie understood this conversation when he couldn't catch more than every other idea. He didn't even know what Blue Hope wanted, although he had researched the planet enough to know that Blue Hope was one of the other agricultural valleys. Temar and Shan had been so careful with operational security that Verly hadn't even figured out if they were allies or rivals.

"Then we talk more," Temar said with a casual shrug before he reached over and caught Verly's arm. "I want to show you a piece I made to thank you for helping us," he said, effectively cutting off the argument.

Shan followed Temar's lead. "It seems like I should have made you something since I'm the one you rescued, but since I doubt you want a refurbished sand bike engine, I had to settle for sitting in the tent while Temar made you something,"

Verly smiled at Shan. Shan was a lot healthier than the last time Verly had seen him up close. The two of them had come through the day he'd arrived, but it had literally been a drive through. They hadn't even taken off their dusty clothes before they'd headed back out again. "It's good to see you up and moving around. That was a serious injury."

"Shan's too stubborn to die. Either that, or maybe his God protects him," Naite said in an unfriendly tone. Several of the workers had started to wander toward the various fields, but Naite still eyed his brother like he expected a fight.

Shan narrowed his eyes, and for a second, the two brothers were carbon copies of each other. "I like to think that the Lord chooses the right people to put in my life."

"I like to think I have a brother who will give me credit when I show up to rescue his pathetic ass," Naite shot right back, and before he had finished his comment, he was striding off toward the fields.

Shan opened his mouth as if to say something, but Naite was already far enough away that he would have needed to shout it. One of the workers laughed. "You have to insult faster than that to get the last word with Naite."

"Not even an ex-priest can talk that fast," another one teased, and with a few last laughs, the rest of the workers started heading out. Cyla, Natalie, and Rula still presented a sort of united front that Verly wasn't sure how to handle, so he focused on the ambassadors.

"What is the conflict over?" he came right out and asked. He wasn't surprised that Natalie narrowed her eyes and considered him coldly, but Temar tugged him toward the house, and Shan moved to Temar's other side, his hand finding the small of Temar's back and resting there.

Temar answered, "They want additional water rights. They have a point… The Valley had a huge share of water when the terraforming started, so if we all share equally now, that will leave The Valley with a significant advantage for the foreseeable future."

"So, you're going to give them what they want?" That wasn't what Verly expected from any politician.

"They also miss the point entirely by expecting that they can claim the same volume as in the original charter, as if the situation hasn't changed," Temar said as he wrinkled his nose. "So, I have to convince them they're wrong on the specifics, even if they are right about the general shape of the piece. Unfortunately, every time we tried to discuss the details, the conversation grew a little too hot for any agreement to take shape."

"Which is a nice way of saying screaming was involved," Shan explained.

"I didn't scream," Temar said with some amusement even as he emphasized the word "I." Shan had his brother's dark complexion, but as they stepped up onto the porch, Verly could see the slight blush on his cheeks. So Shan had lost his temper.

Shan changed the topic. "After everything that has happened, I can't believe they honestly think you'd favor Landing," he told Temar. "If anything, you have reason to want Landing to pay a heavy price."

"Why?" Verly asked.

Shan raised his eyebrows in a Naite-like expression. However, where Naite would have gone nonverbal, Shan was more than happy to answer. "So, Naite hasn't given you our whole sordid tale?"

With a comment like that, Verly wanted to chase after Naite, to prove something by teasing the story out of the taciturn man. Unfortunately, he suspected Naite was better at holding out than Verly was at extracting information. "No. He didn't say anything."

"Coward," Shan said softly. Temar slipped his arm around Shan's waist, and Shan looked down. "He's vocal enough about his beliefs. He can at least admit it when he's wrong," Shan said, but he sounded a little defensive, and given that Temar hadn't said anything, Verly suspected this was another of those old and often rehashed arguments families used to torture each other.

"He has," Temar said softly, but the rebuke was still there.

Shan's mouth twisted into a grimace. "I'd be happier if he didn't spend so much time avoiding the issue of slavery."

"The what?" The shocked words slipped out of Verly unchecked. He knew all about diplomatic missions and not placing your own judgment on other's beliefs, but slavery fell far outside any moral gray area Verly was willing to consider. Slavery was a disgusting institution, one the breakaway planets used like a sledgehammer to pound anyone who disagreed with the party line while claiming they upheld individual choice and freedom.

Shan stopped and gave Verly a serious look. "Thank you. Normal people are horrified by the thought of it." With that, he gave Temar a slightly less happy expression.

"So I'm not normal?" Temar asked, and his voice dared Shan to say exactly that. Shan physically was the more powerful partner—he had age and size and a certain sharp edge to him that whispered of power—but Temar had a quiet strength that didn't yield. Verly didn't doubt how this was going to end.

Sure enough, Shan's defensiveness slipped, and he looked momentarily confused. "Of course you're normal. I'm just...." Shan stopped. He just stopped. Turning, he opened the door to the house and held it open for them. "I yield. No matter what I say, I'm going to lose this battle, so I am yielding the field before I have a chance to lose. We need to have that wedding ceremony soon because no man should be this consistently wrong unless he's a husband."

Temar stepped close and smiled at Shan. Resting his hands on Shan's chest, he lifted himself up on his toes to give Shan a kiss. "I love you, and you're not wrong. You're only half-wrong, and I'm half-wrong, and we'll figure it out."

Verly frowned, not sure he was following any of this. "Are you talking about working out a plan for slavery?" he asked.

Temar gestured for Verly to go into the house, and Verly quickly moved into the shade. In only a few minutes in the sun, he'd already developed a pounding headache, and the heat outside felt like a weight pressing down. The shade and relative cool of the house was a welcome change, even if Verly was having some rather elaborate fantasies about air conditioners and the ice storms of Delta Seven.

"We can't afford prisons, and we certainly can't afford to feed people who aren't working. So yes, slavery is part of our penal system," Temar explained as he followed Verly into the house.

"Considering that you use sandrats for executioners, that shouldn't shock me, but it does," Verly admitted. The first time he'd seen Temar through the comm viewer on his shuttle, Temar had threatened to take Verly back to Livre and allow sandrats to eat him alive if Verly betrayed them or cost Shan his life. Verly had a lot of respect for the man because he was willing to lay the rules out like that.

However, if Temar had threatened him with slavery... well, Verly might have developed a different opinion.

"The shocking part is that he was a slave, and he still doesn't argue for abolishing the system," Shan said softly. He still clearly disagreed, even if most of the heat had vanished from his voice.

Temar sat on the couch. "Ben abused the system and he abused me, but that doesn't mean that the entire system is broken." He held out his hand toward Shan, and Shan took it and sat so close that their legs pressed together. Verly felt a stab of hot jealousy. It'd been a long time since he shared the sort of intimacy that could survive the light of day. Most of his human contact took place in dark, forgotten corners, but he hadn't thought much of it because being surrounded by military personnel, he didn't get to see much open affection. Seeing it here was a little like being hungry while someone ate a feast in front of your eyes. It made Verly ache in ways that hurt more than his stretched ass.

"Abused?" Verly asked, focusing on the question at hand. His emotions... well, they were simply emotions. If he could find a way to tempt Naite into a second encounter, that was good. If not, this feeling wouldn't kill him.

"Ben raped me," Temar said in a matter-of-fact tone. Verly's stomach dropped.

Temar threaded his fingers with Shan's, and for a second, he stared down at their intertwined hands. "He was a sick man who did sick things. But for most people, slavery means they work for a landowner for a certain period of time in order to work off debts or learn to act like a responsible adult when they aren't."

Shan's jaw muscle bulged so that Verly feared for the man's teeth. Given Shan's deep feelings for Temar, Verly understood the wealth of anger there. After hearing Naite's description of desert justice, Verly suspected that this Ben hadn't survived long.

"That sounds more like indentured servitude," Verly said slowly. He had to make reports, and he didn't want to send back a report that included a hot-button word like slavery. Verly wasn't fool enough to believe the PA would keep it secret, and civil-rights groups would be picketing the government to get them to intervene on Livre.

Temar tilted his head to the side and then made direct eye contact with Verly. "Indentured implies you have a choice. Slaves don't. They're convicted by the council of some crime—either an intentional crime against property or a negligent crime against a person. They don't have a choice. Someone pays their fines, the money goes to the victim, and the person has to work for whomever paid the money. No choice."

"Like Ben paid for you?" Shan asked, his voice almost shaking with all those dark emotions that danced across his face.

Temar turned toward Shan, his voice steady. "Yes, like Ben paid for me, and like I paid for Naite. Sort of." Temar made a face.

"For Naite I'm willing to make an exception and call slavery morally justified."

"Whoa. Wait." Verly held both hands up. "What are you talking about? Naite?"

Shan's eyes got large with surprise. "Naite didn't tell you any of this?"

"No."

Shan seemed bewildered. Temar didn't look confused as much as thoughtful—like he was carefully considering something. The last time Temar got that look, Verly had ended up in the middle of possibly the most disastrously stupid plan in all history, and he still wasn't sure how it had worked. After a second, Temar shook his head, and the expression cleared.

"We had heard that you and Naite were... well... getting along."

"Words like naked were mentioned," Shan agreed. Verly's face heated up. Sex was a perfectly normal part of human experience, and he didn't feel any need to apologize for that, but he felt like a fool for not understanding the undercurrents with these people. Maybe he was arrogant, but he'd expected life on Livre to be simple and straightforward, and here he was trying to figure out if the ambassadors were ready to kick him off the planet for putting his boots under the wrong bunk, not that boots had come off or bunks been used.

"It's good that Naite's spending some time with someone," Temar quickly added.

"Good for him, not necessarily good for the person who is more than likely to get dropped like a sandrat picked up by mistake," Shan added quietly. These two had sibling rivalry that put some wars to shame. Temar put his elbow in Shan's side. "Hey, I would go to his wedding if he would find someone and settle down. I'm simply warning Verly that the odds of that aren't good," Shan defended himself.

"Can we go back to the discussion of slavery and leave any relationship discussion alone?" Verly asked. At this point, he'd beg if it got them back on topic.

"Naite's serving a slave sentence," Shan said casually, and for someone who claimed to hate slavery, there wasn't a lot of emotion there.

"It's complicated," Temar said.

Verly focused on Temar. "Complicated in what way, because I consider slavery very close to that moral line that has no room for compromise."

Oddly, Temar smiled at him. "And like Shan, you are half-right. In Naite's case, I don't think he should serve this sentence. He was on the committee that sentenced me to serve for a number of years, and I probably deserved them. My stupidity led me to pull a stupid stunt— one that wasted a lot of water, water that is necessary for life."

"By accident?"

Temar leaned back against the couch. "It wasn't on purpose, but it certainly wasn't an accident because I should have seen where my stupidity was leading."

"Cyla was leading, you were following," Shan corrected him.

"Either way, I know what I did was wrong, and when I learned that I was only going to serve time as a slave, I was relieved."

"But...." Verly shook his head as he struggled to understand. He was starting to miss the PA and their obsessive-compulsive need to write out every rule and regulation. "You only damaged property, and they enslaved you?"

"I wasted thousands of gallons of water. Without water, people die, Verly. I expected to be exiled to the desert."

That made Verly's skin crawl. He didn't care what Temar had done, the man didn't deserve to die for it. "You mean executed?" he asked coldly.

Temar cringed at the same time he nodded. "There was a chance. So when they sold my contract to Ben, I was grateful, all the way up to the point that I figured out that Ben was a raping, lying water thief. However, the council who sentenced me believed they needed to pay a penalty for not investigating Ben enough and for not checking on me. They were ultimately responsible for my safety, and they let me get hurt."

Verly sat in the nearest chair. Either he wasn't understanding Temar, or the logic circuits had not closed in these council members' brains. "So they enslaved themselves?" That sounded unbelievable, unless some high-powered weaponry was pointed at their backs at the time.

Temar shrugged. "Most paid fines. As an unskilled worker, Naite didn't have a lot of spare money, so he set his sentence at three years of service."

"So, he can't quit?" Verly felt a wave of nausea. Someone as independent as Naite should not be trapped.

"Sadly, no," Shan said. "Well, actually if Naite weren't here, Cyla would be trying to run the farm, so maybe that's for the best. He is good at running the farm."

"And he could leave if he wanted because I'd free him in a second if he asked me to," Temar added. "He said that he felt guilty and that he needed to feel like he was making up for having left me vulnerable. After a year of fighting with Shan and Cyla, he might be willing to give up the guilt and ask to have the slave sentence cut short." Temar gave Shan a look full of both affection and a weary sort of frustration.

Before Shan could answer, Temar pushed himself up. "But I want to get your gift, so stay here, and I'll be right back." Temar jogged up the stairs, and Verly was left with Shan. He didn't know Shan all that well, and honestly, he found it a little uncomfortable to look at a man who looked so much like the lover who had used Verly hard and left him broke down at the side of the road.

Shan cleared his throat. "We were surprised you came."

"Why?"

"We know that Natalie's people sent her because they think she's spying, but she said that your government would ignore us as unimportant. She didn't think you'd come, and when you sent word that you were landing, she had some rather creative solutions planned."

Verly thought about his welcoming party from Naite and Natalie. "Yeah, I can imagine."

"So, why are you here?" Shan asked.

Verly leaned back and tried to figure out Shan's game. If Natalie told Naite, she would have told the ambassadors. "My people aren't that forgiving of mistakes, and I've made some large ones."

"We've all made large mistakes."

"Mine cost lives."

Shan took a slow breath, and Verly wondered how deep he was digging his own grave. "I've made choices. I've stood by while things happened that I questioned—including watching Temar sentenced to slavery. But I was so afraid of being arrogant that I didn't speak up, or in the case of Temar, I spoke and spoke and spoke, and I chose such poor words that I didn't convince anyone. We all have pasts. Luckily, there's forgiveness."

Verly pursed his lips. Maybe on Livre forgiveness existed. Most of the universe had a longer memory.

"Here we go," Temar called as he came down the stairs. He had a beautiful piece of glass with colors swirling within colors. For a second, the vivid shades of blues and greens distracted Verly, and he didn't see the delicate shape, the curved wings and narrow body. "I know it doesn't replace flying, but...."

"It's stunning," Verly said as he reached for the delicate shuttle. He'd never owned such a beautiful piece of art.

"I'm working with glass again, but I don't seem to be doing anything particularly useful," Temar said with a self-deprecating shrug.

"I love it."

Temar might have been a powerful man, but he offered up a shy smile. "I'm glad," he said softly. "I know you gave up a lot to come here."

"I didn't give up anything that I'll miss," Verly said. It was a small lie, but maybe if he told himself that lie every day he could make it true. Today it certainly felt a little more true than yesterday. Temar rested a hand on Verly's arm, and Verly focused on the cool glass in his hands.

"I assume your people would like reports on your time here," Temar said, and the warmth in Verly's heart retreated.

"Yes," Verly said. If these people refused to give him access to a communication station, he didn't have any way to force the issue. "I don't think they expect much out of me, but they will expect some communication."

Temar glanced over toward Shan. "Can you run him over to the relay station?"

Shan nodded. "Easily. Are we going to talk about what he's going to report?"

"We should," Temar said. For all their warmth and easygoing nature, these two were still the dangerous ambassadors. They might give him access to communication, but they weren't fool enough to give him free rein. Verly only hoped that same caution applied to the two AFP agents as well. Verly didn't have a mission here other than to get out of his commanding officers' sight—the same wasn't true of those two women.

chapter
nine

NAITE TIGHTENED the connection between the water tank and the irrigation pipe as he watched Verly cross the dusty field. He carefully picked his way around the tender plants, but he didn't look local. Most locals had skin darkened by the sun. A few last remnants of the fair-skinned genome survived in people like Temar, Cyla, and Lilian Freeland, but Verly clearly didn't share that gene pool.

His broad shoulders and square jaw didn't have any of their delicacy. He was much more masculine than that family tree. Naite had trouble believing Temar had threatened the man because Verly looked more like the sort that issued threats rather than enduring them. He didn't have the muscle mass of a worker, but he had strength in those long limbs.

The memory of Verly's legs wrapped around him so tight that they left bruises distracted Naite. He had to resist the urge to press a thumb against the tender flesh.

"Hey," Verly offered when he got close. Naite grunted and waited for the man to catch the hint and go away. Clearly Verly was not that bright because he leaned against the water tank right next to him. Workers were off in the east fields today, so only two people were working—Hannah was replacing some nails on the barn, and Kibwe walked the edge of the field.

Naite finished the connection and then set the water release for the line. He didn't have anything to say, at least nothing Verly wanted to hear. For some time, Naite worked in silence, his back getting more and more tense as he waited for Verly to either say something or move on.

"So, does that control the whole farm?" Verly finally asked. He ran his hand over the collar of the tank, a rotating piece that could turn and then connect to any of the various irrigation lines that ended here.

"Yep."

"The scientists back home assumed that Livre would have returned to the desert by now. They said there weren't enough resources for the surviving colonists to have maintained food and water supplies, but I have to say that you guys are pretty damn capable."

Naite grunted again.

"The slavery system… that would shock them, though. Temar says you're serving a term right now."

Naite stood and eyed Verly coldly.

"Of course, if that's true, then your slavery system is nothing like the sorts of slavery I know from history or from the AFP."

"The AFP have slaves?" Naite didn't know why he was surprised, but he was. He'd gotten the impression that the universe was more about manipulating each other rather than coming out and being direct. All Shan and Temar's stories suggested that, anyway.

Verly gave one of his crooked smiles, like he'd earned some victory just by getting Naite to talk. Naite rolled his eyes.

"The AFP don't call it slavery," Verly explained, "but if children can't afford food, the AFP will feed and house them, and record every coin spent. They don't believe that the government should tax one person to pay for another's care, so every coin spent has to be repaid. If a child is orphaned at three, then when they reach adulthood, they have to repay every credit spent on a piece of clothing, food, the roof over their heads, even their education."

Naite couldn't say he approved of that. On Livre, people took care of their own. If a person got old, they lived on the farm where they'd worked, and family and friends cared for them. If a child lost his parents, then someone else stepped in, either a family member or some friend, and whoever owned the land where they lived would make some allowance to help care for their needs. Despite his general sense of unease, Naite wouldn't go passing judgment on other people and their system.

"A person should pay his own way. I wouldn't ask that of a child, but if others do, I wouldn't call it slavery." If Naite said that to Shan, he would expect a lot of moralizing and unproductive discussion of God to follow. Verly's mouth quirked into a frown, but he took the time to think Naite's words through. Between Cyla and Shan, Naite was about fed up with people who dismissed him out of hand, so he appreciated that gesture.

Finally, Verly asked, "And if the state chooses to send the child to an expensive school to train to be an assassin? Should the child pay for that?"

"They have schools for that?" Naite couldn't believe it. Maybe Verly was trying to provoke Naite to get some sort of response out of him.

"Several," Verly agreed. "The breakaway planets have a strange definition of education. The PA may have certain branches of the military that have training in carrying out executive orders, but they certainly don't send people below the age of majority to school specifically to learn that particular skill."

"But you both train assassins," Naite pointed out dryly. If someone ended up dead, Naite doubted it mattered to them whether a sixteen-year-old orphan or a thirty-year-old soldier did the killing. That said, Naite certainly did find one more objectionable than the other.

"Both sides do a lot of things," Verly said.

"And you're telling me this because?" Crossing his arms, Naite waited to see how far Verly would take this streak of honesty. Natalie had told Naite to expect the PA representative to show up with a lot of lies and slick talk. So far she'd been wrong across the board. Verly struck Naite as a man who cared more about actions than slick talk and who tended toward the truth. That's why he'd refused to listen when Natalie had tried telling him about Verly's past. Naite had a past of his own, and he sure as hell didn't want others judging him on it. The least he could do was extend that same courtesy to others.

Verly shrugged. "Why wouldn't I?"

That sort of glibness annoyed Naite. "It'll be awkward when you go back."

Verly's face lost all expression, and his skin pinked up. Naite didn't figure embarrassment had anything to do with it, so that left anger. Interesting. Verly didn't retreat, though. That was both interesting and annoying. Naite didn't like it when emotions lurked under the surface. He worried about what he couldn't see.

Naite decided to poke a little more. "Natalie insists that your people rig elections, interfere with local politics, tell people how to live their lives, and force them to send their children to schools that teach things people don't want their children learning."

Again, Verly seemed to think about that. "Lots of that is probably true," he finally agreed. "But we don't kill people for being gay, force our religion on others, turn children into weapons, or make people disappear in the middle of the night, so I think we're better than the alternative."

"Natalie's not a big fan of her own side either," Naite agreed. They stared at each other, and the darker emotions pressed close. Since he didn't have anything more to say, he headed back toward the bunkhouse. The last set of storms had loosened some of the overhead netting, and he needed to grab some tools and head up to the top of the valley walls.

More than that, he needed a little distance. It'd been a long time since he took a man out back, and most of the time, he chose partners from other farms so he never had to deal with the aftereffects. He shouldn't have fucked Verly. That had been so stupid that it was something Shan would have done. Well, except that Shan was more the type to deny himself any sex for years as he pretended to be a priest. Idiot. Naite could have told him that was the wrong path.

"So, what are we working on today?" Verly followed after him like some sort of half-wit apprentice. Naite graced Verly with his least friendly expression. Most men fled at the look. Verly's crooked smile made a reappearance.

Naite had any number of responses that he could've given, but he chose to walk away. It was the most polite option.

Verly kept on with his attempts at conversation. "Cyla was complaining that she couldn't find you this morning."

"Good for her." The last thing Naite needed was to add a dose of Cyla to his already fairly crappy day.

"She's an interesting one."

Frustration made Naite a little more honest than he intended. "She's a sharp-tongued bitch who can't pull her head out of her ass long enough to see where she's going," Naite corrected him. Maybe Naite should give her more credit; after all, she had some difficult knocks in life. Still, the woman made it a personal mission to annoy Naite, and he did not like to be annoyed.

"Like I said, interesting."

Naite grunted.

"So, are you two doing some dysfunctional courting display, or do you simply hate each other?"

"We hate each other. Not that it's any of your business. Laying down together once doesn't give you any rights over who I might choose as a partner any other night," Naite warned him. Sleeping with Verly had been a mistake. The man didn't have the good sense to go away.

"I agree. It's absolutely none of my business. I wanted to make sure I wasn't ground zero for any breakup."

"You won't be. I'm smart enough to know to avoid someone with that many issues." Naite made sure to give Verly a meaningful look that implied that Cyla wasn't the only one with issues. That took some of the shine off his smile. Naite headed back for the bunkhouse. Considering that Verly had a perfectly good room in the main house and that he didn't have any chores to complete, Naite wasn't sure why he was even bothering to come out here. Naite didn't plan on asking for any more help in the fields. It was not like Verly's hands would be able to stand up to that kind of work.

Instead of catching a clue, Verly continued to follow Naite. "So, do you want to fuck again tonight?"

Again, Naite stopped and turned. Men typically didn't ask for a second night. Naite suspected that had less to do with his sexual prowess than it did with his habit of growling at his partners two seconds after he was finished. Most people preferred sweet talk, and Naite understood that full well. That's exactly why he growled.

Naite took a deep breath. "There are days you don't come across as particularly bright."

Verly's smile returned full force. "Oh, you have no idea how not bright I can be. So, is that a yes? I would love to return that very large favor you gave me last night." Verly arched his back a little, enough to let Naite know he was still feeling the aftereffects of that hard fucking.

Naite raised his eyebrows. As much as he generally avoided going out back with men, he definitely avoided spreading his legs for any of them. Actually, he couldn't remember the last time someone even suggested it. Crossing his arms, he gave a cold look. "What makes you think I'm interested?"

"Because I'm very good, and because you really enjoyed it last night."

"You're assuming a lot."

"I'm assuming that when a man grunts through an orgasm and makes a face like he's sucked a sour lemon that means he enjoyed it."

Naite studied Verly up and down. This man broke every rule Naite knew about how people treated each other. He was not particularly fond of walking on new territory, and this was new territory. "You're annoying me," Naite warned.

"And yet you still haven't said no."

"You have a very high opinion of yourself."

"Actually, I don't," Verly said with a shrug. "However, after last night I think you have a very high opinion of how good sex is between us. So when you say no strings, no games, just sex...."

Naite narrowed his eyes and searched for some sign that Verly was being dishonest. The fact was he had enjoyed the sex. A lot. But enjoying the sex didn't mean he was ready for all the tangled emotions that normally came with sex that happened with the same person more than once.

When Naite thought about Shan and Temar, he was happy for his brother. Those two might be giant pains in the ass, but they deserved some happiness. Naite couldn't imagine himself in that same position, though. He wasn't the sort of man that got all soft and dewy-eyed every time he looked at someone. He didn't do relationships. "Just sex?"

Verly held both hands up. "Absolutely. Just sex."

Naite weighed his options. His prick wanted to pound into Verly right now, but Naite generally listened to his bigger head. That head had some real concerns. Caught between two desires, Naite finally sighed. "Fine. I'll meet you by the pomegranate trees."

The second the words came out of his mouth, Naite half regretted them. "Don't think this is anything other than sex."

"I don't."

"Good." Naite started back toward the bunkhouse. He needed some space and some time and possibly some alcohol. Either that, or he needed to get his head screwed on straight and cancel this meeting. Even though Verly had gotten his answer, he continued to trail after, that same stupid, crooked grin on his face. Naite fantasized about grabbing Verly and slamming him into something until that grin vanished. Unfortunately, his cock hardened as he thought about where the fantasy might go from there.

"So what are we doing today?" Verly asked the question with the same bright enthusiasm.

"Well, you seem to be busy annoying me."

Verly's grin grew wider. "I do have some talent at that. I could annoy you more by giving you Cyla's message."

"No."

"You people do tend to be direct. That was the first thing I liked about Temar. He said exactly what he was thinking. Compared to people back home, he was unique, but I'm starting to think blunt honesty might be a cultural trait." Verly matched Naite's steps, which annoyed Naite as much as the endless conversation. He liked it when he could use his long stride to either leave people behind or make them trot after him. People gave up quicker that way. Verly matched him step for step.

"Do you mind if I ask a question?"

"Yep."

Naite smiled as that caused Verly to pause. In the moment of silence, Naite walked a little faster. Just because he planned to fuck the man didn't mean they needed to have long conversations. If Verly wanted to talk, he'd picked the wrong Polli brother. Talking things to death was Shan's game, not Naite's. Naite preferred action, and the only action he wanted from Verly would have to wait until dark under the pomegranate trees.

chapter
t e n

WHEN NAITE started climbing up the world's narrowest path, a path that led up the side of the cliff face, a cliff with no guardrail—Verly finally took the hint. If he wasn't flying, he wanted to keep both feet close enough to the ground to avoid dying when he fell. That didn't mean he wasn't annoyed. He was finally making some inroads into the mystery that was Naite Polli, and part of him worried that Naite would take the time apart to repair some of his defenses.

With his primary path of attack blocked, Verly fell back on his favorite strategy. Flank and surprise. He needed information on Naite, and he had a pretty good idea who on this farm might crack like an overheated engine coil.

Verly headed back to the main house. Walking in without announcing himself still made him uncomfortable, but that might have something to do with Rula always hovering in the background. This time, however, everyone had abandoned the house. Shan and Temar had gone to town to discuss the Blue Hope issue with Lilian Freeland who sounded like she was the real power behind the elected officials. Cyla had vanished along with the two AFP women.

With nothing else he could do, Verly pulled out a datapad uploaded with background information on Livre and settled on the sofa in the front room. Bars of sunlight came in through the striped fabric window covers, and Verly shifted so the warm lines fell across his legs. After years of being in space, the natural light felt odd. Sure, he'd spent the required time in reproduced sunlight, but it wasn't the same.

Until Naite came down or Cyla showed up, Verly decided to read all the government documents he could find. The first settlers had mostly signed on for short-term contracts. Most planned to spend five to ten years working the new world and then retire on a core planet.

The Polli ancestor had been an engineer. Pulling up Frente Polli's official documents, Verly wondered if the man was as tough and stubborn as his descendants. Verly figured the man for Naite's great-grandfather. Frente had once held one of the shortest contracts with three years required until he earned his bonus. That would have put him back on a core world before the war, but he extended his stay.

Verly toyed with the idea of asking for permission to access the colony records so he could figure out why Frente Polli made that choice. Having taken command psychology courses, he knew he was displacing his curiosity about Naite, but at this point, he figured he had a better chance of understanding Frente Polli than Naite. That long-dead ancestor had degrees in mining engineering and geology, so he could have found a high-paying job on a developed planet if he'd chosen to go home at the end of his contract. He'd been born on the same planet as Verly's mother, a woman Verly barely remembered. She'd died laying mines to protect the border from AFP raid ships.

With nothing more pressing to worry about, Verly spent the rest of the morning and the early afternoon reading about those early colonists. He found seven Freelands in the rosters and a single woman named Gazer who listed two of the Freelands as immediate family.

"Look who we have here."

Verly looked up to see Natalie standing in the door. Verly sat up, slightly horrified that he hadn't heard her come in. She closed the front door behind her.

"No Rula?" Verly asked. He worried about a soldier less than he worried about this woman with her overly perfect smile and eyes that never stopped scanning the area.

"Cyla is introducing her to some of the neighbors."

Verly glanced over, and the angle of the sun suggested hours had passed. "Is that where you've been?"

Natalie's smile was cold and predatory. "Are you keeping track of my comings and goings?"

"I can't say I am." Verly put his datapad to one side, and not for the first time, he wished the ambassadors had allowed him to bring weapons. He might have followed that rule, but right now he doubted Natalie had.

"Funny. I got the feeling that the PA had a vested interest in making sure that we didn't get a trade treaty with Livre."

Verly shifted on the sofa and studied the woman. "What 'we' are you talking about?"

She gave the barest hint of a twitch and moved farther into the room. "I'm not here for the AFP." She raised her chin, clearly ready to fight about this. Verly hoped she only wanted a verbal fight because he might have a good sixty pounds and six or eight inches of height on her, but he didn't give himself good odds against an assassin.

"Do they know that?"

"Does the PA know you're fucking one of the local slaves?"

Verly smiled. "I doubt they'd worry much about Naite's honor once they met him. I may not understand their slave system, but I certainly don't think it looks anything like my definition of slavery."

Natalie narrowed her eyes.

"But to answer your question, yes. They do know I'm fucking him. Temar approved a message that included that bit of trivia along with some operational details. Although technically, I'm getting fucked by," he pointed out. Verly had the feeling that it was going to take a little more trust building before he got to do any fucking. He was looking forward to the chance to prove that Naite could trust him in that sort of intimate situation, but if Naite was anything like some of the other emotionally closed off and damaged soldiers Verly had known, it would be a while.

"So you are reporting to them."

Verly shrugged. "It's better than burning those bridges. My reports are going to be rather limited. I can offer a report on the daily duties of a farm worker or offer a rather detailed report on Naite's rather considerable sexual skills," Verly said with a cocky grin.

Clearly Natalie didn't have the best sense of humor. She studied him with all the warmth of a schoolgirl getting ready to dissect a snake.

"I'm in a position where I can get away with sending them very little useful intel. If you aren't sending valuable information, your people will replace you," Verly pointed out.

"Assuming they can."

Verly leaned back and waited for some sort of explanation for that comment, but Natalie didn't seem the sharing sort.

"The breakaway planets aren't known for their patience."

Natalie gave him a long, searching look. "And they aren't known for trying to steal from younger planets and sending the resources back to the central worlds either."

"I think both sides played their games."

Natalie's eyes narrowed more. This woman was drowning in paranoia, but then again, if she'd been hiding a homosexual relationship with Rula and trying to navigate the military ranks of the AFP as a woman, she might have some justification. Verly wished she would give him a chance to show that he didn't want to be an enemy, but there was a lot of water under that bridge. Besides, he didn't appreciate that she'd tried to tell Naite about his own dark past.

After staring at him for an uncomfortably long time, Natalie moved to one of the chairs and leaned against the arm, her body still coiled. "They did. But I'll admit that I didn't expect a soldier to recognize that."

"Because we're all idiots?"

"Because you're in the ships. You float over everything, and it's hard to see the truth from the deck of a battleship."

Verly could debate that, but he doubted an argument would improve their ability to share a planet. And this wasn't the sort of well-developed, overpopulated planet that two people could share without running into each other.

"Were you on the ground?"

"Perhaps." She didn't put a lot of effort into denying it, but her body grew unnaturally still.

Verly took a wild guess. "You're from Oneida. You trained there." It would make sense that if she'd come through that version of hell she'd have a high rank, high enough to hide her illegal relationship.

Her voice grew soft. "This is dangerous territory."

"I know," Verly answered. "But do our pasts really matter here?"

"The butcher of Minga wants to be friends." She placed her hand over her heart and offered him a look of mock adoration. "That gives me warm, fuzzy feelings."

Verly felt that same old punch in his gut at the mention of that planet, but he'd practiced grinning through that particular pain for a long time now. "I'm starting to understand why you needed a new start. I'm guessing you don't make friends easily." She didn't react, but Verly didn't make the mistake of assuming she would show her emotions. "This is a new world with new ideas and new people who don't care about your war."

"And do you care about it?" Natalie demanded.

"I don't want the AFP here. I care about that," Verly said honestly. "I don't think anyone has a right to train children for their own wars."

"And your schools don't fill you with righteous indignation for anyone who chooses to be different?" Natalie gave a mirthless laugh.

"I don't want the PA down here either," Verly admitted. "I don't think that PA laws work for this world."

"Capital punishment, slavery, families making their own choices about what they want for their children… that breaks every rule the Planetary Alliance holds dear."

"A planet full of homosexual relationships, churches that don't use religion as a weapon, and a belief that people shouldn't be allowed to starve. The AFP would be devoutly offended," Verly shot back with just as much unctuous sweetness as she was using on him.

For a second, she blinked at him, clearly surprised. Then the moment passed, and Natalie settled down onto the seat of the chair. "Yes, they would be. They'd want to reform the planet, only I think that Temar scared them a little."

"He scared my officers a lot," Verly admitted. "They couldn't get a psych profile on him."

"Ironic." She leaned forward, resting her elbows on her knees. "I can't get a psych profile on you. I don't trust you, not you or your judgment."

Verly nodded. His own government had busted him from senior commander down to a lieutenant commander—three whole grades and the loss of every bit of respect he'd earned. He couldn't expect this woman to offer him some show of faith. "I'll admit that I have trouble trusting you. You loved a woman, but you went along with a government that tortures other people who make the same choice. You can see why that makes me wonder how you define right and wrong."

Natalie leaned back in her chair. "It's simple. If it protects Rula, if it protects both of us, it's right. Do anything to make me think that you're a threat, and that's a wrong that I'll have to correct." Her smile made it very clear she'd enjoy doing that correcting.

"You're a cold bitch."

"You have no idea," she offered. "I wouldn't hesitate to put a bullet between your eyes." Her gaze traveled up and down the length of Verly's body before settling near his crotch. "And I wouldn't hesitate to put one between your legs and leave you to bleed out." With those closing words and one final smile, she stood and headed for the stairs. Verly had to fight an urge to cross his legs. Threatening to shoot a man in the balls might not be original, but it made her point.

"Is Oneida something I should know about?"

Sucking in a startled breath, Verly twisted around to see Naite leaning against the door to the kitchen. Clearly Verly had been on his own in that surveillance shuttle far too long. He needed to pay more attention to his surroundings.

"You heard?"

Naite walked in and dropped wearily into the chair Natalie had recently abandoned. "I saw her coming in, and I wanted to make sure you two didn't kill each other."

"I don't think I have a chance in hell of killing her."

Naite snorted. "I think you could; I don't want you to try."

"I guess I should be complimented that someone still thinks I'm important enough to be a risk. The lack of security around here sometimes makes me feel a little neglected. I expected guards and restrictions." Verly made a joke out of it, but Naite didn't understand Natalie if he believed that.

"What makes you think I'm not your guard?"

"Because you keep trying to get rid of me," Verly pointed out. "If you were ordered to keep me under control, you'd use your very impressive talents in bed as leverage to make me play nice."

Naite laughed, but after a mere second, he stopped and looked at Verly in horror. "Sandcat prick on a stick. Tell me that does not happen."

"What? Fucking the enemy to get an advantage?" Verly asked. From Naite's expression, that's exactly what he meant. "It happens all the time, Naite. If you use an attractive agent, it's called a honeypot."

"You people are fucked-up. Hell, you make Ben sound downright sane."

"Ben?"

"The asshole who raped Temar. He's dead now. So if I were you, I wouldn't be bragging about how you people treat sex like a weapon."

Verly nodded. Naite was an interesting man. He was uncomfortable getting a compliment from a lover, but he could comfortably have a conversation about rapists being killed and assassins.

If Verly were a psych officer, he could write interesting reports on the people of Livre. He wondered if the people here were all shaped by this harsh desert world into some alien psychopathy or if Naite and Temar and Shan were particularly strange, even on this world.

"You know, sometimes you act like a farm worker, and other times I can definitely tell you're a council member with a good deal of power." Verly gave Naite his best grin. "It's a little sexy."

The look Naite gave him in return made it clear that Naite questioned his sanity.

Clearing his throat, Verly changed the topic back to a safer subject, like assassination. "So, Oneida. Leadership theory says that a good leader can adapt to different situations. But a chaotic situation is the best way to get people to accept quick change and charismatic leaders. Put people in a panic—blow up a spaceport or release a bioweapon—and the population will embrace the most top-down military dictatorship you can find. If you are the person standing out as a pillar of strength when the world crumbles, the people are yours."

"And that happened on Oneida?"

"During the war, they were the center of some of the worst fighting. Their entire capital was leveled when a battle cruiser took a full nuclear hit in orbit and crashed into the heart of the city. After that, they started turning out some of the most vicious, unrelenting fighters in the war. After the official truce, they accused the PA of a number of atrocities including a biological attack."

"Were you guilty?"

"Personally? No. I've never been near the planet. Was the PA involved in the attacks?" Verly sighed. "The first one or two, maybe. Probably. But after everyone figured out what was happening on the ground, the PA didn't want to add fuel to the fire. The rumor is that when the PA backed off, Oneida engineered their own terrorism."

"Engineered?"

Turning away, Verly pushed the edge of the curtain aside. Workers quietly moved about their business, laughing and chatting as they walked. A woman sat in the shade of the bunkhouse, her feet up on a barrel as she worked something in her hands, and two men ushered goats from one pen to another.

"They wanted the people of Oneida angry—the word is that the AFP had units dress as terrorists and attack, both on Oneida and on other planets. They attacked their own. It's a way of making sure people are afraid and willing to accept the dictatorship that offers protection. It's an old game, Naite, and one the AFP plays to win. Or at least the upper leadership does. They've limited information so much that I'm not even sure their upper-level officers are aware of how commonly this strategy is used. State-controlled vid service certainly doesn't bring up the possibility."

Naite wrinkled his nose. "And here I thought Ben was as evil as they got."

Verly shrugged. "Oh, you have no idea what evil looks like. No matter where orphans are from, if they have certain talents or if they are beautiful enough to qualify as a honeypot, they're sent to Oneida. Oneida trains spies that will perform any sex act, any assassination, any act of terrorism in order to defend their world. Oneida is a code word for a type of spy that strikes fear in the heart of wise men. If I got into a fight with an agent trained at Oneida, I would not survive."

Naite stood, and Verly abandoned his view out the window to watch Naite get up and cross the room. Having a man as large as Naite Polli hover over you was not comfortable, but Verly struggled to control that instinct to retreat to a safe distance. "And you think this Natalie is one of those?"

"I thought you didn't care about our pasts."

"I don't give a fuck about what you did. I'm asking about one particular kind of crazy that you people have going on up there." Naite poked his thumb toward the sky. "And I'm asking for your reasons for thinking Natalie is one of these assassins. I will then feel free to ignore anything you say that I don't happen to agree with."

Verly took a deep breath as he thought about that. His gut told him she was. She had a way of moving, a way of always positioning herself in the most defensible corner, a wariness that set his inner alarms off. "She's suspicious."

Naite snorted. "She's not the sort of trusting fool to invite home the first soldier who's nice. That happens to sound more like common sense."

"She clears a room before she comes into it. She keeps close to lines of retreat. She has a control over her body that most people don't—there's not a wasted movement in her whole body, no nervous habits or tics."

"And that makes her an assassin?" Naite clearly didn't believe him.

Verly shifted so he was squared off against Naite, but he didn't stand up. "You run your thumbs over things," Verly said, nodding toward Naite's large hands. Even now he had the fingers of his right hand shoved under his belt, and his thumb rubbed his shirt fabric. "Every time you're uncomfortable, you find something to touch. Shan mumbles, and yes, he's probably praying. He also tends to rock side to side. Temar twists his fingers like he's twirling some invisible stick. Cyla...." Verly huffed, "Don't even get me started on Cyla. That woman has so many nervous tics that it's not funny. She's hurting, Naite. She's seriously hurting. And Rula... every time she gets uncomfortable, she goes ramrod straight, like some officer is going to come in and do an inspection.

"We all have these nervous tics. Natalie doesn't. She has perfect control over her body. Every move is graceful. Every step calculated. That isn't a casual skill. I would never start a fight with her because I don't doubt for a second that she could kill me." Verly stopped. Staring up at Naite, he didn't know how to convince the man to see the world the way he saw it. For a time, Naite frowned as though mentally reviewing memories he didn't generally like.

"Huh." Naite scratched his arm and looked nonplused before he turned toward the door.

"Naite?"

"I've got work," Naite said as he headed out.

Well, crap. The tenuous connection between them strained. Naite didn't want to believe him, and right now Verly didn't care if Naite believed or not. He didn't want to give Naite an excuse to back away from this relationship. Tossing his datapad to the side, Verly chased after the man. "Hey, wait up. I'll give you a hand."

chapter
eleven

NAITE DISLIKED this whole discussion. He'd spent his youth living with a monster, and he didn't want to think that Natalie might be a variation on that same personality. He didn't want to think of a predator using her bright smile to get close to Cyla. But he'd seen Natalie when she'd threatened to shoot Verly. That had not been hyperbole or some empty threat. She meant it.

Verly called after him, offering to help, and Naite barely suppressed a growl. Or maybe he didn't suppress it. Hannah took one look at him, gathered up the leather strapping she was repairing, and fled the area. Now that was a smart woman. Clearly Rich didn't have her intelligence, because he leaned against the rail fence and gawked like Naite and Verly were some traveling show.

"You got some work to do?" Naite demanded.

Rich grinned at him, his white teeth a sharp contrast to his dark skin. "Nope," he said cheerfully. He even had the nerve to look back at Verly and then back to Naite. "I'm good."

Naite gritted his teeth. He could assign Rich another job, but that would be retaliation, and Naite struggled hard to be fair. Fury crawling up his spine, he walked away.

"Man, you have balls, I'll give you that," Rich said behind him, and Naite assumed those words were for Verly who still chased after him. Idiot. The last thing Naite needed was another person poking his issues. Hell, one good poke and Verly was going to get a fucking he wouldn't forget. While they both might enjoy that, Naite didn't like losing control.

Behind him, fast footsteps thumped against the hard-packed ground, and Naite angled off toward the base of the cliff. He'd planned to do the rest of the netting repairs tomorrow when he was fresh, but that didn't mean he couldn't climb up and take a little time off in the shade of some rock. Naite started up the narrow path, his feet close to the cliff face as he walked the dangerous ledge. He made it to the first hairpin bend before turning and looking back. He expected to see Verly standing on the ground, looking up with an expression of horror.

Naite felt a hot flash of some unidentifiable emotion as Verly worked his way up the path. Both his hands clung to the rocks, and his expression was a riot of determination and terror, but he moved steadily up the path. Shit.

"If you start up this, no one can help you down. You finish the trail, or you fall off," Naite warned before Verly got too high. Verly looked up, and for a second, there was a flash of that crooked grin. Then Verly glanced back down toward the farm, and the expression vanished.

"Sounds like life," Verly said, his voice thin and high-pitched.

"It's your funeral," Naite said. Verly shot him an odd look, but Naite strangled the guilt and headed up the path. He could have used the bike path to make most of this trip, but he'd chosen this old trail specifically to earn a little privacy. If Verly fell off it, Naite figured that some of the blame was his. "You can use the turn to get yourself situated and head back down," Naite called, and then he moved into the second leg of the trail.

Moving as quickly as he could without losing his footing, Naite made his way to the top of the valley. The valley was a long slit that had once been one of the rock mountains that littered the planet. Their ancestors had lopped off the top and then used massive machines to carve out the valley before filling it with dirt. It meant a long climb up and out, but once Naite got to the top, there was a gentle slope down toward the mountain. Loose rocks and pipe plants certainly threatened ankles, but sandcats and sandrats wouldn't come up onto the rocks where they couldn't burrow into the sand to hide from the hunting birds that fed on them.

For long minutes, Naite stood at the top of the valley, breathing hard as he listened for a sign of Verly coming up the trail or a terrified scream as he fell off it. Neither came. Naite's heart was pounding hard, and he took a few deep breaths to calm himself as he walked slowly out toward the desert. The sun was dropping, and the windwood trees shivered as the evening breezes blew. The thin, winding branches created a maze of shadows that Naite crossed as he worked his way closer to the desert. The silence up here often calmed him when nothing else could.

The stillness of the desert seeped into his heart and gave him enough peace for him to look at his own thoughts. As much as he hated to admit it, Verly was right that Natalie had a different set of physical reactions. Naite had chalked that up to growing up on another world, but when Verly laid all the evidence out, it did seem like they had allowed a sandcat into their house.

Only it wasn't Naite's house, and he didn't have a right to disinvite anyone. He could take it to the council, but disliking a woman's past didn't seem fair, especially given that she'd called Verly the butcher of Minga. If he tried to have Natalie sent off-world, he suspected she would retaliate by taking Verly down with her. Verly might be a pain in the ass, but he wasn't a butcher, and it bothered Naite to think of the man living in a universe where that's how people saw him.

Maybe he'd killed the people who had taken him hostage and raped him. In that case, Naite was more than supportive of a little human butchery. Some human beings deserved to end up sandrat food. Naite's memory summoned the image of Ben Gratu crying, begging for help as he clawed at the rats that clung to his legs. That morphed into an older image, one constructed out of imagination more than reality.

"Fuck." Sitting on a boulder rubbed smooth by blowing sands, Naite pushed all the thoughts aside and buried his face in his hands as he tried to simply feel the stillness of the desert, the softly blowing winds and the rustle of the windwood branches rubbing against each other.

"Remind me to never do that again."

Naite twisted around, and Verly stood behind him, his brown hair dark with sweat and his skin paler than usual.

With a huge sigh, Verly sat on a smaller boulder next to Naite. "That is an unpleasant path." With that, Verly leaned back on his hands and studied the Livre desert.

Naite stood. "What are you doing here?"

When Verly gave him one of those boyish grins, Naite felt a new flash of hot emotion.

"If I wanted company, I would have fucking invited you," Naite growled.

"You didn't uninvite me."

Naite closed his eyes and struggled with his own emotions. The sharp scent of the desert and the musk of the windwood trees soothed him. This was his sanctuary, but Verly had followed him, even here.

"You're playing with fire," Naite said without opening his eyes.

"I'm a big boy. I can take care of myself," Verly said with the sort of confidence that grated across Naite's nerves. He didn't want Verly confident. He wanted him fleeing, retreating, running to the bunkhouse to complain about Naite's unpredictable temper and his horrible after-sex manners. He wanted something familiar.

A hand brushed across Naite's shoulder, and Naite's eyes flew open and his heart raced. Grabbing Verly's shirt, he yanked the man around and slammed him into the boulder where Naite had been sitting. "What the fuck do you want from me?"

Verly lay still... either that or Naite had driven the wind out of him. Naite leaned closer, trapping Verly against the rock. Even then, Verly lay quiet, and Naite put his hands on either side of Verly's head and leaned in so close that he was practically lying on Verly, their cocks pressed together. "What the fuck do you want?" he demanded again.

Verly reached up and grabbed Naite's shirt. "I want Naite. I want to know the real you."

"No. No, you fucking don't."

"Oh, I fucking do." With that, Verly yanked hard. Naite hadn't expected the move, and Verly got one hand around the back of Naite's neck and pulled him close enough for a bruising kiss. With a growl, Naite pulled back, but Verly held on so that Naite pulled him up.

Naite grabbed Verly by the neck. His hands were large enough to wrap around Verly's neck, but the idiot raised his chin and waited.

"Go away," he ordered, and he gave Verly a shove back toward the path. The second he let go, Verly rocked back on his heels and then pressed closer to Naite. Grabbing one of Naite's arms, he pulled him in for a hungry kiss. Lips and teeth and tongue all assaulted Naite, and while he tried to retreat, before Naite knew what he was doing, he opened his mouth and counterattacked. Catching Verly's lower lip between his teeth, he gave a hard nip as a warning, and then he took charge of the kiss, devouring Verly's mouth.

Maneuvering Verly back to the boulder, Naite pinned him against the rock. Verly responded by opening his mouth farther and digging his fingers into Naite's hips so hard that pain sang along Naite's nerves.

"Fuck yes," Verly cried when Naite thrust forward, grinding their cocks together. Naite pressed forward again, his prick hard and aching. Verly writhed, shifting his hands until he caught Naite's neck and pulled him down again. Tongues attacked, and Naite's lips grew warm from the force of the bruises. This felt right. Sex. Simple. Hard. Uncomplicated. Sex. Naite panted as he jerked his hips against Verly's groin. And that was a little too much pain.

Turning his head to the side, Verly gasped out, "You're going to break me."

"Good," Naite responded, and he nipped at the arch of Verly's neck. This time Verly thrust up. Naite smirked. Now Verly had that twisted and pained expression of ultimate bliss. While Verly was temporarily distracted, Naite pulled at the buttons of his shirt. Naite wanted skin. He wanted to see those small, hard nipples, the line of muscle running down Verly's stomach, the sparse hair that led to the belly button and then to Naite's ultimate goal.

The buttons popped open, and Naite spread his fingers out over the warm flesh. Verly pressed up into the touch, soft moans starting. His head rolled first to one side and then the other as he continued to thrust up into Naite's body. Leaning in, Naite let his lips brush across Verly's jaw and then down his neck. Pressing his head backward, Verly presented the arch of his throat, and Naite found the soft spot at the base of the neck and sucked hard.

"Fuck! Oh fuck." Verly's legs locked around Naite, trapping him, and Naite sucked harder. Reaching between their bodies, Naite fumbled at the zippers and buttons, but before he could figure them out, Verly was pushing him away. Naite's control nearly snapped, but he stepped back, only to have Verly desperately open his own pants. Verly's cock pressed up against his underwear, and Naite grabbed the pants, underwear and all and yanked it down. Verly started kicking to get the loose pants to slide down over his boots, but the second Naite had opened his own pants, he stepped back in, pinning Verly with hands on his thighs.

Closing his eyes, Verly gave a long grunt and tried to thrust up, but Naite enjoyed this. He liked seeing a lover pinned down, hungry, needing. All the dark emotions Naite kept carefully contained pushed up and out, and Naite pressed into Verly's thighs until white islands appeared around each of his fingers. Tomorrow Verly would have ten perfect bruises.

"God yes. More. Fuck me, dammit," Verly demanded.

"Without gakka? Not a chance in hell."

Verly gave a pitiful moan.

Naite pressed close and wrapped his hand around both their cocks at once. Verly nearly bucked up off the rock. His legs tightened around the back of Naite's legs. This man wasn't asking for sex, he was demanding it, and Naite felt the last of his doubts vanish under a sandstorm of lust.

Verly stretched up and caught the back of Naite's neck and pulled him in for another kiss, only this time it was slow. This time the heat built, the teeth nipped and slid over the hot skin instead of biting. The gentleness made something uncomfortable stir in Naite's gut, and he broke away. Leaning over, he sunk his teeth into Verly's shoulder. The man shouted, but Naite had already started sucking. He hadn't bit hard enough to break skin, but he would leave a vicious bruise, and that's what Naite wanted. He wanted bruises. He wanted to give them and get them.

Verly pressed his fingers into Naite's arms so hard that the pain started to sing again, and Naite tightened his hand around their cocks. Painfully slow. He started stroking them both painfully slow. Verly nearly choked, his face turning red.

Panting, Naite sped up. He lost himself in the heat, the dance of sunlight over his skin, the smooth, firm body writhing under him. He tingled, and pleasure made every muscle tighten as he moved faster and faster.

"Please, Naite. Please." Verly's fingers dug into his arms, his body trembling.

Naite obliged, jerking them both with fast strokes that bordered on painful. He thrust his hips forward, and a shudder went through Verly's frame.

With a cry, Verly came. He arched up off the rock, and his come splattered against his pale skin. The extra slickness made Naite's cock slide through his hand, and he started coming, shouting Verly's name as he drove himself forward into the man.

They collapsed together, both panting. Verly's arms were thrown wide, and Naite let Verly carry his weight. The blood rushed through

Naite's head so fast that he couldn't hear anything except the beating of his own heart and the way they gasped in air.

For a moment they rested there. Finally Verly broke the spell. Reaching up, he stroked his fingers down Naite's arm. Weary to his bones, Naite pushed himself up and grimaced when he realized that their combined come had stained his shirt. He would hear about that.

Backing up a step, Naite tucked himself in and started zipping his pants as he considered Verly's form. His shirt was open and pushed to the sides. His pants were still caught around his ankles, and smears of white come decorated his stomach. His neck, however, looked like a favorite chew toy. Deep marks at the base of his neck and on his shoulder left very little to the imagination, and his lips were bruised and full.

"That was worth the climb up here," Verly said in a sated voice that Naite hadn't expected.

"I left marks," he said carefully.

Verly reached up and fingered the marks around his neck. "Oh yeah, you did." Sitting up, he still had a stupid smile on his face. "You definitely left marks. So, what are we doing up here?" he asked with the same sort of bright smile. The man was a moron.

chapter
twelve

NAITE WALKED toward the desert, still tucking his shirt into his pants, and Verly watched him. If Verly knew anything, he knew that Naite liked him, but that block was still there. He might have cut loose during sex, but trying to get at the real Naite Polli was like trying to burrow through the sand of the planet—all your tunnels collapsed in before you could finish.

At least it didn't feel like some great gulf was opening up between them anymore. Nope, Naite was back to looking at Verly like he had sustained brain damage somewhere along the way. Truth be told, that was a great deal nicer than most of Verly's lovers. Ever since Minga, Verly didn't have a shortage of lovers. Men got a perverse pleasure out of fucking the butcher of Minga; however, they wouldn't look him in the eye afterward. They certainly never gave him that exasperated look Naite seemed to love.

Since he didn't want to push Naite too far, Verly silently followed as he buttoned up his own shirt. Naite moved downslope, weaving his way through the loose shale to a spot near the open sand. Verly slipped on a few rocks, sending them rolling down the hill, and he was starting to wonder if he would have to camp out on the top of the slope. Between the energetic sex and the climbing, his leg muscles trembled. He couldn't get back down that hellacious trail without falling eight stories to his bloody death.

Naite stood quietly, and Verly went to parade rest and waited. Soft winds brought a scent Verly associated with heated metal, and the barchan dunes slowly drifted as the wind stole grains of sand off the top of one dune to deliver it to the next. The whole desert looked like folds of fabric with each dune fading off into the next.

The low angle of the sun created sharp angles to contrast against the soft curves of the dunes.

"What do you see when you look out there?" Naite asked.

If this were Shan or Temar, Verly would be tempted to talk about the stark beauty. Instead, he answered, "Sand."

Naite snorted a quick laugh. "That's an answer I can get behind." Picking a wide flat rock, Naite settled in on the end, leaving more than enough room. Accepting the tacit invitation, Verly moved to his side and sat next to him.

Looking out at the wavering lines of the barchan dunes, Verly tried to find another answer that might help him reach the inner sanctum of Naite Polli. "It's beautiful. It's quiet... a place where people don't kill each other for stupid reasons."

"We kill each other down here," Naite quickly corrected him.

"But not for stupid reasons."

Naite looked at him, and again he had that expression that implied he questioned either Verly's intelligence or his sanity. "We try not to, anyway," Naite admitted. "But don't go assuming this place is some sort of paradise."

"Compared to where I've been, it sometimes feels like it. Hell, I just had great sex without the risk of a drill siren interrupting in the middle. That's as close to paradise as I need."

With a snort, Naite turned his attention back to the desert. "You have a streak of twisted romance in you, don't you?"

Verly grinned. "Guilty as charged. I simply think a man should get complimented when he's that good."

"You see those squiggles down there?" Naite pointed toward the sand.

"Where?"

"This side of the wisp grass, see them?"

Verly found the blades of thin, almost gray grass rising from the desert and searched the sand near it. "Yeah. Those don't look like wind marks," he said slowly. The marks had the same curving lines, but they were small and irregular, unlike the giant dunes slowly shifting their way across the planet.

"They aren't. That's a sandrat nest." Naite got up and started threading his way down the rocks.

"If you're trying to show me a sandcat prick, I'll skip it," Verly called after him.

That earned him another of those deep Naite-laughs. "Nah, those aren't any fun unless you've got a thirteen-year-old girl to chase around with it." Naite paused. "You know, saying that sounds wrong. It sounds like I'd go torturing a kid now, and you know I wouldn't."

"I know what you meant. At least I hope you meant you'd have to be thirteen to get any amusement out of it." Verly got up and started following Naite down, trusting Naite to explain how any of this related to Naite's quicksilver moods.

"Sixteen at most," Naite agreed. He pulled a handkerchief out of his back pocket. "Grab a rock."

The sheer number of options made Verly hesitate. Whatever had blasted this part of the valley had turned solid bedrock into a mass of rubble. "Head-sized, fist-sized, pebble-sized?"

"Fist-sized," Naite said as he eased out onto the edge of the rock. "We're going to convince them a raptor put down looking for food."

"Okay." Verly didn't see the point of this, but he scooped up a nice-sized rock and delivered it to Naite's outstretched hand.

Naite kept his gaze on the sand, and Verly inched closer. He felt a little like a victim in a horror vid… as if some diseased alien was about to jump out of the sand and chew his leg off. Maybe that was Naite's intention—to make Verly uncomfortable. God knows he'd tried every other trick to drive Verly away. Well, every trick except one. He hadn't said "no." Maybe a therapist would accuse Verly of projecting his own insecurities and loneliness onto Naite, but Verly refused to give up until Naite used that word.

After swinging the rock a couple of times, Naite carefully lobbed it toward the edge of the nest. The sand erupted in movement, a small cloud of dust rising from the ground. Naite kept one boot on a large stone that protruded into the desert, and his hand darted out so fast that Verly couldn't even follow it. For a big farmer, he had some serious moves. Just as quick, he retreated back to the rocks as the last of the sandrats turned and buried themselves again.

"What was that about?"

"This." Naite held up his hand with the handkerchief, and Verly could tell there was something in it.

Living on ships, Verly had developed a hatred for all vermin. He said with disgust, "Don't tell me you grabbed one."

"Yep. It's something kids do out here on dares. You miss, and one of these can rip your hand up good. Do it right, and you can show off and terrify your friends by threatening to drop it down their pants." Naite smiled as if remembering a happier time.

"You make me very happy I didn't grow up on this world."

"I figured you'd like to see a real sandrat. The sandcats are the same species, just a bigger version of their little cousin here. They're more solitary hunters, although sometimes you'll find small groups of three or four hunting together." Naite rearranged his small bundle, moving slowly, and Verly wondered if this wasn't a set up for some sort of joke—a native hazing. Well, he'd survived worse. He'd survived a lot worse than a practical joke or two.

Slowly Naite pulled back the edges of the handkerchief, and an animal emerged. The back legs were oversized with wide feet at the end, and the front legs had two "fingers" with an opposing thumb in the middle. It had large black eyes, a tapered nose that ended in a dark brown tip, and two huge round ears. Naite held it firmly by the body so all four legs stuck up in the air, and while Verly watched, the animal pulled its big hind legs in close and did something to make its ears close up and fold back.

Verly moved closer. "It's cute."

"First settlers thought so," Naite agreed slowly. "There's a story the kids love to read in school. I suppose it's supposed to teach some moral, but mostly we loved stories about the first settlers. Anyway, a number of them caught sandrats and apparently they thought they'd make good pets."

Verly looked at the small animal in Naite's hand. "It looks cute, but I wouldn't trust it in my bunk space with me."

"Yeah, settlers didn't think like that, though. This one will be quiet as long as he's caught good, but if he smells a chance to escape, he'll turn mean. Do you have something on you like a stick or something made of leather?"

"No. I could go back and get a stick," Verly offered.

"Nah, not worth the walk. I'll show you." Naite reached in and squeezed the sides of the rat's head and held both hands tilted to the side to show Verly. The rat was pulling back its lips now, either in pain or because Naite had pressed some pressure point, and Verly could see two rows of teeth on the bottom of its jaw, the front longer than the back, but they all looked needle sharp, like some piranha from earth.

"Holy shit." Verly swallowed as he thought of how much damage those teeth could do.

"They grow new ones as fast as they lose the old. So the settlers take them in, and the first time the things feel comfortable, they take off little Johnny's thumb."

Looking up at Naite's face, Verly tried to figure out what this demonstration was about. If Naite was trying to impress him with acts of bravery, he'd missed the point. Right now Verly figured Naite had been dropped on his head once too often as a child. That was the best explanation for his sheer stupidity in handling the rat. "And you're holding it?" he demanded.

Naite gave the handkerchief a flip, tossing the rat out so it fell several feet away. With a chattering sound, it buried itself back under the sand. "This place isn't that peaceful," Naite pointed out. With that, he shoved his handkerchief in his pocket and started climbing back up toward the valley's edge. Verly watched the rat trails meet and diverge in the sand, not sure what was more interesting, sandrats or Naite Polli. It was a close call, but he knew which one he liked better. Turning his back on the desert, he started climbing after Naite.

"So, does everyone get that lecture?"

"Any migrant who starts looking at that desert like it's beautiful is going to get it out of me," Naite said. Verly smiled. Aw, Naite worried about him. Naite glanced over, and the aggravation was etched into his face, but Verly couldn't stop smiling.

"It is beautiful," he defended himself. "That doesn't mean I don't see the dangers."

Turning to face Verly, Naite crossed his arms over his chest. "If you aren't careful, you'll end up bringing a sandrat back and calling it cute."

Verly tilted his head as he tried to sort this tangle of emotions. Was Naite suggesting that he was the sandrat, that chasing after him was dangerous, or were they talking about Natalie? "I was a soldier long enough that I wouldn't do that," Verly said carefully, still not entirely sure what they were talking about. "I would, however, say that a sandrat is interesting to watch although I would avoid getting within twelve feet."

Naite started climbing up the slope again. "Fifteen or twenty."

"What?"

"Those back feet of theirs make them jumpers. That's how they take down raptors in packs. They all jump on it when it's trying to grab a rat for dinner, so you stay fifteen or twenty feet back."

Verly grimaced as he considered the range those little things had. "Understood."

"I hope so," Naite said. "Because I've seen that desert kill plenty of folks smarter and stronger than you."

"Maybe," Verly agreed, "but I've survived worse than this desert. But now that we're on the topic of avoiding death, I have to say that I cannot go down that trail tonight. My legs are too worn out to risk on that sort of cliff."

"I'm surprised you made it up at all."

"I'm a determined bastard," Verly explained. Naite's mouth almost twitched into a quick smile.

"Well, we can take the main trail back down."

"The... what?" Verly crossed his arms as he processed that tidbit of information.

"You don't think we use that old trail every time we have to come up and fix the netting, do you?" Naite gave Verly a very smug smile. "No, that was a special trip for you. Most of the time we use a trail carved into the mountain rock. It's wide enough that Shan drives his bike through it." That smug smile widened even more, and Naite took a twenty-degree turn to his right and started heading for a place where the rock rose up higher.

"Shit," Verly muttered. So when he'd suspected that Naite had come up the trail to get rid of Verly, he hadn't been imagining things. "I'll get you for that."

"I doubt it," Naite said over his shoulder. "Move your ass, or I won't stick around to show you the topside entrance."

That was a threat to get Verly moving. Tired legs or not, he started trotting up the slope after Naite.

"So, hey, are we still meeting after dark for a quick fuck?" Verly tried to keep his words casual, as if it didn't matter to him one way or another.

Naite looked back over his shoulder. "Well, that's a romantic offer."

Verly grinned. Yep, he simply needed to find the right bait. "If you're looking for romance, you asked the wrong person," Verly teased. "I'm looking for uncomplicated sex, and you are remarkably good at providing it."

"Huh. I never thought of officers as the sort that got up to that."

"Oh, trust me, we are," Verly said. "I didn't know you spent all that much time thinking about Planetary Alliance officers and our potential sex lives."

"I don't like surprises. Since Temar dragged your ass home, I thought I'd read a little war history."

"Reconnoiter the target to assess danger and target possible vulnerabilities," Verly said thoughtfully. "Good strategy. So are we still on for sex tonight?"

Naite stopped near a spire of solid rock. Turning around, he eyed Verly hungrily. "Hell yes."

chapter
thirteen

VERLY TRIED wiping the stupid grin off his face before walking into the house, but it wasn't easy. Today had been more than sex—today Naite had tried so hard to reach out and make a connection, and even if Verly had no idea what danger Naite wanted him to avoid, a person didn't make that kind of effort for someone unless they had some feelings involved. The evening had grown dark enough that Verly navigated his way through the yard by the light spilling out the house windows.

The bunkhouse sounded more inviting. Verly missed the camaraderie of a few dozen soldiers all sharing one communal space. Every rank he'd worked through up to lieutenant had meant living in communal spaces. When he'd been busted back, he'd almost hoped for a full drop to lieutenant and a chance to live among a group of soldiers that he could prove himself to. He wanted to reconnect with someone. Anyone.

Instead he'd been demoted to lieutenant commander and sent out on scout ships. Alone. He'd rendezvous with a ship, get a psych eval and a quick fuck, and then he'd spend another two months wandering the black. So a huge part of Verly wanted to follow Naite back to the bunkhouse and get to know people's names and laugh at the stupid jokes.

But he suspected Naite needed a little more time to adjust, and Verly was well aware this relationship was on shaky ground. So he headed for the main house and the yellow light spilling out the windows.

"Oh my God. What happened to you?" Cyla demanded as Verly walked in the back door.

Verly stopped. Temar, Shan, Cyla, Rula, and Natalie all sat around the table, and two empty spots set with glass plates waited on the end closest to the door.

"I think I know," Shan said. "Naite needs a teething ring."

Verly reached up and fingered the mark at the base of his neck. The skin was hot and swollen. Even without a mirror, Verly could tell he had the world's biggest hickey. Well, he hadn't planned to hide their relationship, so hopefully Naite felt the same. If he didn't, he should have chosen a more discreet place to mark his territory.

Natalie carefully balanced her fork on the edge of her plate and watched him with a blank expression, but Rula smiled. "Well, he's as enthusiastic in bed as he is with the weeding. Somehow, I'm not surprised."

Shan was grinning from ear to ear. "A second time with the same man? I think that's a record for Naite. He hasn't gone back to the same person a second time for at least...." Shan made a production out of trying to remember.

Temar gave him a shove on the arm. "Be nice. You are charitable toward everyone in the universe except your brother."

Shan looked a little sheepish and dropped the subject.

"I can't believe Naite did that," Cyla said. Disapproval dripped from her voice, and Verly wondered again if there wasn't some attraction there that Naite had managed to miss.

"I don't think Verly was complaining." Natalie made the words sound sweet, but Verly couldn't ignore their afternoon conversation.

"Well, I don't plan to put the details in any reports if that's what you're worrying about," Verly offered just as sweetly.

The whole room went silent, so Verly suspected he had poked the sore center of some problem. The smile fell off Shan's face, and Temar rested his hand on Shan's arm.

"Is there a problem?"

"No," Natalie said.

At the same time, Temar said, "Maybe." Verly had a lot more trust in Temar's judgment than in Natalie's. Now that he was paying attention, he could see the stress in everyone's faces.

Shan was the first to offer an explanation. "The AFP wants some sort of report."

"What kind of report?" Verly focused on Natalie, because she would be the one submitting any reports they asked for. That was, assuming she didn't defect completely. For the briefest of moments, Natalie met his gaze, her face impassive.

"A complete tactical assessment?" Temar looked at Natalie as if waiting for a confirmation that he'd gotten the wording right.

"Crap." Verly ran a hand over his face.

"That was Natalie's reaction when we brought the message," Shan said. "Apparently we're better at breaking codes than the AFP suspected, but we're still trying to figure out exactly what this means."

"This might not be the time to discuss it," Natalie said. The woman had more control over emotions than anyone Verly had ever seen. If Verly had been asked for that report, he would be a bundle of nervous panic. That was the sort of report a general asked for while preparing invasion plans.

Temar tilted his head and looked from Natalie to Verly and back again. Verly could almost see that tactical brain sorting through the evidence. "Verly is not the enemy," he offered after the silence had dragged on for an uncomfortably long time.

Natalie shot Verly another look. "Excuse me if I have some trouble believing that."

"I understand that you have history," Temar said gently, "but that doesn't change the fact that this is our world and our decision. Verly isn't a threat here. And if we want to protect ourselves, we have to work together because there's more than one enemy."

"If you knew what I knew…."

"I know everything I have to know about them," Temar said, his voice taking on a sharper edge. That was the Temar that Verly knew and desperately didn't want to cross because he was a little scary. Even Natalie fell silent.

Cyla, however, jumped into the fray. "She's trying to look out for us. The universe has these people who do terrible things to each other. You don't understand how dangerous that place is." Cyla kept shooting Natalie these glances as if trying to figure out how she could best back Natalie's play. The alliance there was developing into something formidable, but Verly had to trust Temar to notice that his sister's loyalties were somewhat questionable.

"I do understand, Cyla," Temar said, his voice even sharper.

Cyla sucked in a breath as if she was about to launch into a good long tirade.

"Maybe we should all calm down," Shan suggested. "We do understand the danger, Cyla. We were in the middle of the danger.

Hell, I got taken hostage and blown up. I think that gives me some insight." Shan colored his voice with humor, but no one was laughing.

"You only saw one terrorist action," Natalie pointed out, and she looked at Verly, her gaze calculating. He knew exactly what was coming. What he didn't know was how Shan and Temar might react to the news.

Before she could say anything, Temar leaned toward her, both his hands coming down on the table. "Natalie, turning on each other is not going to make the world a safer place. If you want this world to be yours, then you have to learn to live by a different set of rules."

"Are you so sure that your rules are going to work? You people had decades, entire generations even, without wars or terrorists or political machinations. Are your rules going to stand up to all of that?" Natalie's façade fell away for one critical moment, and Verly could see the anger and the fear behind it.

"Our rules are about doing what's right," Shan pointed out. "What's right doesn't change even if the circumstances do."

Natalie took several deep breaths. "And then the people who do right get killed by the people who do whatever it takes to get power."

"That's a rather cynical way to look at the world." Shan sounded more like a man comforting her than correcting her.

"No, it's a realistic way. If they want a tactical report, that means they're considering taking tactical action."

Feeling like his legs might give out at any time, Verly sat heavily in the empty chair that was waiting for him. "I thought the AFP had decided not to make demands here. I thought they couldn't get a good psych profile on Temar and that they had decided it was safer to trade rather than to risk losing the resources." Verly glared at Natalie. "Isn't that what you said this afternoon?"

She drew herself up a little straighter, and Verly had the impression that she would love to hit him. "That's what I was told," she said archly.

"Well then, we have to find a way to bend that report to our advantage," Temar said. Despite the rising emotion, he kept his calm.

"Our advantage?" Cyla's voice was dangerously high. Verly could almost feel the stress fractures forming. "How are we supposed to have an advantage over people that have spaceships? They could cut us off from trade, and where would we be then?"

"We would be a lot better off than we were a year ago," Temar said. "Two tanker deliveries of water, and we could go for another six or seven generations before we needed more. Our backs aren't up against the wall, even if theirs are."

"So trading with them essentially means keeping them in business," Verly summarized. He couldn't approve of that. The AFP had done too much damage to the universe. If their house of cards was ready to fall, he was more likely to give a good push than he was to try to prop it up by trading vital supplies. He could only hope Temar felt the same.

"Refusing to trade with them means they come down here and take what they want," Natalie argued.

"They can try," Shan said with some amusement. "It's not like we haven't had other people try their little games."

"The PA could offer protection. They can bring in a lot of resources, and for a planet with this many raw materials, they would bring a whole fleet." What Verly didn't add was that if they had any idea that protecting Livre meant cutting the AFP off from vital supplies, they'd bring two fleets.

"And then Livre would belong to them," Natalie said in a cold tone.

Temar gave him a long look that dared Verly to disagree with her. Sadly, Verly couldn't. That would be the cost of asking for help.

Cyla gave a half sob, half laugh. "Great, so either way we look at it someone is going to come barging in here treating us like unskilled workers on our own land. This is ours. We worked for it."

"And we're going to hold on to it." Temar had a calm to him that settled Natalie somewhat. Cyla pressed her lips together into an angry line, clearly not willing to accept anything he said. Never before had Verly had so much reason to be thankful for his own lack of siblings.

"Shan and I are going to go back to the council." Temar moved right into the solutions phase of the conversation. "Natalie, Verly, we'd like you to come and explain the realities of life up there to our council. I think we'll need to invite the other council members in as well."

Natalie lost a lot of her color. Verly felt some sympathy. The AFP were suspicious bastards, known to interrogate their own officers if those officers had been out of their control for any length of time. If she helped a foreign government and then went home, her life expectancy... well it might be mercifully short or unbearably long. But either way, she would suffer.

"We came here to get away from those people," Rula said.

"I didn't expect us to have to throw ourselves in the deep end quite so quickly." Natalie gave her lover an apologetic look. Rula smiled back and leaned closer. For a moment the two women seemed to draw strength from each other, their hands touching. Clearing her throat, Natalie sat up. "I don't know exactly what you expect us to say."

"The truth," Shan said. "We can figure the rest out as long as we have the truth."

Natalie gave him an exasperated look. "I think you have a rather optimistic view of yourself."

"I think there are a lot of people who would agree. So far, we've been right and they've been wrong," Temar pointed out. "One way or another, we'll figure it out."

"The good Lord provides. We have to recognize the opportunities He offers," Shan agreed. He twined his fingers with Temar's.

"Then we have to start looking for it," Temar agreed.

"Has anyone told Naite all this?" Verly asked. From the blank stares everyone gave him, he was guessing that was a no.

Temar stood. "I'll talk to him." Shan tried to stand as well, but Temar rested a hand on Shan's shoulder and urged him back down into his chair. "Seriously, I think this will go better without you around to aggravate him."

"I don't aggravate him."

Temar raised an eyebrow.

Shan changed his answer to "I can be polite."

"The way you breathe tends to annoy him. I have this," Temar said. Verly opened his mouth to volunteer, but then Temar added, "I think he'll take the news better if it's me."

Verly closed his mouth. Well crap. Verly suspected he'd just lost his chance at a night under the pomegranate trees. Potential interplanetary invasion tended to ruin the mood.

chapter
fourteen

VERLY HAD a few doubts about whether he was in the right place. The "trees" in this sheltered grove looked like bushes on steroids, but Rich's directions had been specific. Rather than worry about it, Verly settled down on the ground, leaning back against a rough-cut stone. He ran his fingers along the tool marks on the rock.

"I didn't think you'd show." Naite stepped out from the deep shadows. Only the redder of the two moons was in the sky, so the night was darker and somehow more ominous.

"I wanted to come with Temar to tell you about it."

For a long time, Naite didn't answer. Taking a step closer, he loomed over Verly. Few men had the height or the bulk to loom, but Naite had both. "Why?" he finally asked, sounding as closed off as he had that first day. Verly sighed. Clearly he'd lost any momentum he'd managed to gain.

"I thought you had a right to know...." Verly paused. Honestly that didn't explain why he had wanted to go with Temar. "I thought you had a right to ask me questions."

Again, silence fell on the grove. Naite stood in the dim light doing his tall, dark, and pissed off impression, and Verly stretched his legs out in front of him and waited. He'd had so many fantasies coming here. Maybe he had expected too much. Naite didn't owe him anything, and right now, Verly figured he was more likely to get locked in a room to keep him out of the way than he was to get fucked.

"So, ask your questions," Verly said. He was weary down to his bones, and he couldn't continue this emotional push-pull. It was time to offer up what he knew and accept whatever consequences came from it. He didn't have the energy for any other plan.

"Will Natalie's people attack?"

"You're asking me?" Verly laughed. He was the last person to offer an objective opinion on the AFP, for any number of reasons. "I'm the one they captured and tortured for routing information. Don't ask me to think rationally about them or to analyze their motives."

"I'm not. I'm asking for your opinion."

"Have you asked Natalie for hers?"

"I will." Naite moved in another inch, and Verly had to tamp down on the urge to pull away. "Right now, I'm asking for your opinion."

"They're cowards. They attack outliers, the weak, people who can't fight back. They target children, Naite. If they understand this world, they'll steer clear. Maybe you could give them your sandrat speech." Verly tried going for the boyish grin, but Naite didn't seem in the mood for a joke. "I'm not the AFP, Naite. I don't know what you want me to say."

"Cyla is suggesting that we call your people for protection."

"Oh." Verly blew out a breath. "In the kitchen, she sounded like she wanted to veto that plan."

"Nice to know you had a long discussion without me." Naite did not sound amused, but he had to know that Verly hadn't been consulted on that decision.

"I walked into the middle of it. But Cyla was against asking for help. She said that she didn't want to be treated like an unskilled worker on her own land."

"That sounds like her. She doesn't own any land, and there's nothing wrong with unskilled work. Without it, everyone on the planet would starve." Picking out a boulder some distance from Verly, he sat. "So, how likely is it that your people are engineering this to get us to ask for help?"

Now Verly felt like he was being interrogated. Pulling his legs up under him, he sat cross-legged on the ground. "I don't know. I'm not exactly welcome in strategy meetings."

"So, it could be a trap, a way of regaining control of Livre," Naite summarized.

"Maybe." Verly wished he could defend his government, but now that Naite asked the question, Verly didn't know the right answer. "I'm not working for them."

Naite snorted. Turning, he took one step back the way he had come, and Verly stood. "You do know that I'm not going to give up, right? I mean, I'm a stubborn bastard that never walks away from a fight."

Naite turned to him. "Is this a fight?"

Verly wished he could read minds because Naite's words sounded dangerously calm.

"Yes. Yes, this is. I like you, and I don't think that's a secret. So this is open warfare, and I don't plan to lose. I think there's something worth fighting for here."

Naite tilted his head to the side. "Then this is me disengaging from battle." If he had said that and walked away, Verly would have paused. He would have reconsidered his position. Instead Naite made that announcement and then stood there, waiting. He wanted someone to fight for him, Verly knew it. Either that, or Verly was utterly wrong and talking his way into a council complaint of harassment—one or the other.

"Oh, someone's been reading the battle reports. I love it when you use soldier-talk," Verly teased.

"I have been reading battle reports, reports from Minga, specifically." Naite crossed his arms, and Verly's stomach dropped. It shouldn't bother him so much, not after all this time and all the people who had demanded answers. Unfortunately, Verly had put too much faith in Naite's claim that the past didn't matter.

"Okay." Verly kept his voice as neutral as possible.

"You opened fire on a ship of refugees." Oddly, Naite sounded equally unemotional.

"Yes, I did." Verly waited for the condemnation, for the arrest, hell—maybe this precious council of theirs would decide that getting busted down three ranks and exiled to the edges of the universe wasn't enough. Maybe they'd mete out their own justice.

As much as Verly had fantasized about a planet cut off from all communication, a planet full of people who weren't likely to have heard anything about him, he'd had an equal number of nightmares about what might happen to him if people did find out. The service was a shield for him. The PA might delight in punishing him, but they protected him from the worst of the hatred.

Naite took a long time to answer, and Verly held his breath. "What? No defending yourself?"

"Would it work? I have to tell you, it never has in the past."

"You haven't explained yourself to me." They stood no more than six feet apart, but the larger moon was only now peeking over the horizon, and Verly couldn't read Naite's expression. The man was difficult and prickly and closed off under the best of circumstances, but right now, Verly felt like he was flying a minefield without instruments.

"If you read the report, then you know why I thought it was a terrorist attack."

"Because they didn't answer your hails."

Verly took a deep breath. "That and because of the nuclear signature from the loading bays, and because the flight path put it on the far side of the moon from the closest defensive array. I made a call. It was a bad call, and I live with that."

"And three hundred and seventeen refugees don't."

"Yes. While you're poking that button, you should probably mention that ninety-seven were children. I killed ninety-seven children because I made a mistake." If they were going to go wading through the mud of Verly's life, they might as well get it all out there.

"The report said that your capture and torture had made you overly suspicious."

Verly ran a hand over his face. "Hell, I don't know what you want me to say, Naite. Was I fucked-up in the head after that? Probably. They gave me a fucking promotion because I got captured and tortured. I wasn't in a good place."

"Do you even feel sorry?"

Frustration—rage—helplessness and regret. It all surged forward, and Verly closed the distance between them and hit Naite in the chest hard enough to make him stumble back. "Don't suggest you know how I feel. I feel guilty every day of the week, but beating myself up won't change the fact that those people are dead and that I never intended to harm civilians." He hit Naite again, and damn it felt good.

"I needed to protect my men, and if that had been a nuclear terrorist, it could have destroyed my ship and sent radioactive chunks raining down into the atmosphere. I made a choice. It was clearly a bad choice, but you don't get to judge because you don't know how I feel." Verly raised his hand to hit Naite a third time, but Naite caught his wrist. Those worker's hands were far stronger than Verly's own, and after a quick struggle that Verly lost, he quieted and waited to see what Naite would do now. The ball was in his court.

"Yes, I do."

"You do what?"

"Sandcat pricks. Yeah, I know what it feels like to kill."

Verly sucked in a breath, but he didn't interrupt. He waited, and Naite's fingers were painful around his wrist, but he still waited.

"Shan left the council, quit the priesthood and the council before Ben and his group could come up for judging. Maybe love for Temar was part of that, but he didn't have the stomach to send people out to die. They tried to kill him, Ben raped Temar, and the whole lot stole enough water to seriously jeopardize lives, but he still couldn't be part of killing them. You look at Shan and Temar like they're smart enough to figure all this out, but they…. Shan wouldn't even do what needed to be done." Naite breathed fast, and Verly worried that the man was losing himself in his own miseries and memories. Verly had done it often enough to recognize the signs.

"You did, though. You killed," Verly prompted him.

"Hell yes. I condemned those people, no doubts and no second thoughts."

"Naite, that's not a mistake. That's not murder. That was you being part of a group that applied a law. Not the same."

Naite shook his head. "I was on the council that condemned more men in one month than in the rest of Livre history. I voted to exile every bastard who conspired with Ben Gratu to steal water, and I watched them beg for mercy that they sure weren't willing to give others. I'm not going to claim my hands are clean on that count."

Verly tilted his head and struggled to figure out what piece of the puzzle he was missing. "Did you kill any of them? Did you pull the trigger?"

Letting go of Verly's wrist, Naite whirled around so that Verly had a nice view of his back. "No. I watched Ben Gratu, though. The sandrat started walking like he could make it to the relay station and call for a ride back into space. Even barefoot in the desert, he was a cocky bastard."

"How long did that last?"

Naite looked up at the sky. "Until the second night. That's when he started begging. He started calling on Temar to save him, the bastard. He'd raped Temar, tortured the man, and he was calling on Temar to save him. The worst part was that Temar probably would have." Naite gave a mirthless laugh. "Too bad for Ben, I was the only one out there."

"Those children... they didn't even have a chance to beg, Naite. I think back. I've reread my own reports over and over. I've reviewed every bit of sensor data, and I still don't know if I was making the best call I could or if I overreacted... if I saw an AFP ship and I wanted an excuse to open fire. I would have landed in a prison for the rest of my life, only my lawyer argued that the PA should have known I was still a little nuts. I was crazy. That's what saved me from prison. Well, that and condemning me would have made the AFP very happy, and we can't have that. Hell, the AFP ambassador fought to get me extradited to an AFP world where I would have faced execution by torture."

Naite looked over his shoulder. "And now it looks like either the AFP or the PA is trying to take over. Where's that going to put you?"

"Screwed," Verly admitted. "Either way I'm screwed. If the AFP takes over, I'm going to be screaming for an unmercifully long time before I'm also dead. Hell, if the AFP takes control, I'd consider it a favor if you took me out quick, maybe breaking my neck or slitting my throat." Verly raised his chin and fought down the fear of death that had always kept him from considering suicide. However, if the AFP took over, it wouldn't be suicide as much as choosing a quick death over a slow one.

"And if the PA takes over?"

This time Verly turned away. God, he'd wanted so much to find a corner of some world where he could be anyone other than the butcher of Minga. He wanted to sit with people at a table and laugh. It was a ridiculous fairy tale. "I'll go back to space. If they can assign another representative, they will. I'm only here because Temar wouldn't allow them to send anyone else." Verly wondered if he could do it—go back to a universe that hated him, men who fucked him and then laughed, officers who searched for any mistake that would allow them to punish him. Verly hadn't realized how desperate he'd become, not until Temar had shown up and treated him fairly.

"Whether it was justified or not, you aren't a butcher. You didn't mean to hurt anyone." Naite's voice was close, and the pity was harder to handle than hate. During the trial, he'd gotten vids proposing marriage and congratulations notes from nutcases who argued the entire AFP should be nuked. People who supported him were worse than people who hated him.

"You executed a rapist. Don't pretend it's the same. I killed children, Naite. How are you supposed to overlook that?"

"Because I killed my father."

Verly whirled around, and he expected... laughter maybe. He expected Naite to be making some elaborate joke at his expense. Instead Naite stood so close that Verly could smell the musk and the dirt, and his eyes shone in the moonlight.

"I killed him," Naite repeated, and this time Verly knew it wasn't a joke.

chapter
fifteen

VERLY OPENED his mouth, but he couldn't think of one thing to say, so he closed it again. He had an indifferent relationship with his own father, and his mother died before he had more than vague memories, but Verly had assumed that these people with their geographically close families had tighter relationships. Clearly he'd assumed wrong.

Naite took a deep breath, his face red from the light of the moon. "He was the same sort of asshole as Ben. Oh, he used pipe juice as his excuse rather than a sense of moral superiority, but they were two halves of one nut."

"Do you mean...?" Verly tasted bile. "Sandcat prick on a stick." He whispered the words, shock robbing him of any volume. He knew Naite had suffered rape; that much was clear in every reaction. He hadn't expected this.

Naite gave a rough laugh. "Yeah. Exactly. So don't pretend you're the only person to make some fucked-up decisions."

Verly struggled to come up with something to say. "He hurt you?"

"Raped," Naite corrected him. "And I was a stupid kid who didn't know to tell someone what was happening. Fuck. Half the time, I believed him when he said that he did it out of love."

Verly knew the psychology of rape. His own post-capture therapists had spent a lot of time talking to him about identification with abusers and emotional damage. Still, Verly doubted what he'd gone through could compare to having a parent do the raping. "What happened?" he asked.

Naite looked at him, and Verly sat. His legs were feeling a little shaky, but more than that, he didn't want to hover over Naite who had staked out his own bit of rock to sit on. Eventually Naite shrugged. "I guess it's only fair since I know about your big secret."

"My big secret isn't much of a secret. I went on public trial, and I got demoted for showing a lack of good judgment. Most days, I count myself lucky for not ending up in a jail cell. Other days, I think they should have thrown me in one and lost the key."

"Yeah, but people here don't know. That's why you came here, isn't it?"

Verly nodded. "In part. Before Temar, it'd been a long time since someone asked for my opinions about a problem. Temar... he trusted my judgment—not blindly but because he heard me out and believed I had the right answer."

"I'll keep your secret, but don't put Temar on a pedestal."

"And don't underestimate him. He may look young—"

"He is young. I remember when he was running after the candy sellers," Naite interrupted.

"Well, I remember him intimidating an AFP captain, taking on a terrorist, and making it clear that he would kill me if I tried to double-cross him, so he's not that boy anymore, Naite. He made hard decisions, and he stuck with them."

Naite gave him a look that questioned Verly's intelligence, and Verly decided to change the subject back to something that wouldn't cause a fight.

"And as much as I appreciate your offer to keep this secret, I won't hide what happened. I may avoid the discussion, but if Natalie starts telling people about my past, those people who died deserve better than to have me deny them. I knew it would come out eventually, but I did hope that people would get to know me before hearing the story. I don't want to have people hate me for making an honest mistake."

"People are judgmental sandcats," Naite agreed.

"I take it that's pretty much why you've kept your secret?" Verly didn't know for a fact that this was a secret. The rest of the planet might know, but somehow he doubted it.

Naite nodded. "Yeah. My brother would have Catholic epilepsy if he knew the truth, and the rest of Landing... they'd pretty much think they had to exile me."

"Exile... you mean execute you?"

"Yeah, pretty much." Naite sounded fairly calm for a man admitting his friends and neighbors would want him dead if they knew his secret, but then Verly understood how mistakes could weigh on the soul. He understood better than he'd ever wanted to.

"Would you even protest if they did?" Verly asked softly.

Naite took his time before answering. "Nope. I've agreed to exile people because their actions could have caused people's deaths. It'd be a sort of justice to get exiled myself."

"I think it would be an injustice."

Naite huffed. "You don't know what happened."

Verly paused. Naite didn't want trite or easy answers, which was good because Verly didn't have any. "No, I don't," he admitted. "I do know you're a soldier at heart. I know you wouldn't have done it without believing that you had to."

Naite shook his head and turned away. He didn't leave, though. He sat with his back to Verly and seemed to collect his thoughts. "Then you have more faith in me than I do. Most days I think I did it out of anger."

Verly ran his palm over the back of his head as he stared at the ground. He understood that feeling. "What did you do?"

There was another long silence as Naite studied the twin moons. The larger moon was now moving above the horizon, inching closer to the slower moving red one. Verly waited. Naite would tell him or he wouldn't, but that was a decision Naite had to make. "I'd been slaved out to Tom, one of the other landowners, for a few months, and I gave him all kinds of grief." Naite started slow and then ran out of words.

"I can imagine," Verly said with some humor. Naite wasn't the most tractable of men.

"No, you can't. He never could get out of me what happened to make me so cussed angry, but I think he suspected the truth." Naite leaped to his feet and moved away. With his back to Verly, he said, "He'd have to be an idiot not to, and Tom's no idiot. But he kept waiting for me to come around before he went to the council and made any charges he couldn't prove."

"But he never had the opportunity to go to the council," Verly guessed.

"Hell, do you think I wanted to drag all that out for the world to see?"

Verly thought about coming home after his capture. Everyone kept wanting to shake his hand and tell him what a great job he'd done, and all he could think about was how they'd never want to touch him if they knew what he'd done to survive. He'd spent months in therapy before he could start talking about it, and he'd been a soldier. His training had prepared him to understand the way torture and rape twisted a person's head around. If Verly understood the fragments of Naite's story right, he'd been a child when it started.

"Is that why you killed him? To keep the secret?" While Verly had never approved of execution of prisoners, he would make an exception for child rapists.

"Hell, I don't know. Maybe," Naite said without turning around. "If so, killing to keep a secret... that's what I condemned Ben's crew for doing. I watched Ben get eaten alive, so if I——"

"So, is it still a secret, what your father did?" This time Verly interrupted. Letting Naite beat up on himself verbally wouldn't help anything.

Naite shook his head. "When Tom came to tell me my father was dead, I told him all about the abuse." Naite took a long and uneven breath. The whole valley was unnaturally silent, so Verly could hear each scuff as Naite shifted his weight and each unsteady breath. "I loved Tom, and I lost him right there because I can still remember the panic on his face when he realized how bad it had all been. He didn't know how to deal with that, and I dumped it all on him."

Verly pointed out the obvious. "Then you weren't trying to protect a secret."

Turning around, Naite studied him for a second. "Do you think it's that easy?"

"Fuck no. I know how hard it is. Do you know how many times some officer asked me if I was angry at the refugees? Did I resent the way soldier rations kept getting cut? Did I hate the civilians for refusing to stand up against their own governments?" Verly's anger rose up, and he took a second to push it all back down into that pit where it lived. "They sat me in little rooms and asked me why I resented the world so much that I killed children." A sob slipped out, and Verly closed his eyes tightly. "Yes, I resented all the crap," he admitted, safe in the darkness behind his closed eyes. If he couldn't see the disgust in Naite's face, it didn't exist. "I resented the hell out of the hatred and the attacks and the justifications and the fucking torture. I resented being a soldier when I'd wanted to work in veterinary medicine. And for a while there, they had me so turned around that I wasn't sure why I ordered the gunnery sergeant to fire. But in the end, I believed I was firing on terrorists and saving my ship."

"So, you think that makes it even? I killed my father." Naite's voice rose. "My father. Shan sits next to me when we go into town, and he never knows that I'm the one who ended that sad son of a bitch's life. So that's not the same."

"No, it isn't," Verly quickly agreed. "But those were children—hungry children running for their lives." For some time, they stared at each other, and it was like the entire universe balanced on this one single point. He wanted to reach out, to grab Naite and hold on. But grabbing Naite was about as dangerous as grabbing a sandrat, and Verly didn't know how to do it without getting chewed up. He didn't know how to do it without laying another layer of guilt onto Naite, because he didn't doubt for a second that Naite would feel guilty if he lashed out. "If you killed him, you did it because he didn't leave you any choice," Verly said firmly.

"God damn it. I don't want to dig this back up."

Verly closed the distance between them. "So you bury it and pretend it isn't poisoning the well? I was a soldier too long to think that's going to end well."

"It's worked well so far." Naite gave a dark laugh that made the hairs on Verly's arms stand up.

"Has it?" Verly asked. Naite was too smart to believe that. He was hurting. Hell, maybe that's why Verly had such a strong reaction to him, such a strong attraction. Although to be honest, sleeping with a man the first day he met him wasn't unusual for Verly. Staying around long enough to have a conversation was, though. "Why did you do it?"

Naite threw up his arms, and Verly flinched back, momentarily startled into thinking Naite was striking out at him.

"I saw him with Shan!" Naite shouted. "I broke out of the damn barn at Tom's place, and I went back to the house, and I saw him with Shan. And Shan was fast-talking and dancing all around the subject, talking fast enough to confuse the old man, but how long were words going to keep him away? How long would it take until he got tired of trying to play nice and pushed Shan to the ground and raped him? And I let him do that." Naite's arms dropped to his sides, and his voice fell to a whisper. "I let him hurt me until he thought it was okay. It was my fucking fault. If he'd touched Shan, that would be my fucking fault."

Verly didn't have any more tears for his own pain... his or his victims... but his eyes warmed with tears as he imagined the scene. Naite with his big heart—his utter need to be fair and right and good—it would have torn him to shreds to see that.

"You took action, because you had to. None of that was your fault."

Naite shook his head. "Don't give me that shit. If I'd have run to some neighbor the first time the bastard had touched me, maybe they could have figured out a way to stop him from doing that." He wiped a hand across his eyes even though his voice remained steady. "But what was I supposed to do? Let him rape Shan? Tell the council or Tom and let them do their tiptoeing around the subject until the old man got so frustrated and afraid that he raped Shan anyway? There were days he looked at me, and I knew he'd kill me before he'd let me go. I knew it."

Verly moved in closer. Now they were within touching distance, and Verly could feel the danger, the emotion radiating off Naite. "So you protected your brother."

"I fucking killed my father. Don't try to make it sound pretty. I murdered my father." Naite took a step forward, his hands curled into fists at his sides, and now they were nose to nose.

"How?" Verly asked calmly. Naite blinked at him for some time, surprise breaking that anger circuit.

Naite breathed heavily as though he'd been running, and for a long time he didn't answer. They stared, each willing the other to budge. Verly was a little surprised that it was Naite who finally broke the silence. "I waited until Shan took off on his bike." Naite's voice grew distant as though remembering. "Dad was out front yelling for him to come back when I went in through the side door and put sheep sedative in his pipe juice. I thought if I was lucky, he'd stop breathing."

"But he didn't," Verly guessed.

Naite caught his lower lip in his teeth and bit it so hard that the flesh turned white. "I took him by the hand and led him out to the desert. He smiled at me. He smiled at me like I was some fucking lover come home to him." Naite tried to turn away, but Verly rested his hand on Naite's arm.

"And then?"

"And then I led him out to the desert and sat him down in the sand. I handed him more drink, and I made sure he was so drunk he couldn't possibly get up again. After that, I went down to Ben Gratu's place and stole enough pipe juice from some worker to get so fucking plastered that I didn't even notice when the field hands found me and called Tom out to fetch me back."

"They never made the connection." Verly wondered what these people would have done if they had. Naite wasn't the guilty party here. He'd done what every soldier did—made a horrible decision because it was his job to protect innocent lives. He'd been a better soldier than Verly.

"Hell, I don't even know. Tom might have. Like I said, he's not a stupid man."

"Did the sandrats get your father?"

Naite nodded wearily. "Ate his back out and gutted him. The whole time I watched Ben screaming and flailing as he grabbed the rats and broke their necks, the whole time I thought… I never did give my father even that much of a fighting chance."

"He didn't deserve one. Of course, what you did to him sounds a lot kinder than what happened to Ben, and I'm not sure he deserved a kind end."

Naite didn't answer. The silence filled the night, stuffing Verly's head until he felt like his thoughts didn't fit inside his skull.

"If you want to tell the council, I won't deny any of it," Naite said quietly.

"And they may not understand why you had to act. I do. A soldier on the battlefield makes choices, and sometimes they're good, and sometimes they're not, but they're the best choices we can make."

"I'm not a soldier."

"Yes, you are. So, soldier, just to let you know, I still think you're a battle worth winning, and I don't plan to give up."

A desperate laugh slipped out of Naite. "You're bordering on stalking here."

Verly gave him a crooked grin. "You going to report me?"

"I'm considering it." That might have sounded more believable if Naite's hand wasn't resting against Verly's hip. Verly didn't even remember when Naite had put it there, but it suggested that Naite's words were slightly less than reliable.

"When you do report me, I'll consider myself warned away. Until that day, you can say anything you want, but I'm still going to try to win this fight," Verly said.

Naite frowned. "Why? There are other people who would be happy to bed you. Hell, you saved their precious Ambassador Shan Polli, so I'm not sure most of them will even give a damn about that mess on Minga, even if Natalie tells them. So why are you putting so much effort into chasing me?"

"That's easy. Because a good soldier at your back is worth fighting for, Naite." Reaching up, Verly rested his hand against Naite's chest. When Naite didn't push him away, Verly took that as an invitation, and he leaned in and brushed his lips against Naite's in a gentle kiss.

chapter
sixteen

HE TUGGED at Naite's shirt, pulling it free of his jeans. Naite shifted closer, but he made no effort to help Verly. Before Naite had been aggressive, bordering on violent. Now he reached up and rested his large hands on Verly's shoulders as he leaned in to return a gentle kiss for a gentle kiss.

Finally Verly tossed Naite's shirt to the side and leaned in, only instead of kissing Naite on the lips, he placed a kiss at the base of Naite's throat, right over the spot where he wore a rather vivid mark of his own. Naite grunted and arched his neck out, allowing Verly more access. Accepting the silent permission, Verly sucked at the warm skin, tasting the salt as he left a dark mark of his own.

Verly rolled Naite's nipple between his finger and thumb while running his other hand over Naite's flank. Naite stood silent, but the bulge in his pants grew more and more prominent. Smiling, Verly leaned down to suck at the peaked nipple. After a mere second or two, Naite dug fingers into Verly's shoulders, his breathing loud and uneven.

Verly pulled at Naite's pants. The belt was unfamiliar—an old-fashioned design with a prong of metal that stuck through the leather strip, and Verly fumbled at it a second. Then Naite lost patience. Taking a step back, he pulled his belt and pants loose and shoved both off ungracefully, tugging when they got caught on his shoes for a moment. After spreading the pants and his shirt over the dust under the pomegranate tree, Naite threw himself down and looked up at Verly. His expression was still guarded, but Verly knew only actions would ever convince Naite to trust him. Slowly Verly pulled his own clothes off and did the same. He had to admit that while he hadn't considered sitting on his clothes, they did make the ground more comfortable.

Despite the silence, Naite's large cock jutted up, already darkening visibly, even in the low light of the twin moons. Naite wanted him. That was about the best feeling in the world, and Verly took a second to appreciate how beautiful and how powerful Naite truly was. "God I want you," Verly whispered as he scooted close enough to run his hand over Naite's bare chest. The muscles rippled under the skin.

The words flipped some switch in Naite. He surged forward, grabbing Verly's shoulders, and Verly ended up flat on his back, which was not a problem.

Naite stared down at him, and Verly waited. Whatever Naite needed, Verly would offer it. Fingers pressed deep into Verly's upper arms, and then Naite slowly ran his fingers down over Verly's shoulders and chest. Without a word, Naite leaned closer and placed a soft kiss against the front of Verly's shoulder. Then he worked his way down Verly's body, scattering kisses over his warm skin.

Verly arched his back, his cock hard and throbbing with need, but Naite moved slowly, skimming his hand over Verly's hip. He ran his fingers featherlight over Verly's skin. Without warning, Naite reached up and pulled at one nipple hard enough to make Verly cry out. Immediately Naite soothed the skin, rubbing it gently with his thumb. The gentle teasing left Verly writhing as he moaned low in his throat.

"Naite. Please."

Naite ran a thumb over the head of Verly's cock, and Verly involuntarily thrust up.

When Naite's clever fingers found the constellation of burns down Verly's thigh, they paused. Naite circled each old scar, mapping it before moving to the next. "They hurt you," Naite whispered, his voice dark with some unspoken threat.

"And they died for it," Verly pointed out. He knew because he had shoved the blaster deep into the torturer's stomach and pulled the trigger. He'd felt the blood run over his hand even as the rescuers shouted out signals to each other as they cleared the rooms in their search for hostages.

"What do you want?" Naite asked, the question seeming to come out of nowhere. "What do you like to do with lovers?"

Verly studied Naite's dark eyes. He wanted to make both their pasts vanish. He wanted to wave some magic wand and rearrange reality to meet their needs. He wanted Naite to let him in and trust him, not only with his pain but with his heart. He wanted to believe that this moment would last for more than an hour. He wanted to give Naite one perfect moment.

"I want to suck you," Verly said.

"Really?"

"Yeah," Verly agreed. "I want something more intimate than a fucking. I want something soft and slow."

Naite swallowed, his large Adam's apple clear even in the low light. Slowly Naite slid over to the side. Permission given, Verly caressed Naite's warm skin, feeling the muscles contract and tremble before he slid down to explore Naite's cock. Glancing up, he watched as Naite tilted his head back, the arch of his neck and the underside of his chin curving into each other. The mark wasn't clear in this light, but Verly felt a little flash of pleasure that Naite would wear his bruise tomorrow. More importantly, Naite panted even though Verly hadn't started yet. He wanted this.

Verly kissed Naite's shoulder, mirroring Naite's actions as he peppered kisses down his chest and over his stomach until he reached the nest of curls around Naite's cock. Naite muttered curses about Verly hurrying up, but he did it softly enough that Verly wasn't sure he was supposed to hear them. Taking Naite's complaints in mind, Verly took the head of Naite's cock in his mouth, using his tongue and lips to feel the shape of it, the firmness.

"Fuck yes!" Naite cried out.

Verly slid down until the head nudged the back of his throat. He swallowed, the back of his throat straining around the very end of Naite's cock. With a wordless cry, Naite dug his heels into the ground and thrust up so hard and fast that Verly didn't have time to pull back. Verly's gag reflex kicked in, and he jerked back, but Naite was too far gone to notice. Wrapping his fist around the base of Naite's cock to keep from having another accident, Verly went back to sucking the end, using the tip of his tongue to explore the foreskin and the ridge and the veins that stood out from the skin.

The throbbing in his own balls approached the level of pain, and Verly's lower jaw ached, but he wanted to feel Naite lose control. He needed that. He pulled back and brushed his lips over the head of Naite's cock and then sucked in a breath before going in for another round.

He could feel the second that Naite lost control. Maybe it was the air across his damp cock. Maybe it was the tightness of Verly's hand around the shaft. Either way, Verly could feel as Naite's body twitched and his cries grew wilder right before Naite struggled to thrust up, his heels braced against the ground. With a rough shout, Naite came. Verly swallowed, the salt and musk filling his mouth, and there was something intimate about that act, more than fucking. He'd fucked with plenty of men, but there had been fewer that he liked well enough to want this.

Naite reached blindly for Verly, pulling him up until their bodies slid against each other, sweat making bare skin slide against bare skin. Verly's cock ached, and his balls were pulled up tight, but he ignored that for a second, focusing on the sight of a panting and worn Naite. There was something pure in a man too worn out from orgasm to keep up any façades, and Verly looked at the true Naite, a man so weary and so utterly good that he didn't belong in any world Verly had ever lived in. Maybe he belonged here… maybe these people of Livre were truly so different that they deserved a Naite Polli. Verly wasn't convinced of that yet.

Eventually those dark eyes drifted open, and Naite pulled Verly in for a kiss. Instead of a battle, this kiss was a tender press of lips against lips, Naite's fingers dancing over Verly's hip. Naite's fingers teased, explored, his fingertips brushed against the side of Verly's cock, but still Naite kept kissing him. Carefully, reverently.

Finally Naite pulled back. "You're still hard," he whispered, each word a hot puff of air against Verly's neck.

"Huh. Who knew? I am."

"I don't suppose you could think of any place to put that?"

Verly swallowed. "I know where I would like to put it."

Naite wiggled to the side and pulled something out of the pocket of his shirt. A bottle. Verly's cock got harder as he considered what might be in it. Certainly Naite wasn't planning on topping. His cock lay quiet and soft against his dark curls.

"I want to feel you. I want this."

Verly wasn't sure how he felt about a lover who wasn't sexually interested. Naite's cock wasn't struggling to rise. He wasn't flushed with need or arching his back. But he said he wanted it. Verly's cock softened in reaction to the confusion.

Reaching out, Naite caught his hand. "I need it." Naite pressed the bottle of gakka into Verly's palm.

Verly pulled the oily cloth off the top of the jar and dipped his finger inside. The gakka was cool to the touch and clung to his finger. When Verly looked over at Naite, he had spread his legs in invitation. His cock was still soft and thick as it lay against Naite's curled hair, but Verly shifted to sit between Naite's legs. Naite widened his legs even more. Putting his hands behind his head, he waited.

Verly ran a finger along Naite's quiet cock, ignoring his own or else this would be embarrassingly short. While Verly didn't totally understand why Naite wanted this now instead of waiting until he could recover and participate, Verly's own cock was ready to fire at any point.

Reaching down, Verly stroked over Naite's puckered entrance, first with his middle finger and then with the gakka-slicked first finger. Naite dug his heels into the ground and canted his hips up, and Verly took that invitation to slide the whole finger inside.

Naite was hot. Either that or the gakka juice was heating Verly's finger. He worked it in and out, and with each stroke, Naite's body slowly relaxed. With his free hand, Verly stroked Naite's flat stomach and his bent leg. He felt the power of the body under him.

When Naite relaxed enough, Verly added a second finger, bending it to slip in beside the first. Immediately, Naite's whole body tensed, and Verly froze. "Do it," Naite demanded, but that was the voice of enduring, not the voice of enjoyment.

"You are impatient. Beautiful, strong, sexy as hell, and impatient. If this is what you're like after you come, I don't want to even imagine what you're like when you're sexually frustrated."

"I growl a lot."

"Okay, I think I just figured out something. You're sexually frustrated a lot."

Naite gave his best growl, and Verly pressed his fingers in an inch.

Naite arched his back, his growl turning into a groan. Verly pressed in a little farther. Now he had two fingers in, but it was tight. Verly didn't even want to think about how long it had been since Naite had allowed anyone to top him. The man definitely had not been working this set of muscles.

Jerking his hips, Naite complained, "I'm not made of glass."

"No, just flesh and blood, and I would rather avoid seeing blood," Verly pointed out. He started slowly moving, thrusting his fingers in and out of Naite's ass. Now Naite relaxed, his breathing evening out as Verly moved a little faster. He pressed up into the prostate, and Naite moaned softly, but his cock remained still.

"It's nice and warm now. Add another finger," Naite suggested.

"Bitch, bitch, bitch," Verly complained, but he did add another finger as Naite gave him a dirty look. Verly smiled. "I'm calling it the way I see it."

"I wouldn't bitch if you'd move faster."

Verly thrust his fingers into Naite hard and fast. Sucking in a startled breath, Naite threw his hands out to the sides to brace himself. "Fuck, yeah, only it's not your fingers I want to feel."

"Do you plan to give me instructions every fucking time?"

"If you can't get the job done right, yes."

Verly pulled his fingers out and looked down at Naite. He was sprawled against the dirt, his fingers pressing into the ground and his knees open in invitation. It was a nearly pornographic tableau, and Verly's cock was as hard as it could get.

Despite the fact that he hadn't taken that much gakka, the slick still covered his fingers, and Verly slid his hand up and down his hard cock. "You're going to feel this," Verly warned him.

"Good." Naite raised his chin in challenge and widened his legs. Taking Naite up on that offer, Verly placed his cock at the opening and thrust in. At first he was afraid he'd come before he could get all the way in, but Naite was so tight that Verly's eyes watered. It took some effort to get all the way in, and when he did, Verly leaned forward and rested his hands on Naite's shoulders.

Naite reached up and stroked his hands over Verly's arms. "It feels so fucking good," Naite said, and now he sounded like a man enjoying himself.

The gakka began to tingle, and Verly couldn't stay still. He pulled out and thrust back in, the friction making the gakka tingle even more. It was like almost scratching an itch, and Verly pulled back and slammed in harder. This time Naite had to grab at the base of the tree to avoid being thrust into it. His cock so hard that he ached, Verly pounded into Naite harder and harder, their bodies slapped together, and Naite's legs came up around Verly's waist.

Digging fingers into Naite's shoulders, Verly came with a strangled scream, his body jerking with pleasure. Naite reached up and captured Verly's face, pulling him in for a long, deep kiss.

Collapsing half on and half off Naite, Verly lay under the moons, his body exhausted and his cock still oddly tingling from the gakka. It made him wonder how long it would take him to go for another round. Considering this was his second round today, and he wasn't in his teens or twenties anymore, Verly was rather proud of his performance.

For some time, Verly lay silent, his hand wandering over Naite's overheated body. "You're a good man, Naite Polli—one of the best I know," Verly said softly.

It took Naite some time to answer. "Then you know a sorry crop of men."

"Some days I think I do," Verly agreed. So far, the best human beings he'd met in his life all came from Livre. Considering he'd only heard of the planet less than a month ago, that was rather sad. Again, the silence filled the air. This was comfortable—lying in a tangled knot of limbs and clothing. "I wish we could stay out here, but it is getting cold." Verly sighed. He didn't want to go back to the main house. Not only did he not want to give up this refuge he'd found in Naite, but he didn't want to face the messy reality of their situation… not now. "I suppose I could go steal some blankets from the main house and come back," he offered hopefully.

Naite laughed.

"What?"

"Us. Camping out." Naite still chuckled.

Verly sat up. "Why? Is it dangerous to camp out here?"

Catching Verly by the arm, Naite pulled him close. "No. But a couple camps out when they're serious but not yet ready to share a bunk. It's a sort of courting ritual."

"Oh." Verly leaned back into Naite's warmth. "So I shouldn't get some blankets?"

"People would take it wrong," Naite warned.

Verly smiled and pushed himself back up. "People will take it right. They'll assume that I'm determined to end up in your bunk." Without giving Naite a chance to answer, Verly headed for the house to grab some bedding. He made it two steps before realizing he was naked. Turning back, he found Naite lying on the ground with Verly's pants in hand, holding them up. Verly grabbed them and shoved one foot inside, struggling a bit but pulling them over the boots before he dashed back up to the house.

chapter
s e v e n t e e n

RICH FELL in next to Verly as he crossed the front yard of the house under the slanted sunlight of morning. "So, someone has a love bite that matches that," Rich offered with a wide grin.

"Imagine that," Verly said, not giving the man more than he already knew. The farm must run on gossip because everyone had been giving him wicked smiles ever since Verly had brought the bedding back up to the house. Naite was off in the distant fields, and Verly could barely make out his large frame walking between the rows while a dozen other workers helped. He wondered if they were giving him as much grief. Probably not. The man did know how to give an intimidating glare.

"I never expected a stranger to break through that shell of his. It's good, though. He deserves some happiness. And if you make him unhappy...." Rich started backing away, shrugging in an exaggerated manner to suggest that he wasn't sure what might happen. It wasn't the most subtle of threats, but it made Verly feel good to know that the others cared enough about Naite to threaten people. Naite deserved loyalty.

Verly looked back toward the house to see Natalie standing on the porch watching. He understood that her government had put her in a difficult spot... he did. He also knew that when people were in dangerous spots, they struck out. And they didn't always limit themselves to hurting the person responsible for their pain.

Naite had understood what happened at Minga, and it was time for Verly to man up and talk to Temar before the story spread too widely.

Shan and Temar were prepping a vehicle to go back into town and talk to the council, or Shan was prepping it, crawling underneath to do an inspection while Temar sat in the distant shade watching. Temar had to suspect something. Natalie had been less than subtle, and Temar had an analytical mind. When he'd learned Temar did glass blowing as a hobby, it didn't surprise him. That was the sort of hobby that would appeal to an ambassador—detail oriented, dangerous, demanding all a person's skills and attention. Verly prized the glass shuttle Temar had given him more than anything else he owned. It must have taken time... a lot of time. For Temar to invest that much time in a gift made Verly feel like he owed Temar an explanation.

Passing the machine where Shan worked, Verly headed to the shade of the barn where Temar sat on a low stool. "Ambassador Gazer?" Verly waited for Temar to acknowledge him.

Temar gave Verly a strange look. "This must be serious if you're calling me that."

"I had hoped we could discuss something." Verly was painfully aware of Natalie's gaze as it settled on him.

"About Naite? You really should talk to Shan about that." Temar smiled to make it clear he approved. Verly braced himself because that approval might vanish very quickly after he told his story. But if he didn't, Natalie would tell it eventually, and then it would look like Verly was hiding his past.

"This is more about me," Verly said. "Can we talk?"

Temar's smile vanished. "Sure. Why don't we head up toward the gates?" He nodded toward the tall tunnel that led through the mountain out toward the gate. One branch of the same trail doubled back and led up to the top of the mountain, which was the path Naite had led him back down after Verly had navigated a sheer cliff using about eight inches of stable trail. Verly still didn't know which was worse.... Naite trying to hide behind that dangerous road or his own stupidity in climbing it.

"Sounds good," Verly said with a strained smile.

After giving Verly one more odd look, Temar headed for the arched entrance.

"Shan, I'll be at the gates," he called.

"This may be a while," Shan called back from under the vehicle. Verly wasn't used to ambassadors that fixed their own cars, but there were a number of assassinations that could have been avoided if the PA took up the practice. Mechanics were prime spies, but that wouldn't be the case on Livre.

Verly followed Temar into the tunnel. It still bore the tool marks from the laser that had carved it out of solid stone. Verly's ship-made boots made a clopping sound that echoed down the length of the tunnel, making Verly paranoid about footsteps following them. Here, only Natalie would dare try, and Verly suspected that the woman was more vested in protecting her lover than defending her government. He could respect that, but he didn't want to get between her and whatever job she thought she had to do.

Instead of allowing himself to get lost in his irrational fears, Verly focused on the beauty of the tunnel. Narrow slits cut up through the overhead rock allowed small bars of light to illuminate the path, but the tunnel still felt like deep twilight, an impression reinforced by the cool that radiated off the rock. The laser had cut right through the layers of rock, exposing swirls of browns and grays. Verly let his fingers slide over the cool stone.

"I'm surprised the kids don't play in here," Verly blurted when the silence grew too deep.

"If we had any on the farm, they probably would. They'd have to make sure to keep an ear out for Shan. He runs these tunnels at full speed on that bike of his."

"It's hard to think of him being a priest. He seems more like a daredevil than a saint."

Temar glanced over his shoulder and smiled. "He was a daredevil saint. He was good at caring about people, and when he gave up the priesthood to court me, I was afraid he would regret it. But he tells me that the church was a place to hide… to heal after the damage his father inflicted."

Verly cringed at the reminder of what the Polli men had endured. Although, now that Verly thought about it, Temar was a rape victim as well.

"How common is rape on Livre?"

"Exceptionally rare," Temar said quickly. "The consequences are too severe, so it only happens in cases where the rapist truly has lost touch with reality. Ben thought he was helping me." Temar sighed. "He would have killed everyone on the planet and then claimed that they'd misunderstood his intentions."

"Nutball, huh?"

Temar nodded. "Yes."

"Old man Polli sounds like he was just as crazy," Verly pointed out.

Now Temar stopped and turned around. "I hope you manage to make a real connection with Naite. I happen to think you two are good for each other, and even the workers have commented that Naite growls less with you around. However, if you're looking to get information about his past out of me, I'm not okay with that. If you have questions, ask Naite."

Verly cringed. He'd wanted to do exactly that with Cyla. Looking back, trying a flanking maneuver on such direct people seemed like poor judgment. "I know about Naite and his father," Verly said. "I wanted to tell you something, not interrogate you, although I do know that's how it sounded. I get the feeling that these echoes carry, and I'd prefer some privacy." Verly didn't want Natalie getting a front-row seat to this.

"They do. Anyone in the tunnels would hear us," Temar agreed. "The main exit isn't far."

Turning away, Temar started walking faster toward the far end of the tunnel. The tunnel ended in a solid steel door, and Temar worked a computer panel before pushing the door open. Sunlight streamed in, and Verly looked out over miles of those white sands all folded into graceful curves. It might be a dangerous world, but Verly still appreciated the raw beauty. He stepped out onto a packed path, and Temar swung the door shut. To Verly's left the enormous main doors stood closed, and the narrow path curved around and joined a wider path that led to that blast door.

Rocks cut from the mountain had been dropped to create retaining walls to the north and south of the two entrances, and the tall walls slowly tapered off and then vanished under the sand of the desert.

"Beautiful, isn't it?" Temar asked as he stepped to Verly's side. The man might be a foot shorter, but there was a power that reminded Verly of the desert. Temar was all graceful curve... until he gutted you from underneath.

"I said that to Naite, and he caught a sandrat and offered a lecture on underestimating the desert."

Temar smiled. "That's Naite," he offered with a shrug, "but I get the feeling you don't underestimate much. So, is this about the AFP request for tactical data?"

"No." Verly braced himself and went with the fast and painful approach. "You should probably know that when I was the commander of a defense ship over Minga, I ordered the helm to open fire on a ship. I thought they were terrorists, but they weren't. I killed three hundred and seventeen refugees trying to reach a PA planet to ask for sanctuary."

"I know," Temar said without looking away from the desert. "It's in the file your people sent."

"You... but...." Verly closed his mouth. He'd assumed his officers had sent a sanitized version of his file in order to make sure they didn't lose their only chance to land someone on the planet. Temar and Shan certainly hadn't allowed any other representatives to come.

Temar looked at the blast doors. "Has anyone told you the story of the Aipa group?"

"No." Verly wasn't sure where this was going, but the people of Livre were very good at talking around a point, and Verly had learned to go along until he could figure out what they were trying to say. For a direct people, they were strangely anecdotal and metaphoric with their important ideas.

"The gate had only been up for a few weeks, and people had left the big ships and started constructing homes behind the gate. This footpath hadn't been carved yet. Charles Aipa took sixteen men from his unit to the ship to pull out wiring to use for home construction. They were coming back, and they missed the early signs of a sandstorm."

Verly could guess the direction this was headed. The storms were so severe they could be seen from space. Verly had no idea how anyone could survive being in one.

"I take it they didn't make it back," Verly said quietly. He suddenly felt like he was standing on those lost men's graves.

"They did," Temar said. "They had just come over the horizon when the storm hit. The winds slammed up the slope and right through the blast door and into the valley. People ran for cover, and the men at the gate control screamed for Aipa and his group to hurry. But the sand kept building up near the door, and they were afraid they wouldn't be able to shut the door at all if they waited too long. The people in the valley were being pounded by the winds, and Aipa's group couldn't move beyond a crawl because the winds would knock them off their feet."

Temar stopped, his gaze still on the deceptively calm desert.

"They shut the doors," Verly said. To protect the people behind the gates, he would have done the same. He hoped he never found himself in that position because he carried enough guilt already.

"Yes," Temar agreed. "When the storm ended, Aipa and all his men were found huddled outside the gate, their bodies buried in sand, their arms around each other. They were taken out to the desert and their bodies burned in one funeral pyre. No one wanted to separate the men who had clung to each other in their last moments."

Verly could see the analogy, but it wasn't the same. "That ship had refugees, not weapons. No one was actually in danger."

Temar offered him a sad smile. "What every person on Livre knows is that if those gates had stayed open, everyone would have been fine. If you're caught in a sandstorm and you can't find cover, you stay in the open and let it push you along. Keep your sand veil on and keep your back to the winds. You'll end up having a long walk home because the storm will push you, but you'll be fine. The only way a storm can kill a healthy adult is if it pins them up against something. If you're trapped against something hard, the force of the wind and sand will pin you and crush you."

"If they'd left the gates open...."

Temar nodded. "The wind would have come in on this side and gone out on the other, where the gate hadn't been put up yet. Half-built houses would have taken a pounding, but there's a good chance that the people would have survived."

"Oh God." Verly's heart ached for those people at the gate who'd decided to close it even as Aipa's group tried to reach safety.

"I read all the reports," Temar said. "Your people like to assign blame. You like to pretend that you can control everything. We don't believe that here. I already told Lilian and Kevin from the council that you had been put in a position to close the gates on Aipa, and no one considered that anything more than an unfortunate situation full of victims with no wrong to assign. People die, Verly. My people know that a lot better than yours seem to. We fight like hell not to cause each other harm. We try to protect each other, but in the end, we all die. And if you're Aipa or you're Honor Freeland ordering the gates closed, you can't blame individuals for being human."

Verly stared at Temar, not sure what he should be feeling. Superiors didn't think that way. Mistakes came with post mortems and new regulations and demotions to make sure that the same mistake never happened again. Mistakes always came with blame.

Temar gave him a small smile. "The way Natalie keeps trying to tell people that story—that's another issue, but it reflects on her, not on you. So if she starts telling other people, you tell them that you might regret closing the gates on Aipa, but you had to do what you thought would protect your people."

Turning to the door, Temar punched in a code. "When you're ready to come in, the code is 77942," Temar offered, and then he disappeared into the dark of the tunnel, leaving Verly alone with the desert.

Verly walked the path toward the end of the retaining wall. The sand looked almost soft from here. The folds of the dunes appeared small and close. But after riding back from the shuttle landing with Naite, Verly knew they were steep and dangerous, and the vehicle bucked and lurched as it struggled to gain traction. Any shuttles must have died early because the fine dust in the air would wreck the intakes, and overheating had to be a serious issue.

Verly suspected that his brain was darting off into trivial matters because he couldn't understand the new reality in front of him. He'd grown so used to defending himself... defending his actions... that he wasn't sure how to talk to a commanding officer who didn't blame him. Oh, Temar wasn't technically his commanding officer, but Verly had followed him into battle and come out the other side. He felt more loyalty to Temar than he did to the rotation of nameless officers who accepted his deep-space reports.

If Livre turned into a new battleground in this old war, Verly knew which side he'd stand on, but he wasn't sure how he was supposed to feel about that. Guilty for not loving the government he'd pledged allegiance to? Relieved to get out from under the PA's thumb? Regretful about never again having a long soak in a hot bath? All those thoughts tumbled around until Verly wasn't sure how to feel, so he sat on the edge of a low spot in the wall and tightened the sand veil around his face.

The door opened, and Verly ignored it. He couldn't figure out his own feelings, so he couldn't deal with someone else's, particularly if the someone else was Natalie. How would she react to the claim that sometimes three hundred people died and no one was to blame? Verly didn't plan to give her that line.

"Temar said you were out here," Naite commented.

Verly turned to see Naite, his sand veil still hanging around his neck. "Did he?"

"Actually, he tracked me down in the middle of irrigating the north quarter, so I assume he had a reason for telling me."

"I was just… I was thinking about Aipa."

"Aipa?" Naite looked confused for a second, and then he glanced over at the blast door. "Oh. The gates. I haven't thought about that story since grade school."

"You teach schoolchildren that story?" Verly was slightly horrified. Parents would have sent protests to the school en masse if a PA school taught such a horrible story.

Naite shrugged and sat on the wall so close that their legs pressed together. "What should they learn about? This is their world. If no one tells them how dangerous it is, they'll be the next tragic story."

"Is that really how you see what I did? That it was a tragic mistake?"

Naite gave him a look full of disbelief. "You don't?"

For all the years he'd spent thinking about that day, Verly didn't have an answer. "I don't know."

"You didn't set out to kill people. Yeah. I suppose that's a good analogy." Naite fell silent, and the wind made a strange yowl as it blew across the gates. "So, did Temar tell you the story?"

Verly nodded.

"He's better with people than I gave him credit for. I guess I still see him as a shy waif hiding in the glassblowers' tents."

"I think he's more like the desert." Verly stared out over the sands as they slowly drifted from the top of one dune to the rising slope of the next.

"Maybe he is. He's strong enough to love my idiot brother without strangling him for all his moralizing."

Verly laughed and shook his head. "You two are not particularly nice to each other." Verly thought about what it would have been like for Naite to look at his brother and know that he'd killed to protect Shan and never have Shan acknowledge the sacrifice. Reaching out, Verly caught Naite's hand and held it tightly.

Naite gave him an odd look. "Are you okay?"

"I don't know. I'm better at putting off feelings than dealing with them. My therapist would be very proud of me right now."

Naite tugged him close, and then Naite wrapped his arms around his stomach and held on. Resting his hands on Naite's arms, Verly leaned back into the strength. "How many years did you carry it?" Verly asked softly.

Naite's arms tightened a little more. "Fourteen."

Verly closed his eyes as he imagined the strength it took to carry that load. "It's only been three since Minga."

"It gets easier," Naite promised. "Some days I don't even think about it."

Verly nodded. Therapists had told him the same thing, but when Naite said it, he found he could believe it.

"You're worrying me here."

"I just… I haven't let myself feel anything for a long time, and it's hard to have feelings without getting a little overwhelmed," Verly confessed. If he'd said that to a therapist, he would have been booted out of the service. Then he could have gone into the private sector with very little training other than flying military-grade ships and search for a job with "butcher of Minga" on the top of his résumé.

"It's easier to ignore them," Naite said. "I don't know if it's better, but it's easier."

"The idea of the war coming here… I'm so angry at all of them I kind of want to push a button and blow the whole universe up." Verly stopped. He hadn't recognized his own anger until the words came out, and then it was like they redefined reality, and all he could feel was angry.

Naite chuckled. "I understand that, although mostly I had fantasies of blowing up the valley. It's hard to trade with people that you've blasted into a million pieces, so maybe we should avoid that."

"Yeah, you're right. It's still a nice fantasy."

"Yeah, after hearing the stories I've heard about the rest of the universe, I agree. It's a great fantasy." Naite tightened his arms, and they sat there and watched the desert until they were both hot and sweaty and red in the face from the sun.

chapter
eighteen

TEMAR HEADED back through the tunnels. Sometimes he talked to Verly and Natalie and felt like he was speaking to someone from another species or maybe another universe. It was like trying to create glass with dirt instead of sand and about as useful. He came out into the sunshine of the valley, but Shan wasn't working on his bike. He leaned against the rock.

"Trouble?" he asked.

Temar looked around. Rich was repairing clothes, but he sat on the step to the bunkhouse where he could catch any gossip, and Cyla passed by the windows of the main house. He suspected that if she saw them talking, she'd find some chore near them. "Let's take a walk up top," Temar said.

Shan raised his eyebrows. "I could get my bike."

"Or we could walk," Temar said.

Shan nodded. "Or we could walk." He held out his hand, and Temar took it, allowing Shan to pull him close for a hug before they turned back into the tunnels and started the steep climb. Sheared-off rock made the top of the valley walls, and the tunnels wove through the mountain, angling sharply upward in places. The sounds of their own footsteps echoed against the walls until they finally came out into the hot desert air. The wind gained strength, and Temar turned his back to it to protect his eyes.

Shan spoke first. "I sent out runners to Blue Hope, Red Plain, Zhang, Gambles, and White Hills."

"So everyone?"

"Pretty much," Shan agreed. "If we're going to have to make a decision for everyone, everyone has a right to be there."

Temar nodded.

"You aren't going to argue?" Shan asked.

Temar stopped. "Why would I argue?"

"Because you've been taking a lot into your own hands lately." Shan tugged on him to get him walking again. "I'm afraid that if this goes badly, you're going to blame yourself for being so assertive."

"Do you mean pushy?" Temar asked.

"Maybe." The wind was sliding across the mouth of the tunnel, making whistles and low moans. Already the back of Temar's neck was friction-warmed by the sand hitting it. "Before, you were always the quiet one," Shan said.

Before. Before Ben. Before the abuse. Temar had to admit he had changed, and he still wasn't sure if that was for the better or worse, but he couldn't go back to who he'd been in the past.

"Lilian may want you for her heir apparent on the council, but you don't have an obligation to her or to the council."

Temar weighed his words. "I followed Cyla, and we ended up arrested for the damage we did. I followed you on the world's worst plan, and if Naite hadn't shown up to rescue us, we would have died, and Ben would have stolen the very water we need to survive. I rejected everything both those governments told us and followed the plan I believed in, and I saved you."

"So you know better than everyone?" Shan asked. And that was the tone that made it very easy to believe he'd been a priest.

"No," Temar said quickly. He kept his voice low even though the roar of the wind would hide his words. "No, I don't, or I wouldn't have asked for Lilian's advice on whether I should have lied to Aiden and the others at Blue Hope. If you remember, she congratulated me on that move."

"Lilian is ruthless." From the way Shan said that, he did not mean it as a compliment.

Temar could see the long shaft of light cutting through the air and highlighting all the motes of dust that floated through the tunnel. "She has the best interest of her planet and her family in mind."

"And you do too. I know that." They were almost to the top, and Shan didn't say anything until they'd climbed out into the sunshine. He held his hand out to help Temar over the last step, which was steep for Temar's much shorter legs.

Shan took a second to look around before he chose a bit of rock that gave him a view of the open desert. "I know you're trying to do the right thing here, but this could all backfire."

Temar stood in front, and Shan wrapped his arms around Temar's waist and pulled him close enough to rest his head on Temar's shoulder. "I know," Temar said as he ran his fingers through his lover's hair. "Verly tried to confess to the Minga disaster."

"Confess? Did he do something worthy of blame, then?"

"No. But he seems to have the same brand of insanity as his people. He misunderstood the situation, so he must be guilty. I told him the story of Aipa."

"I can see the similarities," Shan said after a slight pause.

Temar leaned forward and let Shan hold his weight. "I'm afraid that I'm going to be the next Honor Freeland to close the gates on innocent people."

"Then stop," Shan said. "You aren't a council member. You shouldn't have to make these decisions."

"Then who will?" Temar asked softly. Shan had been the religious representative on the council at one point, but he'd given up his seat and his power. Technically Temar had no power at all. Their people had given them the dubious distinction of being ambassadors without understanding how the rest of the universe would interpret such a role. "If we don't make these decisions, who will?" As far as Temar could see, there wasn't another individual who had seen the insanity that had gripped the universe firsthand or had the attention of those powerful giants.

"The councils," Shan said firmly. Maybe his belief in God allowed him to put his trust in the council, but Temar knew how disastrously wrong they could be. Worse, they had no idea how these strangers thought. Every time Natalie or Verly spoke, Temar could see the shadows of the people he'd met in space—people who had not impressed him.

"Will they understand why Verly is terrified about people finding out about Minga?"

"Why would he be terrified?"

Temar pulled away from Shan. "Because he blames himself for making a mistake. None of these people seem to believe in forgiveness."

"Paulists are more about the damnation and condemnation, so I'm not surprised that Natalie and Rula have trouble truly forgiving, but do you really think Verly is a rat from the same nest?"

Temar nodded. He sat on the rock next to Shan and leaned his shoulder into Shan's. "Yes. He expected me to get upset."

"He might benefit from talking to a priest, one that puts Christ before Paul. What does this have to do with you taking all this on yourself?"

"The others won't get it," Temar said softly. "They won't understand that mindset." He stared at the desert. "Every night the wind blows all the sand to the east, and every morning the wind blows it back to the west, and every day the land is new—every mark of another's passing erased. For the people in space, they put their faith in the permanence of material things, which are not permanent. Whatever sin we committed to make the AFP feel that they need to invade—they won't give that up easily."

Temar reached for Shan's hand, weaving their fingers together. Temar's hand was pale and his fingers far more slender than Shan's larger, scarred hand. Shan tightened his grip.

"We may have no power in this."

"Perhaps," Temar agreed. "Or winning may require a higher price than we're willing to pay. At least you and I understand the battlefield. People like Bari and Ebi don't. They expect that the rest of the universe will act in a way that is logical."

Shan gave a soft laugh. "I think the universe believes that it is logical, and we're the ones who don't understand reality. Given that your idea of a rescue included nearly killing me, that's not entirely without cause."

"It was Verly's plan."

"Which he wouldn't have tried without you, and I'm glad you did. It was the right call, but it was a risky move. It took something that dangerous to win in a chess game against these people."

"And if we lose, we will all be standing outside of Aipa's gates," Temar agreed. "I understand that, and I know that we may have to do something equally dangerous to make them understand that we will not bow down to them, but...."

"Temar?"

Temar tightened his hand until he was holding on to Shan with all his strength. "I have to know you're behind me in this. I don't know how ugly this is going to get, but I talk to Verly, I talk to Natalie, and I can't help but believe that if we lose this fight, neither side will ever forget or forgive."

"They do seem to lack Christian forgiveness," Shan said. "And I know that. But as long as you are acting in a good-faith effort to protect this world, I would never question your choices. I stood by while you and Lilian planned to sneak forged legal documents into the Landing records in order to back up your Blue Hope lie, didn't I?"

Temar smiled. "You did." He'd made several comments about lying and the Ten Commandments, but he wouldn't be Shan without a little moralizing.

"And I will stand with you through the rest."

"No matter how ugly it gets?" Temar asked.

Shan gave him a small smile. "As far as I'm concerned, we are married. I have told you in the sight of God that I will hold to your side for all of time, and I don't plan on breaking my word to you or God."

Temar leaned until he rested his head against Shan's shoulder. "And if people die in this mess?"

Shan took a deep breath and let it out slowly. He was clearly struggling with his answer. "That's why I would rather you let the councils deal with this. Then they can deal with their own guilt instead of making you carry more."

Temar was surprised that Shan was worried about him rather than the sixth commandment. Or was it the fifth? "So, it's not because you think I can't handle it or that we have no right to ever kill?"

Shan sandwiched Temar's hand between his two dark ones. "I think you can handle a lot more than I can. Honestly, I'm glad I was the one with the gun to his head and you were the one making the rescue plans. Had it been the other way around, I'm not sure it would have turned out as well. I may put my faith in God, but God leaves me to sort out my own problems, and I'm not always good at that."

"What if someone dies?" Temar asked. "These people are so absolute, so determined to place blame and accept blame that I don't know how to negotiate with them, and I'm afraid something far worse than a few forged documents may be required."

Again, Shan needed some time before answering that question. "You nearly killed me last time, and if I had died, you would not have been to blame. I'll stay by your side no matter what happens." Shan disentangled one of his hands and draped his arm over Temar's shoulders. "Of course, I still plan to point out every potential problem and every moral question that comes to mind."

"I wouldn't want it any other way," Temar said. He closed his eyes, and for a time he let himself just feel Shan's strong arms. For now, that's all he needed. Soon he would have to face the rest of the universe, but that could wait for ten minutes while he summoned the strength to deal with their insanity.

chapter
nineteen

NAITE STOOD in the corner as the other council members listened to
Natalie's description of the coded request she'd received from the AFP.
The room was crowded with visiting council members, and he'd been
happy enough to give up his seat. He'd rather stand and watch the
strange goings-on. Ebi and Aiden from Blue Hope kept giving Temar
looks like they wanted to drop him in a sandrat nest, which wasn't
normal. Usually it was Shan who made people that angry. Ninya from
Gambles had arrived looking frayed already, her sand bike smelling of
hot metal and her skin wind burned. The rest looked some variation on
disquieted.

And then there were the otherworlders. His eyes kept wandering
back to Verly.

The man knew everything. He knew Naite had murdered in cold
blood, and Naite had given his word that he would deny none of it in
front of the council. Verly only had to make one comment, and Naite's
whole life would end right here. Instead Verly hovered near the door,
looking like he was trying to fit his six-foot-something frame into the
smallest space possible. Given that Verly was an inch or so taller than
Naite and only about thirty pounds shy of him, that wasn't possible.
Naite had tried and long ago given up any attempt to disappear. That
strategy worked better for men like Temar.

Of course, now that Naite was paying attention, Temar did less
hiding and more watching ever since he'd returned from his trip into
space.

Lilian let out a long sigh and steepled her fingers in front of her,
tapping one trim fingernail against her lips. She was another watcher.
For the first time in Naite's memory, she appeared unsure. Perhaps that
was the illness. She seemed less substantial than usual, her skin mottled

with brown spots and her gray hair thinning. Naite didn't like thinking of a world where she wasn't around to bully people into getting along.

After Natalie's report, Bari Ruiz was the first to speak. He was pale, and he gripped the edge of the council table as if he could hold off any invasion through sheer will. "If you don't answer, what will they do?"

"They'll send someone else."

"Not while I'm alive they won't," Lilian said with uncharacteristic bluntness. While everyone knew her word was law on the council, she herself rarely acknowledged the fact. Even the other councils' members were more than willing to let her make that declaration.

"They'll find a way," Natalie said firmly. "They are committed to making sure the PA doesn't cut them off from supplies."

"We aren't cutting them off," Verly interrupted, and Naite felt an unhappy twinge. A man couldn't work two farms or serve two masters, and yet Verly spent half his time talking like a PA soldier and the other half claiming he wasn't one. Naite got the feeling that he was going to end up on the losing end of this relationship sooner or later.

Natalie whirled around and pinned Verly with a nasty glare. "You want to."

"Is that a 'you' as in me personally, or are you blaming me for the political position of the entire Planetary Alliance?" Verly gave her a cocky grin that seemed almost calculated to annoy.

"Both," Natalie snapped back.

"Enough, both of you," Kevin shouted over them. He brought his hand down on the table in a resounding slap that echoed off the walls of the small room. Unlike most of the buildings in Landing, this one used old plates from the hull of one of the colony ships. Naite always felt a little like he was buried alive in this building with all its echoes.

Lilian chuckled. "Yes, having you two in here is reminding me of when both Polli brothers served on the council. Some people are happier as strangers. You two may wish to cultivate that particular skill."

Naite rolled his eyes. He never pretended to be diplomatic. If they didn't want him on the council, they could damn well ask him to leave.

Pulling herself up into a stiff-backed posture, Natalie glared at Verly. "Given Lieutenant Commander Black's background, I would be more than happy to cultivate that skill."

Naite grimaced. That was a mistake. Maybe Temar's talk this morning had done some good, though. Verly stiffened up instead of cringing back like a man afraid of the dark. A whisper of confusion crossed Natalie's face, so she had expected her taunt to hit harder.

"We can discuss my background if you like," Verly said, his words stiff, but he did make eye contact with her. "Do you want to discuss how I was tortured by AFP forces or the incident at Minga?" Several of the visiting council members traded confused looks but seemed ready to wait for some sort of explanation.

"Incident." Natalie spit the word out with more venom than Naite expected, and Lilian's eyes narrowed as she studied the woman. This wasn't some item from the news for her, even Naite could tell that, and he wasn't the most astute when it came to people.

"What incident?" Ebi from Blue Hope finally asked.

Verly swallowed and squared his shoulders, but Naite answered for him. "Verly shot down a suspicious ship. It turned out that it was full of refugees running away from her side." Naite poked his thumb in Natalie's direction.

Lilian nodded. "He made the same choice my grandfather did, and I suspect he carries the same guilt Honor took to his grave."

Naite felt the dark emotions circling the room, and all the people of Livre grew quiet for a moment. Rula looked around, clearly trying to understand, but Natalie was losing her façade of control.

"He murdered over three hundred people." Her voice got higher.

"He made a mistake," Temar corrected her. "A terrible mistake, one that shouldn't have happened, but the war is to blame for the atmosphere of suspicion and hatred—Verly isn't."

Natalie drew her body up and lifted her chin. "So, all the sacrifices people made... all the underground rebels who died to protect that ship, to get those people on it... all those people who risked their lives to try to make it to a better world... all that is a silly little mistake. 'Oh, I'm so sorry. I didn't mean to murder all your people.'" Natalie was hissing mad now, and for the first time, Naite felt like he was seeing the real Natalie. Despite all her deadly calm, she was as fucked-up as the rest of them. He didn't know if that was a comforting thought or not.

Rula stepped forward and rested her hand on Natalie's arm. "Nat," she said softly. Natalie pulled her arm away and strode out of the room, her head high and a trail of pain following her.

Rula stood in the middle of the room looking uncomfortable. She offered Kevin and Lilian in the center of the council table an apologetic smile. "There were people on the ship... people Natalie talked into running."

Verly turned his back, and Naite itched to go over there and.... Naite's imagination was rather limited. He could either hold the man tight or slap him upside the head for feeling guilty for something he couldn't control. Instead of doing either, Naite watched the room.

Lilian rested her chin on her hand, and Kevin pushed himself back in his chair. "Tragedy is part of war," Kevin eventually offered. He was a woodworker, a man who worked with hard tools to shape the tough, thin trees of Livre into something beautiful, and he wasn't normally the first to jump in with words of comfort.

"And I would rather that tragedy not follow us back to Livre," Temar said in a not-subtle reminder that they had important work here.

Verly turned back around to face them, and the pain was etched deeply into his face. "God. I am so sorry that you're getting dragged into this."

"I rather doubt that you have the power to drag an entire planet into a war," Lilian chided him gently. Verly blushed, but then he should. Naite had no idea what they learned in school up there, but arrogance must have been on the curriculum. Maybe that's why Natalie held such a grudge. People who thought they could do anything expected everything of themselves. Naite had a miserable childhood, but he wouldn't trade his father's abuse for a lifetime of feeling like he had to control the turning of the planets and a lifetime of feeling guilty because he couldn't.

Temar turned to face Rula. "Natalie talked people into getting on that ship. Does that mean she was part of the underground?"

Rula blushed. Naite assumed that was a "yes."

Lilian sighed. "Given that, if she refuses to provide the information, she might be best establishing herself here. Advise her to consider taking work."

Rula was silent.

Naite should probably keep his mouth shut, but the only group they could walk into without any sort of apprenticeship or resources was his. "They're welcome in the unskilled workers, if they're willing to do that sort of work." Given their friendship with Cyla, he wasn't sure his offer would be welcome.

Giving him a smile, Rula nodded. "Honest work in a field is a lot better than some things we've needed to do. I should go check on Natalie." Ducking her head in a quick acknowledgement of the council, Rula headed for the door.

Naite scratched his arm as he stewed on that reaction. He had trouble enough with people whose history he understood. For example, he knew Tom had never turned him in even when he must have suspected the truth because Tom felt guilty. The man was a tender. He tended his animals, and he'd tended Naite when Naite came to him as a teenager—angry and striking out at anyone who happened to be in his way. Tom likely felt bad that he never realized how bad old Yan Polli had gotten.

He understood Shan, even if he didn't approve. As a child, Shan had closed the doors and failed to even see what their father did. He'd thrown immature fits about Naite being the favorite without ever thinking about the price Naite paid for holding that position. As an adult, he'd fled the house, hiding in the church when he'd first suspected the truth, and now he vacillated between that same head-in-the sand approach and a wild recklessness fed by some need to prove his head wasn't in the sand.

However, what did it do to someone to serve a government that forced them to kill? Naite had very little doubt that both women did that. And Verly was an utter mystery. He seemed to think making an honest mistake was worse than leading your father out into the desert and letting him die. Naite still half expected Verly to say something to the council.

"They think we're too close to the PA," Temar said softly.

Lilian gave a little hum as her answer.

"Personally, I don't like any of them." Kevin ran fingers though his white hair.

"But they wouldn't come down here, right?" Aiden, the Blue Hope landowner, asked with a desperate sort of voice. No one gave him that assurance.

Dee'eta Sun, the glassblower, had sat silently through most of the meeting, but now she leaned forward. "It's our glass they want. Our glass and the chemicals we collect off the desert. If they can't reach those, we're of no use to them."

Lilian slowly turned to look at the woman.

"I say we order all glassblowers into hiding. White Hills has caves that the strangers will never find. Without us, let them try to find the glass sands in that shifting desert."

"Glass blowing in an enclosed space can be dangerous," Temar objected. He would know more than the rest of them.

Dee'eta Sun gave him a smile. "No more than insisting on staying in the tent during a sandstorm because I would not abandon a beautiful form at the moment it appeared in the glass. Being an artist means you take on some risk. Besides, the new glass ovens you brought will work better in the caves." Ignoring the others, Dee'eta Sun turned to look at Lilian for an answer.

"The masters should move, but the lower-level craftsmen are needed in the towns. We can't afford to become a people who spend their lives moving goods from one point to another," Lilian said, and Naite could feel the room shift. By tomorrow, the master glass craftsmen would be packing up their supplies. Naite appreciated that she was being more direct. Sometimes the woman tended to wander around a point instead of getting to it.

Verly spoke up. "Will that give White Hills an unfair trade advantage if they have access to the best glass?"

"What?" Yenson from White Hope asked, the word clearly startled out of his mouth.

And there was one more piece of evidence that proved Naite did not understand Verly. How could a person give an advantage to a town? Dee'eta Sun would have the advantage no matter where she lived; however, if she moved from Landing to White Hills, that wouldn't change much else. Well, it would remove her from this council, but Naite suspected she would consider that a bonus. If it weren't for the fact that Naite was slaved out to Temar, he'd consider moving before the next election just to get off the council.

"We don't calculate power the same way. I am not worried about the possibility," Lilian said kindly. "You have a better view of the rest of the universe. You understand the PA and AFP in a way we cannot. How would you solve this?"

The moment Lilian asked, Naite could see the panic in Verly's eyes.

"Not that we'll follow your advice blindly," Naite warned. "If you have a stupid idea, we're likely to call it stupid."

Shan's mouth came open, and Temar planted an elbow in his side.

Before Shan could recover enough to say something stupid, Verly laughed. "I do trust you to call a spade a spade, although I guess in this case it might work better to say that you call a sandcat a sandcat."

Naite grunted. If Verly could make jokes, he had found his balance again. "It's better than knowing someone's an idiot and not telling him." Naite let his gaze slide over to his brother. Now Temar glared at Naite, and Naite suspected that Lilian would have that same expression, which explained why he intentionally did not look at her.

"I am steering clear of that conversation," Verly said with some humor.

"Smart man," Kevin chimed in.

"But if I were an AFP officer, I would be very worried about—" Verly cut off so suddenly that Naite was afraid something had happened. Naite looked over, and Verly was slowly turning red.

"What?" Naite asked.

"I...." Verly cleared his throat. "Perhaps I shouldn't have said anything. Forget it."

"Forget what?" Naite asked, suspicious now.

Temar said, "I think he's wondering if his new relationship is private or if he can publicly claim to have caught the attention of a council member."

"Really?" Bari turned around in his chair with the widest smile Naite had ever seen in his life. Naite scowled at the man. The last thing Naite wanted was other people involved in his private life.

"I didn't say that," Verly hurried to interrupt.

Lilian laughed. "Given your matching markings, I think most of us already assumed as much." Her fingers skimmed over the base of her own neck. "Bari has not had enough sleep if he's not seeing what's in front of him."

"I was blinded by my own faith that Naite's growl was going to keep chasing away every young suitor who tried to catch his eye," Bari said, not even a little offended. In fact, he kept grinning like an idiot.

Verly was turning a dangerous shade of red. "I...."

Naite decided to put Verly out of his misery before the man had heart failure. "Verly has made it clear that he plans to share a bunk, but we haven't gotten past camping at this point."

"Camping? All night?" Bari looked from one to the other. "This is gossip. This is the whole reason I'm on the council. It's been well under a month, and you're actually camping?"

Naite suspected that Shan had been replaced as the person who most annoyed him in the world. "It's better than spending time with the idiots in the house," Naite snapped.

"And no offense to anyone here, and without endorsing the 'idiot' part of that comment, I agree," Verly said. "However, to get back to politics, the AFP is going to assume I'm following an agenda... that I've placed myself inside the council by offering sexual favors."

"You do more receiving than offering," Naite said with an amused look in Verly's direction.

Verly's mouth twitched. "True. I don't think they'll be amused either way."

"How will they find out about it?" Shan asked. "Unless someone tells them, I can't think that it's anyone's business."

"We included it in my report—to make sure that I wasn't accused of hiding it...." Verly bit his lip. "The problem is that most of what the PA knows, the AFP finds out eventually. Neither side is particularly good at keeping secrets."

Naite frowned. "Would your people ask you to try to manipulate me?"

"They'd ask," Verly said, "but I wouldn't try, and if I lost my mind and did try, you'd pretty much have me for lunch."

"And dinner," Shan offered.

"I wouldn't put you in that position," Verly offered. "No matter what they asked. They haven't earned a lot of my trust lately, and I can think of a few reasons why they might have included my full service record, including the disaster at Minga. None of them are good."

Lilian rested her chin on her hand. "Such as?"

Verly sank down on a bench against the wall. Part of Naite felt like going over there, but he wasn't going to turn into the sort of man who needed to be touching all the time.

"I expected people here to be angry. I didn't know anything about Aipa, so I assumed you'd hate me. They must have assumed the same."

"Then why send you?" Shan asked.

"Good question." Verly pursed his lips. "To get rid of me maybe. They had the recordings I took of Temar when he first contacted my ship, so they know Temar made it very clear that if I betrayed him he would drag my ass back to Livre and let the sandcats eat me alive as I screamed."

Naite watched as every head swiveled around to look at Temar. The man Naite had known a few years ago would have blushed red and hidden his face by ducking his head. This Temar returned the disbelieving gazes without even flinching.

"But maybe that's paranoia. Maybe they didn't want to be accused of hiding my past—maybe they were trying to avoid giving the AFP representatives more ammunition."

Lilian sighed. "I sometimes wonder if I didn't live a little longer than I should have. Your people and their machinations are not good for my digestion."

"Or mine," Kevin added. "At this point, I say we treat both sides as disagreeable boars we need to keep separated from a drove of pigs." Most of the council members were nodding at that suggestion.

"Agreed," Yenson added.

"It might not be that easy," Verly said softly. "Both sides will expect reports, and at this point, I don't know what's safe to say. If the AFP has the intelligence on my relationship with Naite, they will not feel comfortable letting issues continue. But I don't know if they would even believe a report of our relationship ending. They might see that as proof that I had found an even better target and was working on it."

"Could you say nothing?" Bari asked. "Could you simply stop sending reports?" The man's easy humor of a moment ago had vanished.

Verly shrugged. "If I wanted to trigger a military invasion as they attempted to 'rescue' me, I might. Of course, their definition of rescue would likely include a lot of troops on the ground and a territorial governor to keep the peace until democracy could be restored. I would rather not give them any excuses, especially since Livre is on the edge of the two territories."

"Charming," Kevin said in a weary voice.

"There is one way," Verly said slowly, but then he quickly added, "but it might not be wise."

"Let us judge wisdom," Lilian said, leaning forward. "I want to hear this idea of yours."

Verly took a deep breath, and Naite almost told him to stop. Whatever Verly was about to say, part of him wanted to avoid it. "If I was disgraced… arrested… they would not lift a finger to try to help me, and that would explain why my reports stopped."

"Arrested? For what?" Shan asked.

Again, Verly shrugged. "I don't know. I would rather avoid being accused of another massacre." It was a poor attempt at humor, but the stiff line of his back made Naite worry about him. Verly might pretend to be at ease with this, but he was clearly upset. The rest of the council were idiots if they couldn't see it. After his poor attempt at humor, Verly added, "If I had followed Natalie and Rula somewhere forbidden, that would be enough to warrant an arrest. With all three of us arrested, our officers couldn't expect any more reports."

"We don't have places that are forbidden, not unless you're talking about walking into someone's bedroom, and that's another sort of crime," Shan pointed out.

"But they don't know that." Verly gave one of his crooked grins. "For all they know, you retrofitted the asteroid blasting lasers from your colony ships." He frowned for a second. "Actually, your ancestors probably did do that, but I think that's where some of this rock carving came from. None of the equipment on the ship was designed to do this sort of heavy terraforming. But if I were to drop a few code words that suggested that this location where I was caught was both hidden and tactical in nature, it would make the PA think twice about what you might have. I know the code words for that much."

Naite pursed his lips and thought about that. It was a smart move. It would also isolate Verly from his people, and Naite could admit that he selfishly wanted that. He wanted to keep Verly away from all the idiots who expected him to be able to read minds and magically know the difference between a refugee ship and a terrorist ship. "You said that if the PA knows something, the AFP hears about it eventually. Will they invade a world if they don't know which weapons it might have?"

"It they're smart they won't, but the AFP hasn't always been smart in the past."

Naite smiled. That tied up a number of loose ends, and Verly would have to stay with them. If he claimed to have been arrested, he couldn't take the next shuttle to space and vanish.

"We can't," Temar said, and Naite felt a flash of hot anger. "I'm sorry, but we can't force Natalie and Rula to give up their ties. We can ask them, but that's not a decision we can make for them."

Naite wasn't so sure about that. "If they aren't AFP spies, they should be happy to have an excuse to stay here."

Surprisingly, it was Verly who spoke up for them. "The AFP sometimes holds family members as hostages, and Natalie has a high enough rank that I think it's likely. If she gets arrested, they may consider that a failed mission and execute any of her family. Temar's right. We can't make that decision, and they may not be willing to take the risk."

Naite thought about Natalie's reaction to the refugee ship. For all her games, she cared deeply, so Verly was right. She might not be willing to risk anyone she had back home.

"Ah," Lilian said, her voice bright with realization. "Young Verly is found in a restricted area, and he claims to have followed Natalie and Rula. However, we find no evidence of the two women. We are most displeased with the PA... perhaps we even refuse to allow another ambassador to come down until certain assurances are made."

Verly nodded. "Which makes the AFP even more secure. They'll believe they have the inside track with you." His smile faded. "But if you cut the PA out, they may... I don't know. You may find you have a terrorist problem of your own. FFA—the group that kidnapped Shan— are known to do the PA's work."

Lilian waved her hand. "You can solve that problem later, when my ashes have been safely scattered to the wind and I no longer have to worry."

Kevin gave her a weary look. "Great. Thank you. We appreciate you leaving us the mess."

"You're like children," she said with an indulgent smile, "always looking for mother to pick up your things. You'll be fine, and I won't have to be here to listen to you whine about it."

"We don't whine. We complain in a high-pitched voice," Bari said softly. Several of the others laughed, but Naite only snorted. They whined. They complained less without Shan on the council, but they were still guilty of it.

"Are you sure you want to destroy your life back there?" Naite asked Verly. As much as Naite wanted exactly that, he wouldn't let these people back Verly into a corner.

Verly gave him a boyish grin. "There's more for me here," he said, and he didn't sound like he had any doubts about that.

Temar cleared his throat. "So, we go to the communication relay, call the PA and tell them that we arrested Verly. I can—"

"You can deal with the more immediate question of the water delivery," Lilian interrupted him. "And there are a number of legal issues that Temar has asked to address. As long as we have members from so many councils together, this is the perfect time."

Naite didn't know of any pending legal issues, none that would make Aiden turn quite that shade of gray, anyway.

Temar frowned. "But I should talk to the PA."

Lilian shook her head. "Naite can handle that. In fact, in this case he might be the best person for the job." She smiled at him, and Naite felt the edges of some trap close around his ankle, although he didn't understand it.

Naite didn't miss all the alarmed expressions at that little proclamation. Hell, Naite was feeling a little alarmed himself. "You want me to talk to those idiots?"

"Yes," Lilian agreed. "And if you could call them idiots, it would probably make our point even more clearly."

"You want me to be rude?"

Lilian offered him a conspiratorial smile. "I want you to show them all the warmth and charity their behavior deserves."

Verly gave a snort that sounded suspiciously like a laugh.

chapter
twenty

NAITE LOOKED at Verly for a second, but then the hauler reached the top of the dune, and he had to focus on the treacherous slide down the sands. The engine noise fell off as gravity took over for solar-powered motors. Wind whipped past the windshield, and Naite judged the bottom of the dune, steering them at an angle so he didn't drive the nose of the hauler into the ground.

The engine growled to life again, and the tracks flung up sand as they drove the hauler forward. Verly gave him a confused look. "Are you sure about this?" Naite blurted.

"About what?"

Naite glared as the hauler started up the next dune, but Verly's eyebrows moved down in confusion. "About ruining your name and getting labeled as a criminal," Naite pointed out. The first time the council had convicted him of vandalism and slaved him out to Tom, he'd been so ashamed that he couldn't look anyone in the eye. Of course, not long after that, he'd started acting out every chance he got, leading to longer and longer slave sentences. That had more to do with an adolescent crush on Tom and a feeling of safety at his house than it did any comfort level with getting convicted, though.

People saw criminals differently. Even when he'd voted to slave himself after Temar's abuse came to light, he'd still hated that feeling… that sense that he'd failed so miserably that he deserved to pay. The others must have felt the same because they'd paid some miserably steep fines.

Verly rolled his eyes. "I don't have a good name."

"No, but you wanted to keep your job with the PA. If you do this, will they let you keep being a lieutenant?"

"Lieutenant commander," Verly quickly corrected him. "You people keep trying to demote me more than the PA did. However, I don't think this can hurt me any. The PA has tried to get rid of me for over two years now, ever since the trial ended."

Naite cursed as he misjudged an angle and the hauler started sliding sideways down the dune. Downshifting, he fought the wheel until he got the nose of the vehicle pointed the right direction again. He never understood how Shan could love riding these dunes. While Naite had no interest in most of the technology Verly's people worshipped, he would love to have a nice flat paved road. But given that the face of Livre constantly shifted as millions of tons of sand moved one grain at a time, that wasn't likely. About halfway up the dune, Naite finally breathed easy as the top approached.

"I thought you had your own ship," Naite said.

Verly made a spitting sound and reached up under his sand veil to wipe his mouth and do some more spitting. "I fly a long-range surveillance ship. Naite, is there any chance I could get a driving lesson?"

The hauler reached the top of the dune, tilted up into the air for a second, and thumped back down onto the ground. Naite hit the brakes and disengaged the engine so they perched on the top edge where miles of sweeping dunes spread out in front of them.

"This isn't like driving in space."

"No, that would be called flying. But long before I could get a license to fly, I was driving anything with more than one wheel. This looks like a challenge."

"You get the angle wrong, and you're going to wreck the hauler, and there aren't any communications out here."

"None?" Verly sounded mildly alarmed.

"Nope. Shan keeps saying he wants to get some communications running again, but so far the only thing he's done is fix the interplanetary relays and land us in the middle of a universe full of people who are all crazy as fuck."

"No offense taken," Verly said in a sarcastic tone.

Naite didn't respond because Verly did seem a little on the crazy side most days. Hell, Naite figured anyone who asked to camp with him was missing a few brain cells. He knew his own faults well enough to admit that.

"Give me a chance. Look at it this way: if I wreck the hauler, you can say 'I told you so' for the next decade. Think how happy that would make you."

Naite didn't look amused.

"Good. Move over." Verly jumped out of the hauler and squawked as he vanished.

"First rule, make sure you know where the ground is before you get out," Naite yelled. He could hear the cursing somewhere below him. Naite waited until Verly had crawled his way up to the driver's side. His sand mask had slipped, and it hung under his chin, giving Naite a good look at a very unhappy Verly.

"Second rule, don't move around much when you have one of these things on the top of a dune. Sometimes the sand shifts faster than you think, and you can send it crashing down on top of anyone stupid enough to be walking on the sands directly below you."

"Thank you. Lessons one and two acknowledged and understood," Verly said. He still sounded a little grumpy. Fixing his sand veil, he watched as Naite slid over to the passenger side.

"If you wreck this, I really will enjoy calling you an idiot," Naite warned.

"You call me an idiot now."

"Because you act like one."

Verly settled in behind the driver's seat, but interestingly enough, he didn't disagree. For long miles, Naite pointed out angles and explained how to keep from plowing long troughs of sand at the bottom of each dune. Verly learned faster than Naite expected, and by the sixth or seventh dune, Verly had started to grin on the downslide, the corners of his eyes wrinkling.

Naite waited until they were crawling up the side of a dune before picking up their conversation. "You said that you flew a surveillance ship like that wasn't a good thing. I thought you liked flying."

"That ship meant I was isolated for three or four months at a time. I didn't have anyone to talk to, and I couldn't monitor story-vid or planetary broadcasts because I was too far from any planet. I couldn't even monitor government broadcasts because I didn't have access to codes. After all, I could be captured, and they didn't want any sensitive information on my ship if the AFP got ahold of it."

Naite might not be a huge fan of humanity, but that sort of isolation would make him meaner than a hungry sandcat. "No offense, but your job sucks."

"Yes. It does. That's the sort of job that makes a pilot quit, and that's why an officer does one tour in long-range surveillance before rotating into another position."

"But they weren't looking to send you anywhere else? If you were a worker, I'd say they wanted you to quit." Naite wasn't sure the analogy fit, but that was what it sounded like. "Does your military work that way?"

"Normally, no. Most of the time, you can only leave at certain benchmarks. Everyone is drafted for a one-year tour, but if you score well on certain aptitude tests, you're drafted for five years." Verly's fingers tightened on the wheel, and Naite thought he remembered something about Verly wanting to work with animals when he was younger. On Livre, he had a right to apprentice with anyone he could either pay to take him or impress enough to earn a spot without payment. It seemed like the PA wasn't quite that fair.

Verly took them down the next slope so fast that for a second, Naite could almost imagine Shan was driving. He grabbed the rail and tried to bite back the curses that nearly slipped out. Generally he avoided cursing out the driver until they stopped the hauler on a nice flat bit of ground.

"If you go for promotions and enter certain kinds of training, you can't request an out for ten years. When I got pulled in for five years, I decided to go for a twenty-year tour and get as much education out of it as I could." Verly's voice had lost a lot of emotion.

"That sounds a whole lot like slavery."

"Funny. Until now, I would have disagreed. Now, I'm not so sure because what you call slavery doesn't seem all that bad."

Naite grimaced. "Usually it isn't. Lately, though, we've had some rather spectacular failures." They hit the bottom of the slope, and Verly slowed as he checked the instruments like Naite had shown him.

After a second, he glanced over and offered one name. "Temar."

Naite wished that was the only example. He wouldn't feel so guilty if Temar were the one exception to the rule. He wasn't. "Most recently," he said. "The worst part of that is that Shan warned us all. I hate it when he's right."

"But it sounds like he's wrong more than he's right."

Even though he had no idea whether or not Verly was saying that to get on his good side, Naite agreed. "You have no idea. So, are you a slave to that military of yours?"

"I've put in twelve years, so I should be locked in for another eight, but if I asked to leave, I don't think anyone would try to stop me. They'd be happy if I went somewhere else and quietly disappeared into a bottle."

"A bottle of what?"

Verly gave Naite a double take. "Of alcohol," he said. Naite nodded. They'd had that when the settlers first landed, but people on Livre had better things to do with food than turn it into an intoxicant. Most morons—like Naite's father—used pipe juice, which gave a nice buzz if diluted and killed you otherwise. "If I turned into an addict, they could shove me in the corner of a hospital and pretend I didn't exist." Verly's voice dropped to a near whisper.

Naite snorted. "Your people have issues." Hot anger rose in his chest, and Naite tightened his hand around the grip bar and took several deep breaths.

"This I know. In the last couple of years, I've had a lot of time to think about it. That's all I could do—sit and stare at the walls and think."

"You don't see anyone out there?"

"I don't see anyone, talk to anyone, listen to anyone…. After a while you start to make up names for the stars and have conversations with them. When the stars start talking back… that's when you worry."

Naite stared at Verly until he glanced over.

"I'm kidding," Verly said, and after a second, he added, "Mostly."

"You were close to quitting." Naite figured that was nicer than pointing out that Verly had been close to ending up crazier than a goose.

Verly laughed. "I saw an AFP ship under attack, and I was so space sick that I flew up to them, called them up, and offered to chat. Yeah. I was running out of sanity."

"I didn't say—"

"Subtlety is not your thing, Naite. Even with the sand veil, I can see you wondering how much crazy I have going on up here. And I'll tell you that I don't have quite as much as I did a month ago."

"And your people left you out there."

"My people wanted me to go away."

"The way Temar and Shan tell the stories, your folks treated them like uneducated cousins who showed up on the doorstep with empty food baskets."

Verly took a long time to answer. Naite wasn't sure if he was thinking through his answer or just paying attention to the hauler's long slide down the barchan dune. "That's a pretty accurate description," he finally offered. "Oddly enough, very few soldiers wanted to hang out with me and gossip. However, even I heard a few snickers about how Temar didn't know how to work hair removal equipment and he insisted on shaving Shan. Most of the talk made it clear that they considered Livre technologically backwards and a bit of a joke."

Old anger rattled around in Naite's chest. It'd been a long time since he'd toyed with the idea of punching someone real hard, but he could feel the itch to do exactly that. "It sounds like they're the barbarians. We're the folk who don't have a lot of money and toys."

"That's probably a pretty fair description."

"And now they're going to think we're holding you as a criminal," Naite said, bringing the conversation back to where they'd started.

"Actually, they're probably going to assume that I was attempting counterespionage and I am as bad at that as I was at commanding a defense perimeter ship."

"That wasn't your fault."

Verly waited until he had navigated another transition between dunes before looking over at Naite. "Say that three or four hundred more times, and I might believe you."

"You made a mistake. It's not like you intentionally killed someone."

"I wouldn't be ashamed of killing a man to protect others."

Naite shook his head. "You aren't subtle." While Naite understood Verly's position, the fact was that he'd killed his father, and he could have done a million different things, like tell Tom or encourage Shan to move in with the old priest or confess to Lilian. Naite had more than one fantasy about Lilian Freeland setting her sights on Yan Polli after finding out he was raping his own son. Naite would bet on Lilian in that fight every damn time.

"Really? I thought I was being amazingly delicate."

Naite huffed a quick laugh.

"Now you're hurting my feelings," Verly said with mock indignation.

"You have issues."

"And you know more about me than my last two military therapists, which either suggests that you're very good with people or my therapists were remarkably bad at their jobs."

"I would guess the second because I know the first isn't true."

Verly's voice turned gentle. "You underestimate yourself."

"You overestimate me," Naite pointed out, aggravation erasing the knot of feelings that Naite didn't know how to untangle. Verly was the most dogged man he had ever met, and Naite was including his annoying brother in that.

"We aren't going to agree on this, are we?" Verly asked.

"Nope. So it's a good thing we're only about ten minutes out from the Communication Relay. Otherwise this might get to be an uncomfortable trip." As much as Naite enjoyed Verly's very nicely formed cock, the man talked too damn much.

Surprisingly, Verly fell silent as he guided the hauler over the last few dunes.

chapter
twenty-one

VERLY OPENED another door to find a storage room stacked high with obsolete tech. The Communication Relay felt like a closed museum—with that vague and creepy sense that they were kids walking through some restricted area. This was the only communication receiver on the planet. Considering the size of the sandstorms, that seemed rather dangerous. "Where's the comm tech?" Verly asked as he realized they were alone in the station.

"Standing at his lover's side while they deal with some legal issues I was pointedly uninvited to attend."

Stepping back out into the main room, Verly looked at Naite. "Shan? He's the only tech?" Naite shrugged like it didn't matter much, and Verly shook his head. From his point of view, that didn't make much sense, but the people of Livre were less interested in messages from the rest of the universe. At the very least they weren't interested in getting them fast. "I guess you really don't have a position for an ambassador who doesn't have a part-time job on the side."

Naite turned and gave him an odd look. "Being a mechanic is the full-time job. We only let him play ambassador when no one else wants to go up there and talk to the crazy people."

"If you give them that attitude, they're going to get the idea that you don't like them."

Naite didn't even bother to answer.

"So, do you leave this place empty when Shan's not here?" Verly eyed the equipment.

"Shuttles give us warning before they come down. Shan comes out here to check messages from time to time. How else would you do it?"

"Rotating shifts of technicians monitoring the communications at all times. Planetary coverage for person-to-person communication with a series of secure lines for government officials to use so they can be reached at any time," Verly explained. "In PA space, that would be the absolute minimum allowed."

Naite gave him a very odd look. "That's disturbing. Who needs to talk to someone that often? Unless I'm sharing a bed with someone, I don't want to talk to them every day."

Verly headed back into the main sitting room, letting the door to the equipment room fall shut behind him. "Well, that might explain some of the twitchiness. Both sides probably think you're freezing them out because you're not answering calls quickly."

"Our lives don't revolve around them," Naite pointed out dryly.

"And that is not what they are used to hearing. Trust me, both sides are so caught up in catching each other doing something wrong that they live with one eye on the enemy and a comm within arm's reach. All the time," Verly added. Sometimes talking to Naite was like communicating with an alien species. Certain cultural rules simply didn't translate.

"They'd better learn that we don't run our lives that way." With that, Naite headed for another door. Verly trailed after as Naite headed through a series of rooms set up row style with one room opening to the next. The whole compound was made of two separate rows of rooms that someone had occasionally put doors in to connect. Verly suspected it was the center section of an old colony ship. If he took all the pieces of tech he'd seen, he could probably reassemble the old ships.

"So, what are you going to say?" Verly asked. Now that they were heading to communications, he could feel the butterflies in his stomach. While he didn't have much of a reputation to ruin, listening to his lover denounce him wouldn't be easy.

"You were in a restricted area, and you're under arrest."

"Do you want to...?" Verly held up his hands with the wrists pressed together.

Naite gave him a confused look. "Why?"

"Well, I'm not suggesting we have bondage fun in the middle of the comm station."

"How the hell is bondage fun?" Naite demanded.

Verly's mouth fell open. "You mean, you don't...." Verly had no idea how to finish that statement, not when Naite was looking at him like he'd lost track of several vital brain cells.

"Don't what?" With every passing second, Naite got more defensive and cranky.

"Don't you tie people up when you're having sex? You know, for fun."

"How is that fun?"

"I think any way you have sex is fun," Verly pointed out.

"Prick on a stick. What the hell are you talking about?"

"At this point, I'm not sure," Verly admitted. "I was trying to make a joke because this is a strange situation. But clearly, you don't tie people up when having sex, so this is awkward."

"You tie people down and then have sex with them?" The disgust in Naite's voice was unmistakable.

"Generally I'm more the type to get tied down," Verly said with a grin, but when Naite's expression didn't soften, he cleared his throat and finished, "but yes, I've played a few games with restraints. Hell, we're stuck on a ship for months at a time. It gets boring." At this point, Verly wished he'd never brought the subject up.

"You.... Wait, you let someone tie you down before sex? Why?" The disgust had vanished, but now Naite looked distressed.

"It's a trust game," Verly said with a shrug. "You let someone tie you up, and it's exciting and a little scary. It makes things more interesting. Not that I've invested enough trust in anyone to do that for a good long time."

Naite gave one of his patented grunts. "If you need to make sex more interesting, you're doing it wrong." With that, Naite appeared perfectly happy to ignore the whole conversation. "So, let's get your people on the line."

"Wait." Verly grabbed for Naite's arm as he went to hit one of the controls. "If you don't enable the encoding before you transmit, you're putting your message out for everyone."

"And?"

Verly pulled his hand back. "And that would be strange," he finished weakly. It would be strange for his people, but he was starting to think it would be normal for Naite and the others. Well, maybe just Naite. Temar had the political savvy that he would only publicly broadcast if he were making a point.

"Just sit." Without giving Verly a chance to do that, Naite caught his arm and pulled him down into the chair. After turning on the communication equipment, he quickly worked through the sequence for the PA. Verly was mildly surprised, not because Naite wasn't intelligent enough to learn the equipment, but because Verly didn't think the man cared enough to have learned it.

The conversation with the PA official was mercifully short—so short that Verly barely slipped in the code words for large-scale weapon and AFP intelligence forces before Naite lost patience and disconnected the PA officer in the middle of his offer to send a legal negotiator to argue Verly's case. "If I wanted your advice or your idiot negotiator down here, I would have asked for it," Naite snapped before hitting the kill switch on the communication panel.

Verly stared at the gray screen. That was it. All ties to his past were cut because this would be the last straw. If Verly ever showed his face on a PA planet again, they would push through a quick dishonorable discharge. "Hey, I'm complimented that he bothered trying." Given Verly's past, he'd expected the PA to write him off and forget he ever existed.

"They're not getting you back," Naite said with an unfamiliar fierceness. Verly swung his chair around, and Naite hovered over him, an odd expression on his face and a tension that turned his body into something stiff and alien.

"No, they aren't," Verly agreed. "I don't even want to go back." And that wasn't even taking into consideration that the PA didn't want him back at this point. Verly had gone on the record as the idiot who'd gotten himself arrested and endangered diplomatic relations. The AFP had to love him right now, or at least they would if he weren't a mass murderer in their eyes.

"All his shit about you having a right to go home was pure crap," Naite said.

Verly grinned. That was as close to a statement of affection as Naite Polli was going to get, and it was more than enough for Verly. "Total shit," he agreed. "Let's find a bed and celebrate with sex." Standing up, he left Naite with a gaping mouth as he went in search of a bed.

He was opening a door to a washroom when Naite caught up with him. "You think you can demand sex?"

"Demand is a strong word," Verly pointed out. "But we're alone, and for the first time, we have a chance to have sex on a surface that doesn't leave me bruised." Verly turned and looked Naite up and down. "What? Don't you want to have sex?"

For a second Naite stared, his mouth working although no sound came out for some time. "Considering that my brother lives here part-time, no." Naite's voice took on an alarmed tone.

"Your brother is nowhere near here." Verly opened the next door and found a very nice bed—a big, old-fashioned bed that was nothing like a bunk... or a rock... or the ground. A light violet spread covered the low mattress. "This isn't his bedroom, is it?" Verly asked. He could admit that he didn't want to have sex in the ambassador's room. This room felt vacant, though, with empty shelves and blank walls.

"No, it isn't. But I'm still not having sex here." Naite crossed his arms over his chest and glowered. Maybe that worked with other men, but Verly had his own streak of stubborn.

"Too bad because I am." Verly started pulling his shirt off.

"What the hell are you doing?" Naite took a fast step backward.

Verly plopped himself on the edge of the bed and started pulling his boots off. Sex without boots on... what a novel concept. "I am getting naked right before I have sex, either with you or with my hand, your choice. I'm not giving up a chance of sex on a bed." Verly set his boots aside and pulled off his socks before standing up.

"You're being pretty damn bossy here," Naite accused him.

Verly could only laugh. Unbuttoning his pants, he started pushing them down. His cock had risen to half-mast already.

Naite stepped closer, and Verly sat on the bed again, eyeing the man as he waited for some sort of reaction. "You think you're going to get your way here, don't you?" Anger simmered just under the surface, but Verly was in this relationship for the long run, so he couldn't afford to start tiptoeing around Naite's issues.

Verly leaned back on the bed. "I think I'm going to come. I hope you'll be involved because I would love to have company. However, your participation is not strictly required, Councilman Polli." Crooking his knee, Verly dug his heel into the mattress and shifted his ass to give him the best angle. Naite watched, his eyes wide and dark as Verly wrapped his hand around his cock and started slowly stroking himself.

Tilting his head back, Verly let his eyes fall closed as he lost himself in the feel of his hand—warm and tight—around his cock. After all his time in that damn shuttle, he'd thought he'd run out of patience for his right hand... and his left. But knowing Naite was watching made his skin warm and his cock harden. He cracked his eyes open to look at Naite

Naite's eyes had widened slightly, and the lust built as Naite watched him with open hunger. Naite wanted him. Whatever objections he might make, Naite wanted him.

Sharp little tingles danced up his spine, and Verly caught his lower lip between his teeth. He wanted to give Naite a show, but his need to come pressed close already. Clearly he had a streak of exhibitionism that he hadn't known about. Naite's calloused hand grabbed his knee, and Verly opened his eyes.

Naite stood over him, naked and hard and staring down hungrily.

"Want to join in?" Verly asked in a teasing voice.

"Asshole."

"I have one, yes."

"You are one. We don't have any gakka," Naite complained, "and before you make any stupid suggestions, I am not going to borrow any from my brother." Despite the doubt in his tone, he pulled his shirt off and tossed it aside.

"Well, we'll have to get creative, then, won't we?" Verly gave Naite the most overly sweet smile he could summon. The glare he earned in return made it worth it.

"Shove over."

"Your romantic words make me feel all warm," Verly said as he scooted over to give Naite room on the bed.

"Your idea of romantic seems to include tying people up, so your judgment isn't exactly reliable."

"It's a game. A trust game." One that Verly regretted bringing up. Naite snorted. "There are lots of other things I can think of doing that we might enjoy even more." Verly reached over and ran a hand down Naite's bare chest. The man had a controlled strength that impressed the hell out of Verly. He was used to the power in a soldier's body—of muscles trained until they were hard and well formed; however, Naite's chest had only the hint of the sharp cuts of a gym-conditioned body, and he had twice the bulk. Just resting his palm against Naite's skin, Verly could feel the power—the strength. And yet, unlike all those soldiers Verly had once known, Naite never felt the need to show off to others. This was a form of power Verly had never known existed.

"You plan on doing something or petting me like a dog all day?" Naite asked, and he sounded cranky. Then again, Naite always sounded cranky.

"I plan on taking my time and exploring every inch," Verly said. Leaning closer, he placed a kiss on Naite's shoulder and tasted the salt of his skin before moving down to kiss the inside of his elbow.

"You're in danger of turning sappy."

"I'll take the risk." Verly had lots of quick fucks in his past, but the number of men who'd allowed this slow exploration, he could count those on the fingers of one hand. "Now shut up and let me work."

Naite huffed, but he did shut up as Verly shifted around until he could kiss the hollow of Naite's hip and the curve of skin down to that beautiful, thick cock already darkening in lust. Suddenly Naite shoved himself toward the foot of the bed, and Verly looked at Naite's nipple. Verly pulled his head back far enough to give Naite a disgusted look. "I was enjoying myself down here."

"Get your dick up here."

"Well, if you're going to sweet-talk me like that."

Naite snorted. "I'm not the type to sweet talk, but I am the sort who likes to suck on a man's cock and watch him lose control." Naite raised his eyebrows, practically daring Verly to argue with that logic, but Verly was far too smart for that. Twisting around, he got his feet up toward the head of the bed so that they lay nose to cock with each other.

"Is this—" Verly swallowed his words and his tongue nearly went with them as Naite caught the head of Verly's cock in his mouth and then sucked while using his tongue to tease the slit. In a nanosecond, Verly went from horny straight to ready to explode. "Oh hell." Verly's eyes nearly crossed as Naite pulled back, gave one last little flick of his tongue before looking at Verly and fucking smirking. He full-on smirked.

"That work for you?" Naite asked, smacking his lips. Verly might respect, lust after, and care about Naite, but he couldn't deny one thing. Naite Polli was a bastard.

Instead of answering, Verly leaned down and took Naite into his mouth, pressing in until the head of Naite's rather impressive cock bumped the back of his throat. His whole mouth stuffed full of Naite, Verly hummed as he rocked slightly back and forth. Naite clutched the sheets and cursed colorfully as Verly made his own point. Obviously Naite enjoyed the attention because Verly had slowly worked all the way back until he only had the head of Naite's cock in his mouth before Naite managed to find his own prize.

Verly groaned as Naite's tongue flicked across the underside of Verly's cock a half second before cool air slid over the damp skin, and then Naite closed his mouth and sucked hard, the warmth and tightness of his mouth tempting Verly to thrust. The sensations changed so fast that Verly's body barely adjusted to one very impressive oral technique before Naite shifted into another. Wrapping one hand around the base of Verly's cock, Naite turned his attention to Verly's sensitive balls. Naite's warm breath, the feel of his soft lips and the quick, teasing taps with his tongue all distracted Verly so much that he had trouble focusing.

Not to be outdone, Verly took Naite in his mouth until the head of his cock was at the back of his throat, and then he swallowed. Immediately, Naite's whole body shivered, and Verly took that as an invitation to slip fingers between Naite's legs. He brushed fingertips across the sensitive skin behind Naite's balls before gently palming them.

Naite did something along the underside of Verly's cock, and Verly's toes curled as his balls drew up tight, and before he could catch his breath, Verly came hard. His whole body locked up, and he lost all control as the orgasm shivered its way through every cell and every molecule in his body.

In some distant corner, he realized that Naite had grabbed his own cock, and with only a pull or two, he came. Naite's cum splattered the side of Verly's face, but he couldn't have cared less. If the entire command staff of the PA had shown up nude and dancing a jig, Verly could not have found one spare brain cell to care about any of it. His body was drained, and it took every ounce of energy to flop onto his back, his one arm still between Naite's legs.

One of Naite's hands traced circles inside Verly's thigh, but other than that, they lay silent and still as their bodies slowly cooled. Sweat gathered, cooled, and then dried as Verly studied the pattern of welds on the metal ceiling. Time paused to watch the two of them, and Verly felt caught inside the moment, like a ship at the edge of a wormhole, exempt from time and unable to move. Or rather, the ship could move as much as it wanted without seeming to move from any outside perspective.

That's how Verly felt. He was moving, flailing even. Lying in bed, some small and starved part of himself raged back to life. He wanted this; he wanted closeness and trust and someone who would tease him in bed and still claim him in the morning. He wanted it so much that the need physically hurt. His chest ached with the years and the fear that if he lost Naite, he'd be right back to that empty man again. The silence grew louder and heavier until Naite broke the spell.

"I won," he announced in a grand voice. Verly didn't even have to look at Naite's face to know the man wore a smirk—he could hear it in the tone.

"Asshole," Verly said.

Naite laughed.

chapter
twenty-two

NAITE WATCHED as Verly guided the hauler up the face of a dune. Sand slid out from under the tracks, and they slithered back, but Verly only lost a few inches before he got them moving the right direction again. He had talent with machines.

He had talent with a lot of things.

Gripping the wheel tightly, Verly braced himself for the moment when the hauler hit the crest of the dune, and he had to completely shift his strategy for driving. Naite hated that moment, that point where he was neither climbing the dune nor falling, and he couldn't decide if the idiot machine was going to lurch forward or fall back. Nope, Naite preferred something solid under his feet. He wanted a digging stick in hand as he walked the fields. He wanted to watch water trickle into the irrigation system. He knew himself well enough to understand that his own control issues fueled his discomfort with the unknown, but that didn't mean he knew how to handle them.

There was a difference between knowing that a relationship scared the shit out of you and knowing how to get past it.

Naite still didn't know what possessed him to tell Verly about his father. He'd carried the secret for years, and now some inexplicable need to tell a man he'd known for days had possessed him. And it wasn't as if the secret weighed on him. Naite had done what he needed, and other than a vague desire to pound the stupid out of Shan every time the man talked about forgiveness, Naite had moved past it. They crested the dune, and the engine went into low gear as they started falling down the far side.

"So, what will you do?" Naite asked.

"I don't know. What are the options?" Verly didn't even spare Naite a glance as he focused on the drift of the machine.

"You have any talent fixing these?" Naite asked.

"Nope. I just turn in requests when something breaks. I can perform an emergency repair, but only if I have a datapad telling me which gear to strip or how to crosswire something."

That seemed stupid. Even Naite knew how to perform a few simple repairs if a hauler failed him in the middle of the desert. On Livre, if you had to leave a machine behind and walk off the desert, your survival was questionable, and the planet would swallow the damn hauler whole. In school they learned about the *Ptah*, a mining ship that disappeared whole with the entire crew. Naite had imagined what it would be like, buried alive and waiting for the machines to slowly die. Schoolchildren had passionate debates about whether the air scrubbers or the water recycling would have failed first. At about ten, Shan had even written a truly disturbing short story for English class where the crew all lost their tempers and murdered each other with mining lasers. For a one-time priest, he'd had a rather vivid imagination as a kid.

"Could I learn veterinarian science?" The hauler hit the bottom of the dune, and Verly transitioned smoothly, shifting the engine back into gear with only a slight jolt.

"Doctoring animals? Sure." That was a solid trade.

"Are you sure I'm not too old? Maybe I'd be better off taking an unskilled job."

"I've seen you dig fields. Train for doctoring."

Verly laughed as if Naite had made some grand joke. He hadn't.

"You have a point," Verly agreed easily. "How much would that cost?"

"You let the council accuse you of a crime so we could try manipulating others. I think you can get the council to cover the costs." Two seconds later, Naite grabbed for the handlebar as Verly cut the hauler at a sharp angle that essentially shoved the nose of the vehicle into the side of the dune. Shan pulled stupid shit like that, but most normal people avoided moves with a high risk of rolling a vehicle. Naite glared at Verly.

Reaching up, Verly pulled off his sand veil. "I'm not letting someone else pay my way."

"Fuck. I'm not saying you should. I wouldn't say that." Naite understood that sore spot more than most. After Shan had gone into an apprenticeship to become a mechanic, Tom had offered to pay

Naite's way into skilled work. Naite didn't want sympathy, not Tom's and not anyone else's.

"You are saying that. You think I should let the council pay these fees."

Naite pulled off his own sand veil. He didn't want to have this argument from behind a mask. "Because it's bullshit that you have to give up your good name not because of what you did but because we're playing fucking games with assholes who don't know how to take 'no' as an answer."

"I caused this mess," Verly said in a tone that made it clear he meant what he said, even if what he said made no sense at all.

"The fuck you did." Naite realized why he had so much sex with Verly—sex was easier than talking or trying to understand the man's logic.

"I sent the report that said I was sleeping with you."

"And did you go behind Temar's back?"

"What? Of course not."

"Then he approved it, and you haven't done anything wrong. Unless you plan to count letting me fuck you a mistake." Naite crossed his arms and waited to see if that's where Verly planned to go. This was why he slept with men once and moved on before they got to the camping and screaming stage.

Verly blinked at him, cocking his head to the side like a buteo. "Do you think I would ever call that a mistake?" Verly's tone suggested he hadn't even been in that general area, so now Naite was well and thoroughly confused. Naite felt like he was trying to walk in shifting sand, and he did what he always did when he couldn't find solid footing. He glared.

With a little sigh, Verly leaned back in his seat. "I'm not sorry about us. I'm sorry I told my superiors about us. I was so worried about Natalie and the near enemy that I lost track of the larger strategy, which is a rookie mistake. I should have known that if the AFP heard that I had landed in the bed of a councilman, they would assume I was a honeypot agent who had successfully infiltrated.

"And from there, it's not hard to guess that they'd feel insecure about their position. I put your world in this danger. Fuck." Verly ran a hand over his face. "It's been too damn long since I had to deal with people, Naite. I've been stuck in deep space for going on three years.

Three years. That's three years of not having to think about how other people are going to react."

Some days Naite only wished he could have three years to himself, but after three years of living in close quarters with his demons and no one else, he'd probably be as crazy as his father. "This isn't your fault." Naite wasn't much for comforting someone, so the truth was all he could offer. "Those people seem like they're looking for excuses."

"And I gave them one on a silver platter," Verly immediately countered. This was why Naite didn't do comforting. People were annoying pains in the ass when you tried to make them feel better. Not willing to get into a fight, Naite stared at his idiot lover and waited for something less annoying to come out of his mouth.

Eventually Verly ran a hand over his face. "You may not believe it, but I do carry some of the blame here. I wouldn't let myself get used if I didn't."

Naite snorted again. He didn't believe that bullshit for two seconds. Verly had a huge streak of masochism, and the fact that he kept coming back for more of Naite's own shit proved that.

"Besides, I'm not broke. I spent years locked in a tiny ship with no way to waste money on anything." Verly pulled his sand veil up over his face. "The first time I gave a donation to the refugee commission, it somehow backfired and all the newsvids implied that I was trying to buy people's forgiveness. It stirred it all up." Verly put the loader into reverse to free it from its awkward position. Weariness and wariness colored Verly's every twitch. Life hadn't treated him well.

"How much money do you have?" Naite asked. Apprenticeships could cost a lot, especially if the skill master didn't know a person. Verly would be asking an animal doctor to take the time to train him when there was no evidence that Verly had any talent at it.

"Around 40,000 credits."

"I don't think your definition of credit is the same as ours."

"Probably not," Verly agreed as he got the hauler headed back up the sand slope. They both had to shout over the sound of the engine growls. "I mean, I could get thousands of gallons of water for fifty credits."

Yeah, they had different definitions of "credit." The problem was that as far as Naite could see, Verly had exactly nothing. A Livre credit was recorded in the town center. It was a simple mark of future goods against any debts. Verly had exactly none of those. People on Livre didn't have much use for the holographic, plastic and metal bits the Planetary Alliance called money.

"I wonder if the PA will charge me for transport fees if I ask them to send supplies. Probably." Verly made a disgusted noise.

"They'll send you supplies?"

Verly glanced over. "Why wouldn't they?"

"Because we made them think you're under arrest for spying."

"Actually, you made them think I'm under arrest for being really bad at following spies." Verly gave Naite a long look. "Wait. Are you trying to tell me that a convict can't use his own money?"

"Most times a slave doesn't have any money. That's why he's slaved out instead of paying a fine."

"So if you wanted to get a new shirt?"

Naite shrugged. "I'd tell Temar to buy it for me."

Verly blew out a long breath. "Oh boy. Not to state the obvious or anything, but not everyone is good about taking care of their responsibilities, especially when that involves spending money on other people."

"Hell, I know that. But most people don't want the whole town to look at them like they're pieces of shit. That keeps them honest." Naite fell silent as he thought about those who hadn't much cared about others' opinions, his own father included. Verly was equally quiet, so Naite figured the man knew just as many sandrats, if not more. It did seem like the rest of the universe had an unfair percentage of vermin.

Verly crested the next dune, and for a half second, Naite's eye found a break in the horizon. After a lifetime of walking fields while searching for evidence of pipe plants and sandrats invading the valley, his gaze went instinctively to the ragged, broken edge of a distant dune. Verly adjusted their trajectory as they sped down the face of the dune, and the engine revved as the hauler labored its way up the face of the next one. Naite used the brace bar to balance himself as he stood. Verly immediately downshifted, and the hauler slowed. As they approached the top, Naite could see a ridge a few miles away, the crisp line broken and ragged, as if some giant had taken a bite out of it.

The winds had already started to smooth it all over, but it clearly wasn't natural. Verly slowed and then stopped the hauler at the top of the dune. He stood and looked in the same direction. "What are we looking at?"

"Something that's not right."

"What kind of not right?"

Naite rolled his eyes. "Won't know until we get there. Looks like something went crashing through. Veer off to the right about twenty degrees."

"Now?" In one second, Verly went from curious to anxious.

"Unless you've got a better idea."

Verly gave a little huff. "How about we call for backup? That sounds better."

Naite sighed. His lover was either an idiot or a poor listener. Either that, or it was going to take a long time to break him of the habits he'd learned on those other worlds. "What exactly would we use, and who exactly would we ask to come out here?"

Verly's eyes went down to the dashboard of the hauler, but there wasn't any radio. Most times Naite was just as happy to escape human contact for a while, but he could admit that right now he wouldn't mind a chance to call for some reinforcements. The trouble was that he couldn't. And he wasn't going to go running in the other direction when the chances were that some fool kids had crashed a loader and needed help.

"We could go back to town and get help," Verly suggested.

Naite shook his head. "We don't even know what we need. We might have one fool kid with a broken neck, which means we don't need anything except a pair of strong arms to haul him and any salvageable parts into the back of our hauler. We might have a dozen craftsmen who had a hauler blow up on them, in which case some might bleed to death before we got back. We need to figure out what we're looking at before we go calling for anyone."

Verly frowned, but he didn't disagree as he settled back down into his seat. Naite dropped down next to him and waited for Verly to come to the most reasonable conclusion.

As they climbed the last dune, Naite's stomach knotted in fear. He'd felt this when he'd found Shan's message, the one that had sent him running into the desert to find an abandoned base where Ben and his friends planned to kill Shan and Temar and flee a dying planet. He'd felt this when he'd watched his father smiling at Shan, that drunken leer hiding a world of pain. He'd suffered too damn much fear for a simple worker.

The hauler reached the top, teetered for a few seconds, and then settled. In the valley formed by two dunes, a ship lay on its belly, pieces of it littering the sands and long streaks of oil or gas already smearing in the wind. It was larger than the small shuttles that had brought Verly and Natalie and Rula and thousands of gallons of water to Livre. This ship had boxy wings, only one of which was still attached to the angular body that looked nothing like the sleek birdlike shapes of the shuttles.

"It's a scoop," Verly said, wariness in his voice.

"Meaning?" Naite hated that there was an entire universe of things he didn't understand. A planet full of stupid people who made equally stupid decisions was about all he could handle.

"One of the high atmosphere shuttles. It only flies into the highest atmospheres, grabs the shuttle and hauls it up to the main ship. They don't have the right structure to even fly in low atmosphere."

Naite grunted. Verly spoke the truth there. This ugly caricature of a ship didn't look like it could fly long enough to escape a sandrat nest. "Looks like someone tried anyway."

"It could have been mechanical failure." Verly didn't even pretend to believe that excuse.

"Is there some other reason someone might drive their ship into a planet?"

Verly looked at him incredulously, and Naite got the feeling the man had a whole host of reasons why someone might do exactly that, and they were all rattling around inside Verly's head right now. Fuck. The rest of the universe had sandcat gnawed brains, that's for sure.

"Start at the top of the list and work your way down," Naite ordered.

"Sabotage, espionage, honeypot, infiltration, secondary explosion, provocation." Verly paused. "I could go on, you know."

"I don't even understand half that list, so I don't see the point of you making me even more suspicious of the rest of the universe."

Verly ran a hand over his face and seemed to age in the blink of an eye. The sharp humor and boyish smile vanished under something infinitely older and harder. Naite wasn't sure whether to be complimented at being allowed to see under the mask or furious at the pain etched in Verly's true face. He chose not to react at all, to allow Verly the illusion of privacy in his own thoughts.

"We may have injured down there, people trading on sympathy to set up covers as honeypot agents."

"The way you keep bringing up honeypot agents is making me uncomfortable. How often do your people turn sex into a weapon?"

"Not all that often. They're not usually all that useful because higher-level officials are trained to beware the traps, but sometimes lower-level officials who have access to bookkeeping records are targeted, and sometimes agents will use very specially baited traps. One AFP agent was paralyzed from the waist down, her spine fused so it couldn't be regenerated, in order to be more attractive to a politician. He'd been a soldier permanently disabled in the war, and because of specialized nerve damage, he couldn't use prosthetics."

Now Naite felt old. People who would do this kind of shit should be dumped into the black of space and forgotten, and he didn't like Verly's tone—so matter-of-fact, as though this were normal.

"One of the best ways to inspire sympathy and forge a relationship is to appear weak and needy." Verly smiled wryly. "And if you are psychologically damaged, then I guess it's even easier to inspire sympathy and get a gruff man to look at you twice."

Naite rubbed his face. Verly was right up there with Shan on the subtle front. "You're no more psychologically damaged than I am, and yes, I am aware that's not saying much." Naite focused on the ship. "Run down what some other options might be."

"They might use provocation if they know you have the ability to kill the people or blow up the ship. They get you to attack first, sacrifice the ship in order to have an excuse to come in, and then destroy you with their whole army. Both sides might use that. You may also have terrorism. A primary accident scene attracts people. Secondary explosions wait until military or government people arrive to investigate or rescue people are on scene, and then they blow up the ship in order to take out the highest number of enemy."

"The more you talk, the more likely I am to vote against letting anyone from your universe set foot on Livre sand."

"I can't say I disagree with that decision. But we have a ship down there that might be full of innocent crew who need help, and we might be looking at a trap. We should go back to Landing and get some backup."

Naite looked down at the torn-up ship. If people were bleeding or unconscious, they needed help now, and the problem with the desert was that things moved, even objects as large as a ship. Naite might not be able to get back with help quickly. And if Verly was right, he might be pulling any rescuers into a situation where they became the victims. Naite would take that risk with his own life, but not with the lives of any healers or other members of the council.

"I'm not letting folk die, and if this is a trap, I'm not letting more people walk into it," Naite said firmly. This was his world, and he refused to turn his back on his own beliefs just because the rest of the universe had no morals. Verly stared at him blankly, seemingly unable to understand simple English, so Naite pushed himself up and started into the back of the hauler where he could jump down without sliding down the rest of the slope they perched on.

"Where are you going?"

"Down there."

"Are you crazy? That could be a trap."

"Could be," Naite agreed easily. "I won't know until I get there." He got into the back, but Verly caught his ankle, and Naite had to stop.

"You're not going in there." Verly had a fierceness to him that Naite wasn't used to seeing.

"Are you telling me what to do?"

"Fuck yes."

Naite lost a half second, unprepared for that answer, and Verly pounced on the silence.

"You know the planet, and I have followed your every request because of it. But this...." Verly waved his hand toward the broken ship. "I know this. You are a member of the ruling council. Killing you would be a coup. In fact, they already tried to kill Shan for that exact reason, only this time I don't have a ship to ride in to the rescue. So you listen to me. If that's a real accident, I can help them as much as you. But if that's a trap, you are the fucking last person in the world that should walk in there. Do you hear me? The last."

"And if you walk in there, they'll kill you. You yourself said that the AFP wanted you dead."

Verly pressed his lips together and cocked his head in a way that suggested a barely contained anger. "They'll do worse than that to you. If that's an AFP trap, if that is some terrorist ship carrying out their orders, they'll torture you, record your screams, and play it back for your brother, transmit your image to all the inner planets and desecrate your body. You have no business heading down there."

A cold anger seeped into Naite's bones, and he wasn't going to turn his back on doing what was right, not even if the rest of the universe had turned into sandrats. "I'm not leaving people who could be dying right now."

"I'm not asking you to. I'll go down there. You take the loader back to Landing and get help."

"We can go together," Naite said, even though he knew that was a stupid idea even before he suggested it. If they both stepped into a trap, there wouldn't be anyone left to go for help.

Maybe Verly got that because he didn't even try to argue with Naite. He calmly said, "You need to get the two ambassadors."

"Shan and Temar," Naite snorted dismissively, but Verly caught his arm.

"Those two have forced respect out of power-hungry politicians. The least you can do is give them a chance to do their fucking jobs, no matter how you feel about them personally."

"You want me to give them a chance to get you back from AFP terrorists." Naite's stomach knotted in fear so intense that he had trouble breathing. His hand trembled with dark emotions so that he had to hold tightly to the seat.

"It may be an accident." Verly's gaze skittered away.

"You don't think it is."

"I think the timing is a little too convenient."

"Then we both go back to Landing," Naite said firmly. That violated every rule he'd learned growing up. You didn't walk away from trouble. Ever. If you had to miss your own wedding or leave your most valuable belongings sitting on the sand to get swallowed by shifting dunes, you did it. You never abandoned someone. But he would do exactly that to keep Verly from walking into a trap.

"And if it is a downed ship? If they are in there bleeding to death?" Verly's words were enough to make Naite's stomach get all knotted. Verly nodded. "If this is a trap, someone has to poke it and set it off. Otherwise, the trap is still there to catch someone else." Verly's voice had a desperate edge.

"So you think you should do it?" Naite demanded.

"What are our options? You're a council member. You have political value, but you don't have the ability to talk your way out of this if it is a trap. Shan and Temar are not only ambassadors, but they're the two people who scare the shit out of the other politicians. Temar's name makes them twitch because he has a power they can't understand."

Naite snorted. "Like what?"

"Hell if I know. But Temar walked on my ship unarmed, took command, and made it pretty clear he'd make me regret ever being born if I even tried to undermined his authority."

Naite frowned. Temar had been different since returning, but he still had trouble seeing the man as capable of that sort of authority. Hell, Naite could snap Temar in half if he put his mind to it. Then again, Naite could snap Lilian in half, and the very thought of trying made him slightly nauseous with fear.

Verly ran his fingers through his short hair. "I'm not playing martyr. I would send Natalie in if she were here, but she's not."

"Then we go get her," Naite said, and he tried very hard to ignore how long that would take.

"They've seen us," Verly said. His disgusted tone and dark glare made it clear exactly what he thought about that plan. "If they're injured and we walk away, think of the impression we've made. Worse, they might use that as an excuse to invade. A piece of propaganda about locals leaving some brave soldier to die in the desert... that's worth a fortune in political capital."

Naite pressed his lips together, fighting against a need to scream in frustration. No matter what he said, Verly had some political insanity to counter it. "If they're trying to capture us, and you walk in there—"

"Then we'll know who set the trap," Verly said, cutting him off. "The PA will claim it's a rescue, send me back up there and try to get me to say something to justify coming in with their military. The AFP will execute me for crimes against civilians, but they'll postpone it until they figure out if I have any value to you. So I'm willing to do this and trust you and Temar to get me out of either of those scenarios if it turns out it's a trap. Tell Temar that there is a legal right of local governments to oversee punitive sentences on their world. So if I were to be sentenced to a crime here, the council would have a legal right to demand I serve a sentence here. You might want to avoid the word slavery, though. If it's a genuine crash, some medical assistance would go a long way toward good will in either camp. Just make sure you find a radio somewhere before you come back. I'll do triage and have the patients ready to go."

"This is stupid."

Verly gave him a small smile and rested his hand against Naite's arm. "Most of what I do is stupid, including volunteering to come to a planet with a man who threatened to feed me to sandrats and then chasing after another man who clearly didn't want more than a one-night stand. Stupid is my specialty. However, these people are from my world, and I understand it better than you. You aren't going to talk me out of this particular form of stupid."

"Verly." Naite grabbed his wrist, unnamed fears clutching at his chest until the physical pain burned as brightly as if Verly had punched him.

"Hey, I've done worse and survived. Have you heard the rescue story from Temar? That was so stupid that I told him up front that it would probably fail one way or another."

"And is this going to fail?" Naite demanded. He wanted an excuse to take Verly with him, to save him from this danger. Of course, he also wanted to go down there himself, so his emotions were not the best guide right now.

"Maybe," Verly said. "If it's a real crash, I'll have another chance to try to prove I'm not a murdering bastard. If it's a trap, I still give myself fifty-fifty odds, because you people do tend to react in ways that the rest of the universe has trouble categorizing as sane."

"We're not the ones with sunbaked brains."

Verly gave him a crooked grin. "I know some psychologists who would be happy to disagree."

"If unpredictable is good, shouldn't I go down there?"

Verly shifted his hand so it rested on Naite's knee. "I love you. I am irrationally in love with you. As the person who forgives you your flaws, I can say that you stick both feet in your mouth on a frighteningly regular basis, and I would rather you not talk to the rest of the universe. They'd end up using a nuclear bomb to irradiate us from space."

Naite gave an offended huff, but he couldn't exactly disagree. Most people did classify unpolished truth as putting your feet in your mouth, and Naite knew he tended to share a little too much rough honesty. He'd rather an ugly truth than some pretty, unctuous lie. If Verly had lied and promised to be okay, Naite would have... he had no idea what he would have done because his thoughts hadn't been this chaotic for decades.

"I don't want to let you go down there." That was the only truth Naite knew.

"And you don't want to walk away from people in trouble, and you don't want to bring Shan here and let him spring the trap, and you don't want a potential threat to your planet lying there without any way of knowing what it really is," Verly added.

Naite sighed. He was right.

"Hey, this is my job. I'm a soldier, not just another pretty boy toy." Verly flashed him a bright, lopsided smile that made something in Naite's gut ache. "So, you get backup; I'll go poke them with a stick and see if they moan or snap closed." Verly pushed past Naite, shoving him back into the passenger side as he crawled between the seats to get into the back. "You have a first-aid kit on this thing?"

"Under the driver's seat," Naite answered. He was on autopilot. He couldn't move as Verly went and fetched the heavy box. "You don't even know how to help them."

Verly gave him one of those grins that made Naite ache with longing and now with fear. "I'm a soldier. I know how to treat burns and broken bones and wounds." After hefting the box up onto his shoulder, Verly headed to the back of the hauler. "I'll be fine. If it's a trap, you guys can get me back out again."

Naite wanted to argue, but he didn't know Verly's world well enough to know what to say. He settled for saying, "I don't want you to go. If anyone goes, it should be me."

"A councilman... yeah, they'd love to get their hands on you. Well, if we assume this is a trap, they would. If it's not a trap, I have more experience with field dressings, and you need to go get real medical help. Those shuttles can have crews of up to twenty." Verly jumped down off the back of the vehicle and slipped in the sand, falling to one knee. "Just hurry, okay? Trust me, Temar knows how to handle these people." Verly stood and started climbing toward the crest of the dune.

Naite watched him walk along the top, away from the hauler where he might get crushed if it fell the wrong way down the dune. "Don't get dead!" Naite called after him.

Verly raised a hand and waved, and Naite knew the only way to help him was to hurry back and get Temar and medical help. If this was a trap, he had to get his idiot lover out as fast as possible. He climbed into the driver's seat and started the engine before backing carefully off the ridge and away from the crash. The next time he saw something strange, he was going to drive the other way, he vowed to himself. Considering how much fear was ripping at his guts, he might even do it.

chapter
twenty-three

VERLY WADED through the fine dust-sand. Naite had warned him about the deep desert where a man could sink into the ground like it was quicksand. People who lived in space considered ships and nuclear weapons the ultimate power, but the people of Livre talked about how the desert swallowed entire ships whole. If this was an intentional crash, these people either didn't understand the desert or they were suicidal.

The thought didn't comfort him.

The likeliest scenario included an AFP ship, probably with multiple individuals tasked with establishing a relationship with local leadership. After all, they would assume that an unauthorized landing would lead to interrogation, and that would give their agents access to interrogators and possible politicians who came to see the interrogations. They had no way of knowing that Livre was not any other world.

"Hey! Anyone alive in there?" Verly called. The wreck looked worse up close. The metal skin had peeled back from the edge of a wing revealing the structural supports inside, and the windows were sandblasted to an opaque finish. "Hello?" A long rip in the center of the shuttle allowed Verly to peek inside, and he cupped his hands around his eyes to try to see in the dark. "Anyone in there?"

He was starting to wonder if this was a true wreck—some ship trying to fly over and spy on them only to be caught in a sandstorm. Maybe no one had survived. Or maybe some disease waited inside. Verly had seen both sides use biologicals even while condemning their use. Of course, if that was the plan, they should have crashed in a populated area in order to infect the greatest number possible.

"Hello?" Verly pounded on the shuttle's door. A metallic thunk and a grinding noise answered him. Verly stepped back to let the door swing open, but it only moved an inch before it stopped. "Great," he muttered as he grabbed the handle and pulled for all his might. Whatever else might be staged, the door truly was jammed. It took all of Verly's strength to pull it open a couple of feet. He stopped when his fingers burned with the effort.

"Hello?" he called again as he moved to the opening. The inside of the shuttle was dim and glowed red from emergency lighting, so it took a second for Verly to notice the injured man on the ground. He lay facedown, his fingers reaching for the door, although he had stopped moving.

"Hang on. I'm here to help," Verly said as he stepped over the man and into the downed ship. He put the emergency kit on the ground and opened it, grabbing out water and bandages before he carefully rolled his patient over onto his back.

Shit. AFP service patch. Sometimes Verly hated it when he was right. He could only play his part and hope it bought the others the time and leverage they needed to set things right. As much as Naite liked to pretend that Verly didn't have any blame in this clusterfuck, Verly knew better, and it was his responsibility to help fix this. Yes, Temar had approved his report to the PA, but Temar had no idea that a simple line about Verly's relationship with Naite could have led to this. If Verly had been thinking with his brain instead of feeling some perverse pride in pointing out that someone wanted him, he would have spotted the danger.

Hell, if they'd brought the AFP women in on the conversation about his report, they would have spotted the problem immediately. But no. He had slipped and assumed two people could find a little relief in each other's bodies without it being an interplanetary issue. When one of those people was a councilman of a mineral-rich planet and the other was the butcher of Minga, that wasn't possible. Verly had been an idiot to even dream it might be.

Pushing all those thoughts to the side, Verly concentrated on his patient. The deep puncture wound in his side wasn't faked, and the man was in real danger. If Verly had a field pack, he'd give the man a quick antibiotic, but all he had was local herbs and extracts. He pulled out a jar labeled "deep wounds" and found a thick substance related to the aloe Naite had used on his sunburn.

"I don't know if this will sting or not, but this is what the locals use for open wounds," Verly explained. The man groaned without answering. The blood was still fresh, so Verly could pull the shirt back without ripping any dried blood or scab free. The wound itself appeared clean with deep red blood still oozing out the puckered hole. Any medicine he put on the skin would be washed away, so Verly dipped the bandage in the jar and coated it before pressing it to the man's side.

"Someone has gone for more help. A doctor should be here soon." Verly didn't mention that the doctors didn't have any of the fancy equipment these people would expect.

The man's eyes fluttered open, and he looked around in confusion. "Where?" he managed, his voice little more than a croak.

"We're still on your ship. My landcar spotted you, but we didn't have a radio. The other man went for help, and I stayed." Verly kept his face turned toward the medical kit. This guy didn't need to have a heart attack when he realized a mass murderer was tending his injuries.

"Local?" The word came out as a pained wheeze, and Verly pressed the dressing to the man's side and used his teeth to rip a strip of adhesive so he could tape it in place.

"No. I'm assigned here," he said. While he didn't want to lie, he didn't want to give too much information either. Suddenly someone pressed cold metal against the back of his neck, and Verly froze. With one hand on the injured man's dressing and the other on the first-aid kit, he was at a disadvantage. "I'm not armed," he said, assuming the metal was a weapon.

The man shifted closer, and a knee pressed into Verly's back. "Where did the other one go?"

"To get help." Verly bit down on an urge to say more. He'd been in AFP custody before, and he knew they wouldn't have patience for any babbling. Only now did Verly recognize the terror crawling through his guts. Maybe the horror of Minga had shadowed that older fear, but Verly wished like hell he had taken one of Naite's suggestions. Any of Naite's suggestions. While this plan was best for protecting Livre, it sucked for him personally. His stomach was tight with fear, and he gripped the edge of the first-aid kit to keep himself from doing something fatally stupid.

New footsteps rang against the metal decking, but Verly didn't try to look. Instead he took slow breaths and tried to swallow the stomach acid that burned the base of his throat.

"Your name," his captor demanded.

Verly paused. Lying was stupid. These people probably already knew who he was, and if not, they would recognize him as soon as he stood up. Unfortunately, he didn't reach that conclusion before getting a kick to the small of his back. Verly fell to the ground, his arm twisting as he didn't let go of the first-aid box fast enough.

"Verly Black. Lieutenant Commander Verly Black," he answered loudly, his chest pressed against the decking. A boot landed on his neck, and Verly closed his eyes. He'd survived this once. He had. He'd been a mess, but this time he at least had Naite out there. The man was loyal enough to help glue together any bits of Verly's psyche that might fall apart. He had to hold on to that.

"The butcher," a second voice said, and Verly didn't bother opening his eyes. If they were going to save him from a long recovery by putting a bullet in his head, he didn't want to see it coming.

"Bring him," the original captor ordered. Verly felt hands at his wrist, pulling his arms behind his back, and he forced his muscles to go lax. He didn't want to bring more damage down on himself by fighting uselessly. Once they'd secured his hands behind his back, they pulled him up, and Verly found himself between two AFP guards in black. Neither had any rank or mission insignia, so he had no idea if he was looking at a surveillance crew or a group of assassins.

"Hey, get the doc down here," the injured man called from the ground. Verly's two guards didn't answer as they yanked him toward a door that led farther into the downed ship. "Scoch?" he called out. "Hey, Scoch, get the doc. The bastard put something on my wound."

The guards pulled Verly through a hatch and closed it so that the voice disappeared. Part of Verly wanted to make a comment about them being coldhearted bastards, but that went without saying. They'd leave their crewmate to bleed to death if that's what it took to make the accident scene look good. They moved Verly up a level by shoving him up a ladder and letting him flop onto the floor helplessly, and then they finally pulled him into a room that was entirely too familiar.

In the center sat a chair with a V-shaped indentation in the high metal back. When they pushed him down, his bound arms fit into those slots so that his back was flat against the chair. He didn't comment as they added straps across his neck, shoulders, and stomach. He knew from experience that fighting wasn't worth it. Besides, the real pain only came when they had you naked.

Once his two guards had strapped his legs down, they walked out, and Verly was left staring at a wall. No doubt someone was watching on cameras, but Verly didn't have time to worry about that. Instead he closed his eyes and tried to estimate how long it would take Naite to reach the valley. Naite was a cautious driver, but he'd push the hauler a little faster.

Verly was suddenly worried about what would happen if he pushed too fast. The dunes were dangerous, and he had a vision of Naite rolling the hauler, trapped under it.

But that wasn't likely. Naite was wary. Verly had to believe that, even if his fears were searching for worst-case scenarios right now. The strap across his neck bit into the soft underside of his chin, and Verly tried to angle his head up a little more to take the pressure off.

By the time anyone bothered with him, Verly could feel the sweat gathering under his arms and along his back. He understood this was a standard interrogation technique, but he couldn't escape the ghost images of previous interrogators. He could feel faint impressions of hands grabbing him, of electrical nodes pressed against his skin and sharp knives splitting his flesh. None of it was real. At least not now, and that's what Verly had to hold on to.

The first person to walk in the room was a tall man with rough stubble that wasn't normal for an officer. They were trying to look the part of ragged and desperate victims. Verly just didn't figure the people of this planet would be foolish enough to fall for the ruse. The first man was followed by a second. This one was slightly shorter with one arm in a sling. Verly glanced at each before moving his gaze back to a spot on the wall.

"The butcher of Minga," the first man commented as he slowly circled Verly. His boots rang against the decking and echoed off the walls. The only soft things in this room were the three bodies, and all the hard surfaces made sound bounce and distort oddly. "What? No comment?"

"Didn't think you needed my input for this part," Verly said in the most insolent tone he could manage with his guts tied in knots. When the interrogator backhanded him hard, Verly let his head roll with the blow. The one advantage of having been here before was knowing how to minimize the damage. Verly ran his tongue along the inside of his lip where his tooth had cut it. The taste of blood was sharp in his mouth, but that was enough to distract him from the ghost of the past. He pressed his tongue to the cut and used the pain to anchor him in the now.

"I should shoot you." The hate in the man's voice wasn't feigned. Verly still didn't think they would be foolish enough or merciful enough to do it. AFP people were smart and ruthless, and they'd keep him on-planet as long as they thought it was useful. When it wasn't useful, they'd ship him back to some well-controlled planet and torture him to death and broadcast every gory moment. Verly idly wondered if the PA press would try to drum up sympathy for him or if they'd dismiss him as some fool who had finally found rough justice. Hopefully Temar would find a political solution before any of that happened. And if he didn't... well at least the Livre council would know what kind of people they were dealing with, and the AFP would feel more secure to know that Naite's PA lover was out of the way. Verly had to believe they'd learned about that piece of intelligence—it was the only thing that made any sense.

"Feel free to explain why you're important enough to allow you to breathe my oxygen." The man leaned against the side of the chair until he was nose to nose with Verly.

"There's nothing I can say that's going to stop what's about to happen," Verly said wearily. His counselor had tried for months to get him to believe that, and Verly had always thought he'd learned the lesson. Sitting in an interrogation chair again, he realized he'd still had a kernel of doubt. He'd been carrying around this tiny seed of fear that he'd somehow handled things badly and triggered his captors into more violence. Now he knew that was horseshit. They didn't care enough about him or his responses to change their plan. He could see it in their eyes.

"You could convince us that you have some value." The man stood and looked down at Verly.

Verly ignored him, and earned another backhand.

The second man stepped forward. "What is your mission here?" He had a soft tone to his voice, almost pleading, as if he wanted to find a way to stop the violence.

Ah, so they had decided on using identification with the captor with this guy playing the helpful, sympathetic soul. Verly would have to be far more careful of psy-ops games than straight-out torture. He turned enough to look at the second man. He had reddish brown hair and a field of freckles that made him appear young, but a hardness had taken up residence in his eyes. If Verly was supposed to come to look to this man as his friend and savior, they were going to have to screw him up in the head first. Right now Verly saw him as a very dangerous wolf in a tattered set of sheep's clothing.

"I'm pretty sure the PA wanted me out of the way. They didn't bother giving me one other than requiring me to send back reports on my activities."

The first man said in a derisive tone, "Your activities."

They definitely knew about his relationship with Naite. The government might as well send out news briefs considering how quickly AFP gained access to some of the government reports.

The second man took a more conciliatory tone, which made sense if they were attempting to turn Verly. "And what activities have you been reporting on?"

Verly gave the man a blank stare.

"We can certainly do this in ways that are less pleasant, but I don't see the need, do you?" he asked, tilting his head to the side in a gesture calculated to look less threatening.

"I don't assume that my idea of need and yours are the same."

The "friendly" interrogator gave a soft laugh while his partner stared down at Verly with a face devoid of emotion. The friendly one continued with his soft sell. "Probably not. But you don't need to tell us anything important. You do need to give us a token, a gesture of your willingness to cooperate. After all, you have been exiled from the PA, and now it seems like you aren't welcome on Livre. Where else will you go?" Clearly they'd heard Naite's broadcast about the fictional arrest.

"Hell?" Verly guessed, even though he knew full well that he had a home on Livre for as long as he wanted it. After all, he wouldn't have taken the risk of springing a trap except that he wanted to protect these people. All these people. He wanted to give Temar the leverage and time he needed to work, he wanted to save Naite from having to see the inside of these interrogation rooms, and he wanted to keep Naite from suffering the guilt of knowing he'd sent his lover to his death. Of course, that last one was looking a little questionable right now. Verly had expected more political games, but they seemed to be flying straight toward a speedy execution.

His buddy laughed louder this time. "It's good to see you're in high spirits."

The taller one then added, "The cocky ones always break faster."

"My name is Commander Syle. If you cooperate, I can find you accommodations better than hell... quite a bit better."

Verly chuckled. "Whatever I tell you, you're going to torture me to death when you're finished. I know that, so don't bother lying."

Syle pursed his lips and studied Verly while the big one continued with his stare of death. "Maybe," Syle said, "or maybe you would be more valuable alive and telling everyone about how your government brainwashed you against the AFP. After all, the butcher of Minga on his knees begging for forgiveness while condemning the corrupt dictatorship that betrayed him... that could be useful."

Verly's skin crawled at the very idea. "I think I'd rather go to hell."

"You and I both know that when the time comes to make a choice, you won't choose death. After all, your people turned their back on you, so it won't be that hard for you to turn your back on them."

Sadly, it was probably true. If it were a choice between PA and the rebel colonies, his own people had left him open for a psy-ops attack. He had nothing to go home to. He was disposable.

However, Verly did have things on Livre worth dying for. Not only did he have Naite, a man who knew his past and still looked at him with all the love he wouldn't say, but he also had an entire culture that forgave him, he had sunsets and children playing around the council house, and one day Naite hoped to convince families to move to the farm. Verly could imagine kids running through the cool tunnels and up to the desert where they could play at picking up sandrats, and that would be the most dangerous thing they could imagine. That was worth protecting.

"What is your relationship with Councilman Polli?"

"Good question," Verly said. They were probably wondering if Verly's recent arrest would end their sexual relationship. Verly was wondering if he was going to survive to go home to Naite.

Syle sighed as if Verly were being particularly difficult. "No doubt you worry that your unnatural relationship with him will result in your execution. The inner worlds teach their people that we're barbarians, but if you ask for forgiveness and admit your wrong, the charges can be dismissed. You can be forgiven for lying with another man."

"Do you make your torturers confess and ask for forgiveness after they rape other men?" Verly asked, moving his gaze to the tall man. He was the sort to indulge in a little rape.

The man raised his arm to backhand Verly again, but Syle caught him by the wrist.

"No," he said firmly.

The man scowled, and his face was turning a vivid shade of red. "We make sacrifices. We do the disgusting work that needs to be done to protect our way of life, and that pervert makes it sound like we're the sinners."

"Peace," Syle told his partner.

Verly rolled his eyes at the entire staged drama.

Syle studied him so long that Verly went back to staring at a spot on the far wall. "He's not ready," Syle finally announced. "Take him to a cell."

Verly gritted his teeth.

"You don't like that, do you?" the tall asshole asked.

Verly looked up at him. "Again, I don't have a lot of illusions about how much my liking or not liking something matters."

Syle raised his hand, and the door came open immediately. Two huge men stepped into the room, and a third held a weapon trained at Verly's head. They clearly had an unrealistic view of Verly's abilities. Give him a ship and he could outfly any of them, but in hand-to-hand fighting, he was average at best. And that was when his hands were free. Right now, he had no chance.

Still, they acted like he posed a serious threat. The one kept the weapon pointed at him while the other two freed the restraints and pulled Verly to his feet. Then all three escorted him deeper into the ship. They finally reached a row of doors so close together that they could only be closets… or AFP holding cells. One of the guards opened one and shoved Verly inside.

When the door slammed closed, Verly was in utter darkness. Air sluggishly moved, so there was some life support running, but not enough. The air was stale, and the tilt of the ship meant the cell pitched downward at an angle so the lowest part of the cell was a seam where the floor met wall. Verly didn't have a place he could even sit.

And, of course, the cell was only about five or five-and-a-half feet deep, so he couldn't lie down without having to tuck up into a ball, which was not comfortable with his hands still tied behind his back.

In short, he was screwed.

Still, he didn't regret walking into the trap. Naite never would have walked away from people who potentially needed help. The man might have a low opinion of his own morals, but everyone knew what a good person he was. He would want to help. But if he'd walked into the trap, right now he would be in the cell next to Verly as the others figured out how to take advantage of capturing a local politician.

Naite did not do well facing his own demons, and in here, Verly knew he would have little else to do. With only the dark for company, sooner or later a prisoner's psyche would start conjuring images, and they were likely far more terrifying than anything a torturer would dream up for him. Naite's guilt-ridden mind would bring to life horrors no one should have to relive.

Verly slid down one of the tilting walls and tried to find a way to minimize the discomfort.

At least here the hatred was honest. They wanted him dead, and Verly would never be able to convince them to change their minds. Even if Temar came in and did his diplomatic magic and told them the story of Aipa and the gate, none of them would change their minds. There was an odd comfort in that, even if Verly's psychologists would have put him on medication for even thinking that.

Verly leaned his head back and rested it in the cradle of another angle and closed his eyes. Eventually the perfect darkness would play tricks with his eyes and he would start seeing things that didn't exist. That was, assuming they gave him food and water. If they didn't, he'd make it two days, maybe three. The desert dried a man out, so he wasn't fully hydrated to start with. Whatever happened to him, Verly had to hope someone else could take advantage of the situation and find a way to keep the AFP from declaring war on Livre.

chapter
twenty-four

TEMAR WATCHED as Naite paced the small room. Even Shan had retreated to a corner to give the man more room to work out his energy. It was like seeing an overheated piece of glass and then watching it slowly fall toward some basin of ice-cold water—you knew things were going to shatter, but you didn't know who would get hit with the flying glass. Naite was not only about to explode, he was about to leave everyone around him with deep lacerations as a side effect.

"We should go now," Naite snapped.

"Let Cyla get Natalie and Rula," Temar said, trying to soothe the danger lurking under Naite's skin. People normally joked about Naite's bark being far worse than his bite. Naite was just as comfortable rocking a crying child or wrestling a hog. He had a calm gentleness in his actions, even if he did bark at people. But right now, he was ready to bite anyone and everyone who came near. Temar was concerned that they wouldn't be able to control him.

The front door came open, and Natalie hurried in, Rula close behind. "I heard what happened. Do we know if the ship is PA or AFP?" she asked, cutting right to the heart of the problem.

"We know they have Verly," Naite snapped. Under normal circumstances, Temar would have said that with the exception of Cyla, Naite was the one person who was closest to the two AFP women, but not today.

Natalie looked startled. "Do you have any signals or images of the ship?" she asked. She was clearly choosing to ignore the tone and focus on the issue. Temar was grateful for that because there were already too many sources of heat and pressure on his problem. Too many stressors and too few skilled people working the situation.

Naite grimaced and turned away from all of them. He spoke to the wall, leaving the rest of them to look at his back. "Verly thought it was AFP."

Natalie frowned. "Then why did he stay behind?"

Temar could understand that as easily as a sunrise. Verly was a risk-taker, especially when it came to protecting people. Given that he had rather actively pursued a relationship with Naite and given his own guilt and need to prove to himself and everyone else that he was a good man, sacrificing himself was the only move he could have made.

Naite whirled around. "He blamed himself for sending some report that made the AFP twitchy. He stayed because he didn't want me to go in and put myself in danger," Naite said with enough self-hate in his voice that Temar ached for the man. "So he went to help them while I came for help. So you can either come with me, or I'll go back by myself."

"We need a plan first," Temar said softly.

"We go and we take Verly back. That's the plan," Naite practically growled.

For a second, Temar let the words hang in the air between them. It only took a couple of seconds, and Naite was already deflating. The man knew better. Hell, it was Naite who had castigated his brother publicly for rushing into a situation without a good idea of how to get out of it again.

Temar waited until Naite had time to think about his comment. Then he said, "If the ship genuinely needs help, then we don't have to worry about making plans. They will have accepted help from Verly or asked him to stay out of their ship, but either way, we can address their needs when we get there. That means packing supplies." Temar turned to Cyla. "Would you please pack the main hauler with several large water containers and medical supplies?" Temar nodded toward his sister. Cyla opened her mouth, but then she glanced over at Naite. Maybe she recognized the danger because she tightened her lips and then headed for the door without comment.

"We need more of a plan for how to handle it if it is a trap," Shan said once she'd left.

"We need one that doesn't include you. Your plans are like pipe plant traps—likely to break a man's leg," Naite snapped. He'd already made his opinions clear. Sadly, Temar had to agree. He loved Shan dearly, but the man had no ability to create workable schemes.

"And I suppose you—" Shan started.

"Enough," Temar said firmly. "This is not the time for you two to get started."

Naite gritted his teeth, and Shan refused to make eye contact, but they both settled down.

"We should get the council," Shan said, and that was a rather predictable answer. Just as Verly was ready to throw himself between Naite and danger, Shan wanted to protect Temar from the guilt of his own actions.

Temar curled his fingers around Shan's strong forearm. "We need to plan, but we don't have time for endless debate. In this case, it's best to stew the meat first and ask about recipes later. Now," Temar said with a lot more calm, before studying the group. "We can't ignore anything. If this is a PA ship, what will Verly's own people do to him, and why would they drop a ship onto the planet?"

He looked around, but no one had any easy answers. Natalie opened her mouth, but she didn't say anything. It was Naite who finally answered.

"Verly talked about how his people might try to find an excuse to come down here," Naite said. "He said they may pretend to be a rescue and then try to find some excuse to invade. Given how he reacted to the idea of slavery, I think we can assume that they'd feel that was enough of a reason to take over our planet."

"Great," Natalie groaned. "Once again, Verly Black screws us over."

A look of such pure fury crossed Naite's face that Temar took a step closer to him, putting his own hand on Naite's arm to try to calm the fire threatening to burn out of control. Naite's next words came out so tense and angry that they were barely louder than a whisper. "He put himself in danger to give us time. He's trusting us to get him back."

Temar figured that a few more minutes and Naite was going to totally lose control. In a perfect world, he'd prefer for Naite to stay on the farm while the rest of them went to the rescue. However, if he even made the suggestion, Naite was going to lose what little patience he was still holding on to.

Temar turned to Natalie. "Okay, if the ship is a trap, but an AFP trap, what can we expect?"

"Violence," she said, her voice clipped. She took a deep breath before straightening her shoulders. "They'll want information. If they have Verly, they'll torture him before they kill him, though. He's a war criminal."

Rula rarely added much to any conversation; however, now she spoke up. "Black admitted that his own people might have set traps here. Maybe we can admit that Minga might have been an AFP trap."

Natalie's face turned stark white, and Temar could almost feel the fury rolling under her skin. She turned on her own lover, murder in her eyes.

Rula continued without even flinching. "Those were some of the most troublesome refugees—they had information that could have undermined the AFP, so I wouldn't be surprised if the nuclear signature was planted there and the communications sabotaged."

Natalie shook her head. "I would have known." The words came out angry.

"Not if they suspected that you had people on it," Rula said softly. "We both know they were giving us a lot of opportunities to make mistakes—too many. It makes sense that they suspected something. Now, I'm not saying it's true. I'm not saying that our government caused Minga. I'm saying it's a possibility. Right now, we need to set aside our war and focus on Black as a hostage to recover."

Natalie was absolutely still, and Temar could see the danger running like a thread of gold in the rocks. She was more than a diplomat, but she rarely showed that dangerous side. Clearly Rula had struck close to home for Natalie to react this much.

As much as Temar hated to do it, he had to put Natalie in her place. She might have been highly ranked in the AFP, but she wasn't here. Her hatred and her fear wouldn't affect his decisions. "Verly proved that he would choose Livre over his people. You haven't," he said. "Think about what you need to prove."

Natalie lifted her chin. "I have no reason to show the AFP any loyalty. Neither of us has any reason to go back."

"And yet you can go back," Temar said. "Verly argued that we should avoid discrediting you, and instead he distracted his people by turning himself into a criminal. His actions speak loudly. What are your actions saying about you?"

Natalie suddenly had every emotion buried deeply, and even Rula seemed to keep a safe distance between them.

"What will your people do?" Temar asked, his voice mild.

For a time, Natalie didn't answer. She stared at him, a hard shell hiding her true reactions. Temar had no idea if she was angry or hurting or mentally calculating her odds and trying to decide on a course of action that produced the most benefit. Finally she said, "I don't know."

Despite himself, Temar felt some sympathy for her situation. "I understand that any guess may be wrong, but I need you to make a few guesses so I can start getting a feel for what's possible," he said as gently as he could.

Natalie threw her hands up in the air, and emotion poured out as if it were water in a vessel that had cracked. "They'll hold him in the ship and either record his torture or wait for pickup and transport him to a cruiser. But he's a bonus, a jewel they ran across while trying to steal credits. They want Livre, not a war criminal from a crime three years ago."

"So they'll focus on us?" Shan demanded.

"On Temar," Natalie said. She gave Temar a look that showed pity. "The profile says that you're the real power, and Ambassador Polli was a distraction sent to minimize your exposure. They see you as the threat, and if you're there, they'll focus on you. If you're dead, they'll start trying to figure out who is strong enough to grab for power in the vacuum you've left behind."

"Will they kill Temar?" Naite demanded.

"No," Natalie said, shaking her head. "They wouldn't want to disrupt the power structure unless they had a good feel for who might move up and a good understanding of how to manipulate those players."

Temar wondered if the rest of the universe had always been so morally damaged or if this was some recent development. "So they would want to negotiate?"

Natalie nodded. "Two possible plays—put an officer up front in the negotiations and hope he can talk you into making mistakes or put an agent up front and get them moved in close enough to act when the time is right."

"Meaning?" Temar tilted his head and studied her.

"An agent, an assassin. The trick is to move them in close and have them interact with you regularly so that when they get a feel for who in the second tier of power might be useful, they can kill you in a way to make sure that the most politically vulnerable members move into the key spots."

Temar closed his eyes for a second. "So they won't kill me if I walk in under a flag of truce, but they'll start planning my death even as they smile at me."

"Yes."

"Prick on a stick," Naite muttered darkly. Temar agreed with the general sentiment.

"I am perfectly willing to engage an officer, but I won't have an assassin anywhere near me," Temar said. Of course, he also recognized that he would be unlikely to recognize the difference. For example, even after all this time, he was unsure about whether Natalie was actually an assassin or if she had simply learned to kill in order to complete her missions.

"I can take care of any assassin," Rula said. "We have a few weapons in our belongings, and I have a sharp eye for distance shooting."

"You broke the prohibition against weapons. Why am I not surprised?" Naite asked. "Whatever you want to get, move fast because I'm leaving to go save Verly in about fifteen minutes. If the rest of you are onboard, fine. If not, I'm going out there on my own."

Temar tightened his hold on Naite's arm. "A few more minutes won't make a difference."

"Do you believe that?" Naite demanded. "Do you really believe that a few more minutes of rape or torture won't matter?" He stared at Temar, daring him to say anything so stupid.

Temar wouldn't. He knew firsthand how long a minute could be when someone more powerful had you pinned down and was taking what you would never willingly give them. From the stories Shan had told, Temar suspected Naite knew the same. Rape was exceptionally rare on Livre, but they were two survivors who understood better than anyone else what Verly could be suffering that exact moment.

He looked at Natalie and Rula. Maybe they knew.

"A few minutes will matter in the short-term, but he's strong. He will survive this as long as we have a plan. If we rush in there, Verly won't be the only one to die."

Naite clearly wanted to argue the point, but he kept silent. At least he did for several seconds. When Temar tried to turn away, Naite grabbed his arm so hard that Temar knew it would leave a bruise. "I sent him down there," he said, his voice barely louder than a whisper. His pain was horrifyingly clear.

"And I ordered Verly to blow up the ship Shan was on. He was sucked out into space," Temar said. He understood what Naite was feeling—he did. However, you couldn't let love stop you from taking action. "Sometimes you do the best you can for people. The rest is up to chance."

"Well, chance had better move fast because I'm about out of patience," Naite warned. He shoved at Temar's arm before heading outside. Clearly they had reached his limits.

Temar looked around at the group. "Shan, check the hauler's supplies. I don't want to get out there and find out Cyla left out bandages. Natalie, retrieve whatever weapons you have. Rula, go ask Naite to show you where we have Landing's weapons, and pull anything you think might help. I'm going to go brief Lilian. I hope we've sorted this mess out before they send help." Temar suspected that any help the council sent would be less than helpful. They had no way of understanding these strange people.

chapter
twenty-five

TEMAR SAT beside Naite and seriously considered asking the man to give up his spot at the driver's side. Naite was showing all the reckless abandon of his brother, but the problem was that Naite didn't have the skills with a machine that Shan had. His driving felt less like an exciting thrill ride and more like speeding toward unavoidable death.

The hauler nearly left the ground as he jumped the top of the dune, and Temar risked a glance back to see Shan driving the second hauler. When Temar had insisted on Naite taking lead, he'd expected a somewhat slower pace. Clearly in the conflict between getting to Verly or avoiding death, Naite did not value his life nearly as much as he did under normal circumstances.

"That's it!" Naite called as he eased up on the engine and let them slide down the face of the dune. "I think."

Out here, it was difficult to judge one dune from another, but Temar tended to trust Naite's memory. "Slow down and park us on this side of the dune," Temar said. Naite's hands tightened on the wheel until the knuckles turned white, but he didn't argue. He knew they couldn't rush straight to the ship.

On the next dune, Naite got a little more than three-quarters up the slope before pulling the hauler sharply to the side to force it into the bank. The driver's side was almost buried in the dune, and sand spilled into the machine. It was secure and probably wouldn't roll back down to the bottom.

"I'll check," Naite said, and he was already climbing up the dune, his footsteps sending sand pouring down into the driver's side.

"Don't be seen," Temar called after him. Naite didn't answer, but Temar trusted him to play this smart. While Naite did that, Temar headed over to the second hauler, which Shan had also set sideways in the dune. However, he'd managed to do it without having bucketfuls of sand land inside.

"Is this it?" Shan asked.

"Naite's checking."

Surprisingly, Rula answered. She held up a small device with a screen on it. "This is it. I'm picking up a scoop-sized shuttle on the other side of the dune."

"Any signals?" Natalie asked. She was all business again as she got out of the hauler and slid several feet downhill before she could get her balance and climb back up the dune to the rear of the hauler. There she started pulling out equipment.

"None," Rula said. She looked from Shan to Temar to Ebi. Temar still wasn't sure why Lilian had insisted on sending Ebi, but he wasn't going to argue with the woman. "A ship normally puts out a distress signal so other ships can find them. They could claim that they cut the signal because they didn't have permission to land and they didn't want to be caught, but the more plausible explanation is that they are running silent."

"Running silent?" Temar asked. That sounded ominous.

"It means we have more watcher ships in orbit, AFP or PA, and this ship doesn't want to be seen by those ships." Rula pointed up.

Ebi tilted his head toward the pale blue sky. "There are more up there?"

"Many more, I suspect," Temar said. "They're sandrats who have caught the scent of blood, and we're the bleeding animal."

Rula frowned, but she didn't disagree.

"So, no way to tell if this is AFP or PA?" Shan asked.

Naite came down the dune, sand sliding ahead of him as he hurried. "They're there. I don't see any sign of Verly, though."

Temar closed his eyes for a second. At this point, he counted both governments as enemies, and they had someone he considered a friend. How he handled this would affect not just Verly and Naite but the entire planet.

"What do we do now?" Ebi asked, his voice sharp.

"Kill them," Natalie said, "hopefully without being seen because that will not make us popular."

Ebi stared at her with his mouth open. Temar could see that much, even through a sand veil.

"We try to avoid killing too many," Temar said. Natalie gave him an odd look, but Temar knew one thing—these people feared unpredictability. So Temar planned to be the most unpredictable bastard in the history of Livre. Given some of the people who'd lived here, it was a tall order.

Shan nodded and moved closer to Temar's side. "We don't want to start a full war we can't win, and we can't afford to treat human life as if it were cheap. That's how all your people came to lose their way," Shan said.

Temar wished he was motivated by Shan's right path, but if he had to deal with something more tangible, at least he had Shan to pull him back if he morally strayed too far. "Rula, do you have your long-range weapon?"

Rula turned to Natalie, who handed her a gun that had to be at least as long as Rula was tall. It looked heavy too. So that's what Natalie had been assembling. Temar doubted any of them would have recognized the various parts of a disassembled weapon. Rula quickly checked the weapon and then nodded. "I'm ready to go."

"Can you tell the difference between an agent and an officer who actually wants to negotiate?"

Rula studied him for a second before answering. "Not immediately, but if I have time to watch people talk for a while, I can spot it."

"Do you have a problem shooting an agent?"

"Temar!" Shan said.

Natalie put her hand on his arm. "Temar's right. We can negotiate with officers and politicians, but an agent will follow orders to the end, even if ordered to their own death."

"So we kill them?" Shan asked. "I believe you were an agent, and you found yourself again. We are talking about taking away a person's right to better their lives, to make different choices."

"To kill us all," Naite added dryly.

Shan glared at him.

"What's an agent?" Ebi asked, but he spoke cautiously, as if afraid of falling into the equivalent of a pipe trap.

"I am," Natalie answered. "I've trained to kill since I was six years old."

"So, a soldier?" Ebi guessed.

"You walked away from that life. We're talking about denying someone else the right to do the same," Shan argued. He kept his voice quiet, but he still had a fervent tone that made Naite even angrier.

"They've taken away Verly. What about his rights?"

"Then we demand him back," Shan said.

"Is it the same as a soldier?" Ebi asked with a little more volume.

Natalie spared the brothers an unhappy look before she answered his question. "No. Rula is a soldier, and she trained to kill other fighters in battle. I was trained to sneak into a place and kill someone without warning. My whole task is to kill without anyone noticing that I did the killing."

Temar couldn't quite figure out the expression on Naite's face. He spotted Temar and pulled his sand veil up again.

"You don't give them a chance to defend themselves?" Ebi asked.

Natalie had all her emotions locked under a perfectly neutral expression. "Never," she said, "and many couldn't defend themselves against me even if they had known I was coming. One military commander was known for having a sharp eye for spotting infiltrators. I was sent to kill his baby girl so he would be distraught and distracted at a time when the AFP needed to move agents into an area." Again, she delivered all that without emotion, but the horror in Ebi's face was unmistakable, veil or no.

"And you walked away from that evil," Shan said in an earnest voice. He might have given up the priesthood, but he still had a lot of Shan the priest in him.

Naite leaned forward. "These agents didn't come to get away from the evil. They came to bring it to us. I wouldn't give a thimbleful of water to save their lives, and I'm not hypocrite enough to pretend I would."

Temar stepped in before someone could go too far with their words. "We don't have the ability to handle an agent. If they're here and they try to engage us, that is an attack. If they stay to their own group and observe, we allow them to leave. Rula, if the person who comes out to talk to me is an agent, you need to kill them."

Shan pressed his lips together before pulling his veil back up, but he didn't comment. Temar hoped that after this the universe would give them all some time to adjust to their changing lives.

"Yes, sir," Rula said. "Am I free to choose a position?"

Temar nodded. Rula took the gun and started toward the ridge.

Ebi asked, "What about the rest of us?"

Temar stood a little straighter. "Ebi, you and Natalie stay out of sight. Natalie, if this goes badly, your first and only task is to get Ebi and Naite to safety."

"What?" Naite demanded. "I don't need babysitting."

Temar sighed. "You two are council members. If this goes badly, the councils will have to handle this."

"God have mercy on us," Ebi whispered.

"I'll get them back safe," Natalie agreed.

"Shan." Temar stopped. Shan had stood by him and trusted him through so much, and he needed Shan to follow him a little farther, but he understood what he was asking Shan to give up. "If you would stay on the ridge of the dune, you could relay messages."

Shan considered him for a time before nodding. "I can do that."

"And if something happens, retreat."

Shan caught Temar by the wrist. "I won't do that. We're in this together," he said firmly. Temar's stomach ached at the idea of Shan being injured again. It was easier to face his own death or capture. He struggled to find some argument, but Shan pulled him close and held him tight. "We're in this together," Shan repeated.

A shiver went through Temar, and he nodded.

"We'll get through this," Shan promised quietly, and something in Temar's chest untangled.

"Can we get moving now?" Naite demanded. "And you'd better hope nothing happens, because I don't give a damn what you say. If they do anything to you two, I'm going down there and introducing some heads to some sandrat nests."

Temar appreciated Naite's honesty, and he was right. The longer they waited, the more dangerous this game became. He turned to Ebi. "Could you please bring me one of the water bottles and some jujube fruit?"

Ebi gave him a strange look, but he went for the supplies.

"Temar?" Shan asked.

"It's time to remind them that they don't understand us well enough to predict our moves," Temar said. Naite looked ready to argue, but Temar started toward Ebi. He grabbed a cloth and shade frame. Naite was ready to explode, so Temar headed up the dune before he had a chance to say anything. He could hear the heavy breathing of someone chasing after him, but Temar hit the top of the dune and started his stumbling slide down the other side.

"Temar," Shan called. When Temar glanced back, Shan stood at the top of the dune. "Be careful."

That was ironic. Temar smiled at him before turning back to focus on the ship. The back of the ship was already half-buried in the dune as the wind moved the sand. Temar jammed the frame in the sand and then clamped the cloth to the edge so he would have some shade. That's where he sat. He had no doubt they were watching, so Temar pulled one leg up under him and started eating his fruit.

With the shade up, Temar couldn't see Shan, but he had no doubt that he was standing in the wind, watching with that intensity that only Polli men had. It took longer than Temar expected for the door to the ship to open. He was working on his third piece of fruit, and he kept eating as a small delegation stepped out onto the sand.

One of them had the sense to look at the rear of the ship with some concern, but the other four men all focused on Temar. It was odd to see only men respond, but Temar assumed that meant that this was an AFP ship. Rula and Natalie were both strong women who could handle anything, so Temar wasn't sure how the AFP justified devaluing women, but it wasn't his job to try to understand stupidity. He had a job here.

The five strangers stayed close to the ship at first, but eventually they moved closer, fighting their way up the sand until fifty or sixty feet separated them from Temar. He leaned forward. "Is your ship damaged?"

The whole group stopped, and a man with black hair stepped forward. "Severely, I'm afraid. I have crew that survived. We need help."

"What happened to the man Councilman Polli left behind to help you?" Temar could see the moment's hesitation. He didn't want to answer.

"We arrested him. He is a wanted war criminal that the Planetary Alliance has protected despite our repeated requests that he face trial on multiple counts of murder."

"Then we have a problem, because he is in the custody of the Council at Landing, and we need him returned."

The AFP man, and Temar had no doubt of that now, took a step forward. "In the custody of? Is that a way of saying you've arrested him?"

"It's a way of saying that we convicted him. He is now legally required to follow the orders of members of the Landing Council. We left him here to render aid, and now we expect him back."

"What crime did he commit?"

This was feeling oddly like an interrogation. And the man hadn't yet asked for a name, which meant either he knew Temar's name or he planned to dismiss him. Temar felt dangerously uninformed, but he could only plant the seeds he'd been given. He opened his water bottle and took a drink. "That is not your business. However, your presence on our planet is our business. Why are you here?"

"This was an accident."

"You had to have come here intentionally before accidentally crashing your ship," Temar pointed out. The others shifted uncomfortably.

The man held his hands out. "We were only doing a survey."

"Of our planet without our permission. We have laws, and if you cannot respect our territories and our laws, you may find out how harsh they can be."

The man moved closer, but he angled his body toward his friends. "Ambassador Gazer, I assume."

Temar didn't answer.

"I'm Commander Morris. I would not want to anger—"

A shot rang across the dunes, and Temar had to force himself to stand still as Morris stumbled backward, a red stain growing on the front of his uniform below his neck. He dropped to his knees, and Temar watched the others. Instead of reacting the way any normal person might, Morris's own crew watched with a sort of detachment. Temar wanted to go to the man's assistance as he fell in the sand and writhed in his final death throes. Their lack of empathy horrified him more than the death itself.

Temar stood. "That will attract predators." He took the cloth down from his shade frame and laid it out on the ground before dropping the frame down onto it to weight it down.

Two of the gathered men were busy watching the dunes. Soldiers. However, one man had consistently kept his attention on Temar the whole time. Temar turned to him. "Are we done playing games? The next bullet will go into you, and then we can see if your second-in-command is more reasonable."

The man with red hair and an arm in a sling glanced over at Morris. "He was my second-in-command."

Temar had expected the violence to put pressure on this delicate work of negotiation. He'd feared it would put too much pressure on it, and everything would crack like fragile glass. Instead it had not even provided enough heat to mold the piece—not yet.

"I hope you have a rescue ship close enough to come and get you within an hour or so," Temar suggested mildly.

The man smiled as if amused by Temar's bluff. Unfortunately for him, Temar wasn't bluffing. "All that blood is going to attract sandrats, maybe even sandcats. Get enough of them in one place, and a man can't walk across the sand without getting eaten. But if you don't keep men out here to clear your ship as the winds shift, you'll get buried alive. So right now, you have three choices—a quick and brutal death, a slow and agonizing death, or me." Temar watched as the man considered his options. There wasn't enough heat. Not yet.

Temar shrugged. "I might be back after I take care of business in the next town." With that he turned around and started up the dune. He could image Naite cursing him out, and part of him was surprised that Naite hadn't already come over the crest of the dune. He might have agreed to let Temar handle this, but Naite wasn't one to step back and let others make decisions. He might bitch about being on the council, but he wouldn't let others set the law without having his own say.

Temar had no more than cleared the crest when Naite was there in his face, fists tight and elbows bent. He wanted to hit someone, and Temar thanked God that he was a good fifty pounds lighter. If they'd been even close to the same size, Naite would have taken a swing.

"What are you doing?"

"The only thing I can to get Verly back," Temar said quietly. He wasn't fooled. For all his bluster and denials, Naite loved Verly to an extent that sometimes amazed Temar. Considering how closed off the man was, Verly had done an incredible job of getting around Naite's defenses. Even the other farmhands had commented, and generally they were relieved to see Naite finally make some sort of long-term connection. It wasn't healthy for people to be so isolated, and Naite had made a career out of doing that.

"Verly says you're good at talking, so get down there and talk." Naite could barely get the words out from between clenched teeth.

Temar wanted to soothe him and offer some sort of comfort, but it'd be easier to comfort a sandcat. So far, Verly was the only one who had figured out how to manage Naite's moods without getting stripped of flesh.

"I can talk, but they aren't ready to listen. They think they have the upper hand, and until the desert teaches them differently, talking won't accomplish anything."

Naite looked at Rula who lay in the sand, her weapon pushed into the drift near the top so that the sand hid her and hid the source of the bullet that had killed Morris.

Shan tried to come to Temar's defense. "We can't kill them all."

"Yeah, we can," Naite said in the coldest voice Temar had ever heard him use.

"No," Temar said, "we can't because they don't care who dies. More will come down here. They have to learn a harsh lesson and take it back up there. Now we move the loaders and wait for the sandrats to do some of our work for us."

"We can't leave him," Naite said. He struggled to even get the words out.

"We have to if we want to save him," Temar said. "I am not taking any risk with his life that I wouldn't take with Shan's or my own. But if we don't move these haulers, they won't be the only ones in danger of being taken down by sandrats." Temar caught Naite by the arm. "Trust me, Naite. I understand these people, and until they feel teeth in their feet, they won't feel the danger." He expected Naite to argue, but at the last second, he gave a quick nod.

"Then let's get ourselves out of the sandrats' path," he said as he headed for the front hauler so fast that Temar almost lost his balance.

chapter
twenty-six

NAITE WATCHED the sky. The buteo showed up less than an hour later, circling in the sky and diving down. Maybe the idiots were trying to protect their dead because the birds would then rise up without any meat in their claws. Where buteo went, sandrats followed. If their man wasn't inside the ship before that happened, no way could they defend his body. And if they had taken Morris in, the rats would look for other prey. That much blood would have them whipped into a frenzy.

"We should check on them," Naite said after about an hour. An hour. He hated to even think of what these people could do to Verly in an hour.

Temar shook his head, and Naite wanted to punch something. Someone. Unfortunately, the others believed that Saint Shan and Ambassador Temar had all the answers. The helplessness left a bitter taste in his mouth, but with Ebi and Temar sitting in his hauler, he couldn't exactly take off on his own. Not unless he went on foot.

Naite eyed the sand, but he would die before he got there and he knew it.

"What approach are we taking when we go back?" Natalie asked.

Temar sighed. "We apply enough heat to force them to change the shape of their piece," he said, which didn't make a bit of sense to Naite. Then again, Temar often didn't.

"Meaning?" Natalie asked. Naite was grateful for that because if he had to talk to Temar right now, he was going to say something unforgivable.

"Meaning they need to understand the danger they put themselves in. If they want to come down here, they'll die. They have to believe that. And it won't be the people killing them."

"Not all of them," Ebi said. He'd been pale and shaky ever since Rula had pulled the trigger, and the sound of the shot had echoed and warbled oddly across the landscape. They hadn't even seen the bastard die, although Naite had a few vivid details from Ben's death that he could substitute in for this stranger.

For a long time, they all sat in the haulers with shade cloths pulled overhead and the sand whipping at their faces. This was hell, and Naite probably deserved to be in it.

"Now we go," Temar said unexpectedly. Naite checked the sun and estimated that they'd had close to two hours. The buteo were gone, so either the rats had made their meal, or the idiots had taken the body inside with them. In that case, they would have hungry rats that had traveled and were desperate for the moisture and calories to contend with.

"Finally," Naite said as he started the engine.

"Wait!" Ebi cried. "Can I get onto the other hauler?"

Temar reached over and put a hand on Naite's arm. "Let Shan pull up close so Ebi can transfer over," Temar said.

"Hurry up and get over here," Naite yelled.

"Patience is a virtue," Shan answered, but at least he was moving his damn hauler into position below Naite's.

"Shan, keep your hauler out of sight," Temar said.

At the same time, Rula asked, "Is it too dangerous to even step foot off the hauler?"

"I wouldn't," Ebi said. "Sandrats can attack fast enough to lame you, even if you're only a few feet from safety."

"And I think the AFP learned that," Temar said as he pulled the shade cloth down. Naite was ready to drive away and let the wind rip it off, but he was stuck waiting for Shan to move his damn vehicle.

"Good luck," Shan called, and then Naite put the motor into gear and headed up the dune.

Temar curled his fingers around Naite's arm. "I know you love him, but keep calm and remember that he walked in there because he wants to protect this whole world, this whole way of life."

"I don't give a fuck what he wants right now," Naite said. Personally he was going to tie the man to a bunk to keep him out of trouble. When Verly had joked about tying people up during sex, Naite honestly had not understood why that would even occur to someone, but right now he wouldn't mind tying Verly up and keeping him somewhere safe.

"Don't ruin what he is trying to do."

"Then get him back, and I won't have to," Naite warned as the hauler hit the top of the dune and then tilted wildly forward. Naite quickly disengaged the engine before he tipped their vehicle and they needed rescue as much as Verly. Temar was holding on to the edge of the seat, but he didn't comment as Naite drove past the spot where Morris fell. The only thing left to mark it was the indentation that was left when sandrats or sandcats put too many tunnels in one place. However, there hadn't been enough time for the rats to get the whole body, so either cats had shown up, or someone had wrestled the gnawed remains away from the animals.

The ship showed more signs of trouble. There were shovels half-buried in the sand, where someone had tried to unbury the back of the shuttle. There was also another sunken place where tunnels had undermined the sand.

"Looks like they lost someone else," Naite said with more than a little satisfaction.

"I see," Temar said calmly as Naite stopped the hauler close to the door. Naite watched the hatch and waited for someone to show, but it stayed closed.

"I'm going—"

"Wait," Temar said. Naite gritted his teeth and reminded himself that Temar had the better understanding of these people and he wasn't as emotionally compromised. Still, sitting didn't feel right. They waited close to another twenty minutes before the hatch opened and Commander Syle appeared in the opening.

"I wouldn't recommend you come any farther unless you're choosing to die quick and ugly," Temar said. Naite didn't bother hiding his smirk.

Syle stopped and studied the sand, leaning out to look at the rear of his shuttle, which was vanishing into the side of the dune. "So, how much longer before we're buried?" he asked.

Temar looked at Naite.

"Probably two hours," Naite estimated. "I might be off by an hour one way or the other. I don't usually time things."

Syle tilted his head. "Councilman Polli," he said.

Naite glared at him.

"I understand that legally you had custody of the prisoner. If my ship is buried, he is buried as well."

Naite's stomach ached with all the emotions he kept swallowing, but standing within six feet of this prick, Naite knew he wouldn't be able to bluff this one out of a single credit. Naite had parked so his side was closer to the door, but Temar stood, his one hand resting on Naite's shoulder, which was either him offering comfort or him trying to make sure Naite didn't start throwing punches.

"If that happens, it happens. People die out here. We won't blame Naite for doing what was, at the time, the right thing. However, the AFP would be at a serious disadvantage because you will have not only broken our laws but refused to accept responsibility for what you've done."

"So, we accept your justice, or we die out here."

Temar smiled, but it was a cold expression Naite hadn't seen from him before. "Your three choices haven't changed. So you can get back in that shuttle and die, try to walk out and die, or get in this hauler."

Syle said, "I'm not sure many of us would fit in there."

"I'm sure not all of you will." Temar leaned a little harder against Naite's shoulder. "This hauler can handle twenty people. Naite, Verly, and I will be the first three. You can choose any seventeen others. I would recommend that you choose people who can keep their balance because it will be standing room only."

"And the rest?"

Temar didn't change expressions. "If you don't play any more games, there might be time for us to come back for more. There might not. So I suggest you make your first seventeen choices good ones."

Naite shifted uncomfortably. If they didn't call in the second hauler, the odds of them getting to Landing, dropping these off and then going back for the rest before the shuttle was buried were slim to none. For the first time, Naite hoped Shan's sense of morality got the best of him because Naite didn't want to leave men behind to die.

"Might, so what are the odds that the ones I leave behind will survive?"

Temar made a show of looking at the sand that had already half-buried the shuttle. "Not good, and your odds are falling by the moment. Arguing won't change that."

"You could call in another vehicle."

"No," Temar said, "I can't. There is no planetary defense system. No maps, no roads, no nice signposts that tell you where you are or how to get someplace. If this hauler breaks down, the two of us will die right alongside your crew, although we're smart enough that we'd last a little longer. I don't think that would be a mercy in the end. Naite, how many people died in the desert last year?"

Naite stiffened. "Too damn many."

Temar nodded. "I agree. Too many. In the early days, entire ships would vanish out here. Not shuttles—ships. Cargo ships, mining ships. They sank in the sands with their crews."

"Psy-ops. I didn't expect it of you," Syle said with an admiring nod.

Temar settled back down. "That's what you don't understand. We don't play psy-ops games. Verly told us how you do that, you and the PA, although Natalie is a little more forthcoming on the sorts of games those people play," Temar said, sounding disgusted with the lot of them. "No, we play the cards we're given, and around here, that means a lot of rough justice. I don't think what Verly did was so bad. He protected his home world, and none of us care who he shot down. Now, entering forbidden territory is a slightly more grievous offense, but I wouldn't have him tortured over it, so I would rather let Verly die in that ship of yours than I would let you torture him."

"Maybe we'll call for help."

"Then I'll have to get him back from the PA who seem to think he has all these rights even after the council enslaved him."

"You think the PA would answer a distress call?"

Temar leaned forward. "I would bet on it. That's the only reason why you're running silent right now. And if one of your ships did come for you, we might be unreasonable enough to make sure it never reached you. Now, you've wasted enough time that I can almost promise anyone not on this loader is going to die out here. Are you ready to pick your seventeen men, or are we headed back to the communication relay alone?"

Temar sat back down in the seat, and Naite was holding his breath.

"If we go with you, what are the terms of our release?" Syle asked.

"One tanker of water for every two men, none smaller than 90,000 liters. A tanker for you alone, commander. So, nine tankers of water or the AFP can continue to wonder what happened to you. Or you can try that distress signal, and we can see what part two of this game looks like."

"That seems like a rather low price."

Temar smiled. "We believe in asking for the true value of things. It's a religious mandate. 'No one can serve two masters, for either he will hate the one and love the other, or he will be devoted to the one and despise the other. You cannot serve God and money,'" Temar quoted the Bible, and it almost sounded like he was channeling Shan.

Syle frowned. "I hadn't thought your people that religious."

"Our priests hold places on every ruling council. Now I'm hot, and I'm ready to go in out of the sun. Are you coming or not?"

"We're coming," Syle said. "Give us some time to arrange for the seventeen."

Temar nodded, and Syle stepped back and closed the hatch.

Naite studied it for a second before he shifted so his back was to the ship. "Those others will die in there," he whispered.

Temar nodded. "They may." His gaze flicked over to the dune. So he was hoping Shan would come as well. "If they put themselves in conflict with the desert, we can't change that."

Naite turned back to the front and said in a normal tone, "We might try to pull a sled behind us."

"We might if they hadn't already attracted sandrats. No one is going to walk back there to secure one. You know better than anyone that sometimes people just die out here."

Naite tried to keep his face clear of emotion, but he suspected he failed. He did know how often people died, and right now his fear was that he was going to lose one more to the desert. Temar was playing his game, but Syle wasn't going to give up easily.

chapter
twenty-seven

VERLY LOOKED up when the door to his cell opened. With his hands tied, he was in no position to stand, so he waited for them to yank him to his feet and march him out. He expected to be taken back to the interrogation room, but they didn't go farther than the corridor. One of the men tied a black cloth around Verly's eyes, and then they slammed him chest first into the wall.

Verly tried to stay calm.

"How many of their people died in the desert last year?" a voice demanded.

"I don't know." Verly groaned as something hit him in the kidneys. It wasn't a debilitating blow, but he would be pissing blood. "I don't," Verly repeated.

"Has anyone talked about people dying?"

"Yes," Verly said. Something had changed, and it sounded like Naite or the ambassadors had talked to these people. It would be logical to try to scare these idiots, but Verly didn't know if that was their play, so all he could do was keep silent.

"What have they told you?"

Verly gritted his teeth and waited for the next punch. It didn't take long. He grunted as the asshole hit the same spot. He was definitely going to pee blood.

"Are they bluffing?" a new voice asked. It sounded like Syle, but Verly couldn't be sure.

"Maybe," someone said. Verly nearly went down when the man punched him a third time, even harder. The least they could do was ask a question before hitting him. "Your lover is leaving you in here to die, Black."

Verly took several deep breaths. That was entirely possible. Naite had a responsibility to his planet first. Verly ranked somewhere between camping out and sharing a bunk. That wasn't a commitment.

"Is the communication up yet?"

"No. The sand is doing a number."

"They claim they don't have communication. It could be they're telling the truth."

"Either that, or they dumped this one on us."

Verly braced himself for another hit, but none came.

"I'll take care of the others. Get him outside," one of the voices ordered. Verly had long ago lost track of who was saying what. Someone jerked his arm, and all Verly could do was follow. So they were feeding him to sandrats. It would be a quicker death than Verly had expected. Maybe they were out of time for anything too fancy. Someone got him down a ladder by way of pushing him through the hole and having someone below break his fall before dropping him on the ground. Verly lay helpless until they pulled him up again and pushed him toward a hot wind.

"He should be going back for execution," someone said.

"You take orders, you don't give them," another answered. Verly wondered if they planned to take his blindfold off so he could see the rats or leave it on so he could imagine them coming at him. Thanks to Naite, he had a rather vivid image of them in his mind.

"Here he is. You get him when we have the first of the men loaded."

"Deal," someone said, and it sounded a lot like Temar. Verly stood a little straighter and tried to figure out if his mind was playing tricks on him. All around, people were jostling, and he could hear thuds, like someone throwing things or jumping.

"Enough. Send him over. He's in my custody, and I'm not letting anyone say I couldn't take care of my responsibilities," Naite said. That was definitely Naite, and suddenly it was all Verly could do not to collapse as his knees lost the ability to hold his weight. Naite had come. Naite and Temar. As many times as Verly had told himself to believe they would, he hadn't been able to hold off that kernel of fear.

Someone grabbed the blindfold and yanked it off, and Verly cringed away from the overly bright light. After blinking the world back into focus, he found himself looking at Naite behind the wheel of a hauler, Temar sitting next to him with his sand veil tucked under his chin.

"Move it," the guy behind him said, shoving him forward. Verly didn't have time to get his feet under him, so one foot caught the board the others were using to climb on the hauler, and Verly toppled sideways, falling to the ground.

The panic on Naite's face was almost comical, only Verly had good reason to believe that if Naite were panicking, something was truly wrong. He struggled to get his knees under him, but with his arms bound, it was hard.

Then Naite was there next to him, hauling him up and practically throwing him at the front seat of the hauler. Temar grabbed his arm and helped as Verly scrambled over the center console. But then he didn't have anywhere to go because Temar was there, so he stood with one foot on Temar's side of the hauler and one foot on the driver's side and his back to the front of the machine.

Naite jumped back up into the driver's side, painfully pinning Verly's leg against the machinery. "Prick on a stick," he snarled as he kicked his boot against the side of the hauler several times. Eventually he reached down, and Verly recognized the small rodent in his hand. He'd had sandrats on him. Verly's skin crawled at the thought of how close he'd come to having those wicked teeth in his skin.

"Next time, aim better," Naite said as he threw the animal at the hatch. It gave a little squeak, and several men moved to the side. Suddenly there was a scream and several heavy thuds, and then a burst of gunfire. Naite gave a satisfied grunt. Only then did he notice Verly's predicament.

"Idiot. Say something if you're hurting," Naite said as he scooted closer to the edge of the hauler. He couldn't drive that way, though.

"Verly, kneel here," Temar said, gesturing in front of his seat. If it got Verly out of AFP hands, no problem. He let Naite and Temar help him over the center console and slid to his knees. He had to assume they were still playing politics because neither of them said anything to him, and no one offered to get the keys to the cuffs.

"Got room for six more," Naite said. "But pull another stunt like that, and it'll be five. I'm vindictive."

Syle stood in the back of the hauler watching shrewdly. "Six more, and I'm sure my men will be more careful."

The one who had tossed Verly onto the sand nodded at Syle. "Yes, sir. Sorry, sir."

"As much time as you're taking, we aren't going to be coming back here for your other men," Temar commented. The comment shocked Verly.

"I had assumed. So, where are we going?"

"Communication relay. You're calling your people and telling them they have three days to come get you, and then we're going to start raising the prices."

"I see."

Verly was truly confused. The last of the men jumped onto the hauler, and Naite pulled away, leaving the door to the shuttle still open.

"Everyone on?" Temar asked. He shifted until he had his legs braced on either side of Verly. It wasn't the most comfortable position to be in, but since Verly didn't have the use of his hands, he appreciated any help he could get to avoid falling out.

And that began a truly terrifying ride with Naite making moves that even Verly would have hesitated to make in such an overloaded machine. Once they tilted at such a wild angle that Verly was sure they were going to tip, and Naite yelled for everyone to move their weight to the right. Men struggled to shift, and the loader finally groaned and got over the crest of the dune. They hit the bottom so hard that two men fell off the back. Verly noticed that neither were the injured man he'd first tended when he got on the ship. Clearly he'd been left behind to die.

"There it is," Temar said, pointing. Verly had his back to the front, so he had a nice view of all the AFP men with their dusty faces and tear tracks as the wind and dirt irritated their eyes. He doubted any of them could see any of it. But with his own back to the front and Temar's body shielding him, Verly was protected from most of it.

"Is that the—" Syle was cut off when the loader slid to the right, and all the men were grabbing for handholds.

Naite fought the loader until the nose was pointed downhill, and then he throttled back on the engine. Verly had a front-row seat. Most of the men had very little to no emotion, but a couple of them had looks of abject horror. Verly understood it. When you were used to fancy technology, the site of the Livre Communication Relay building was enough to make you weep.

Naite let the loader coast to a stop near the building. "People are only out here once a week or so. That means sandrats don't generally bother this place. I wouldn't go walking around overmuch, though," he warned. He turned around in the seat. "Oh, and I want the keys to his cuffs." He poked his thumb at Verly.

Syle hesitated long enough that Verly figured he was trying to work out some angle, but he did reach into his shirt and bring out a key. "What are the rules for our term here?" he asked formally as Naite took it. His gaze flicked over to Verly for a second, so he was probably wondering if he was going to be tortured or locked in a small room.

Temar shrugged. "Try not to break anything. We don't have a lot of spares, and we couldn't be bothered to fix interplanetary communication even if we did. Right now, we happen to dislike both your governments rather intensely." He gave Verly a look that made Verly worry about his neck for a half second, but this was Temar, and Verly trusted him to do the right thing.

"Is Officer Aral here?"

Temar frowned. "Natalie? Why would she be here?"

"For extraction."

Temar twisted around. "She was down here before you idiots decided to spy on us. Why would we kick her off the planet with you?"

Syle didn't understand Temar, and Verly supposed that was their best defense. "I suppose you wouldn't, not if you were being fair."

"We're more likely to hold to our word than the rest of the universe," Temar said. "Now get off my hauler."

"What about the sandrats?" one of the AFP soldiers asked as he studied the sand in pure terror. Verly had missed something.

"Move fast," Naite suggested without much mercy. Now Verly knew something was up because he'd walked the sands around here, and Naite had never warned him of any danger; however, the men took Naite at his word. They were slow to get off the hauler, but once down, they raced to the building.

"Let's go," Temar said.

Naite glanced down at Verly, but then he tucked the key into his shirt and started the hauler. Temar's legs tightened around Verly, holding him safe as Naite turned the machine in the direction of Landing and The Valley.

chapter
twenty-eight

VERLY FOLLOWED Naite into the bunkhouse, but it was eerily quiet. None of the help were around, and Naite had gone nonverbal. So far, Verly only understood the bare facts of their operation. No one had seemed interested in discussing strategy or the reasons behind some of Temar's more outrageous moves. They'd been more focused on getting back to the house than having tactical debriefings.

Naite turned. He pulled the sand veil off and threw it at a chair, where it slid across and fell on the ground. And then he stared.

"Naite?" Verly asked. He couldn't read the emotions in the man's face.

Naite took a step closer. "Are you okay?" His voice had a deadly sort of calm to it that made the hairs on Verly's arms stand at attention.

"Yeah," Verly said. "I'm fine. I'm bruised, but I'm fine."

For a long minute or so, Naite stood there and stared at him, his back as stiff as a soldier at attention. Then all the energy went out of Naite and he dropped back onto the nearest bunk. "I thought I'd gotten you killed."

Verly moved slowly. Naite was coming off one hell of an adrenaline rush, and Verly understood a man could be unpredictable in those circumstances. "I volunteered to go in there, and clearly I was right because look. Here I am. And did you leave AFP agents in your only communication center?"

Naite snorted. "With very little water and hundred-year-old equipment. Given how you reacted to our technology, we figure those guys will be just as horrified."

Verly doubted that. The AFP often held its equipment together with rusty wire and Bible pages, but maybe that was his prejudice showing through. He could see why Temar might want them to see why no one was answering any calls. He moved another step closer and rested his hand on the post that supported the bunk.

"I thought you were dead," Naite repeated.

Taking a risk, Verly grabbed Naite's shoulder, braced for him to explode up off the bed. Instead he sagged more. "Hey, I'm fine. They didn't even do more than give me a few bruises and call me a mass murderer. I've had officers on my own side treat me worse."

Naite glared at Verly before standing slowly. He kept one hand on the bunk but advanced toward Verly with a determination that made Verly worry a little. "I thought you were dead!" He shoved Verly in the chest hard. "I thought they were going to execute you." The outburst wasn't totally unexpected.

"We didn't have any choice," Verly said apologetically. It earned him another shove. Verly had the feeling Naite didn't lose control of his emotions very often, but apparently he'd made an exception for today. Given that Verly was already bruised and Naite was going to eventually feel guilty about any loss of control, Verly caught him by the wrist and pulled him close enough to make swinging more difficult. The second their bodies pressed together, Verly felt the tremors that shook Naite.

"Hey, I'm okay," Verly promised.

"I thought you were dead," Naite said again.

"The AFP keep trying, but they clearly don't know how to get the job done," Verly said with a smile.

Naite wrenched himself away and ended up on the opposite side of the room. "I can't do this." He ran his hands through his hair, and Verly's guts knotted in fear. Clearly humor had been the wrong approach. He let his smile fade.

"What can't you do, Naite?"

Naite whirled around. "I sent you in there." Naite stalked closer. "I fucking sent you in there."

Moving slowly, Verly held his hands out. "I'm a soldier, and I volunteered for a job that needed to be done. But you know I will always do everything I can to come back to you." That was as close as Verly could come to admitting to his own feelings right now. Things felt too fragile.

"We should have gone together. I'm not Temar. I can't move people around on a board like chess pieces. I can't. What the fuck is wrong with me? I try to help my brother by walking my father to his death, and then I send the man I love in to be tortured by his enemies. There's something fucking wrong with me." Naite crumbled to the ground.

Verly leaped forward, but he didn't get there in time to stop the fall, so he ended up on the ground with Naite. "Naite, you're scaring me a little. You're supposed to be the angry, logical one."

Naite gave a laugh that turned into a sob, and then he fisted Verly's shirt and pulled him close. "I nearly got you killed," he whispered into Verly's shoulder. Verly wrapped his arms around Naite and held on as tightly as he could.

"I'm not. I'm okay. I promise I'm okay." Verly started rocking gently, and Naite relaxed into his embrace. He'd seen soldiers break before—more than once. After they took on new recruits, at least one was almost guaranteed to explode after their first mission. It wasn't about being strong enough to carry the burdens of war—it was about being ethical enough and intelligent enough to understand the damage you were doing. You weren't pushing buttons on a console or asking a friend to check out a ship; you were putting human life in the path of death.

Verly remembered coming back from flying his first raid. He'd been fine until he'd seen the news vids broadcast the damage his ship had done to flesh and bone. The only people that didn't break were the ones too stupid to understand the cost of fighting or too ruthless to care.

And all he could do was offer Naite his touch and his patience.

"It hurts to love you." Naite let go of Verly's shirt. "I didn't think it would hurt so much."

"Yeah," Verly said softly as he leaned into Naite, "it does hurt. I'm afraid every time I think about you being a council member. Both the governments would consider you an obstacle because you're too stubborn to ever bend or compromise. So if either of them ever got a foothold on this planet, one of their first goals would be to eliminate you." That ember of pain flared to life at the admission.

"That's funny because I feel helpless around all these people with their weapons and their ships and their stories of raising up children to be killers. I can't even understand that much less understand how to fight it," Naite said miserably.

"Hey, Temar's done a pretty good job so far, and honestly, I think this last operation probably has them convinced that he's insane and entrenched in a position where they can't get him out without massive casualties. I don't think they have the heart for that sort of operation anymore." At least Verly hoped that was true. He knew his side wouldn't want to be anywhere near Temar if even part of this story came out. They'd have a team of psychologists fighting over all the potential diagnoses. Hell, it would be like Verly's trial all over again, only this time they wouldn't be able to sentence Temar to a term of hell in a listening ship on the border.

Naite looked at him for a second, those dark eyes studying everything before he pressed them tightly closed. "Fuck. This is a mistake. I don't have... I can't have this relationship."

That hit Verly like a kick to the guts, but he tried to remind himself that Naite wasn't in his right mind. "People leave that out of the love songs." Verly had more profound statements on the nature of love, but he lost them when Naite grabbed his shirt and pulled him forward. Their lips met, and Verly flinched as his lip was caught between their teeth, but then Naite kissed him so hard he forgot to complain. Naite ran his hands up Verly's arms until he cupped Verly's face, and the whole time, his lips and tongue were moving, exploring, pressing in before pulling back in a kiss that came closer to raw sex than anything Verly had ever experienced.

Naite pressed forward, and Verly was suddenly off-balance and falling backward. Naite caught him by the back of the neck, and Verly fell slower, but he was still pinned down on the ground with all of Naite's considerable weight on top of him. And his leg was bent at an awkward angle. Verly tried to roll to the side to free it, but Naite's hands were on his hips, holding him down while Naite moved down to suck at the side of Verly's neck.

Verly arched his back and gasped out Naite's name. Naite ignored him in favor of working his way down Verly's body, unfastening and unzipping and unbuttoning as he went. Verly writhed when Naite sucked his nipples right through the fabric of his shirt. It made an obscene slurping sound that sent shivers of need through Verly's body. Then Naite pulled on the shirt and stripped Verly from the waist up, all before Verly could fully engage his brain.

He reached for Naite's shirt to return the favor, but Naite was already stripping off, yanking at fabric that stretched before something gave with an audible tearing noise. Naite flung everything at a corner.

"I want to feel you," Naite said.

"Huh?" Verly wasn't at his articulate best when he had Naite's considerable weight pressed down on his hard cock, which was still trapped in pants and his leg bent awkwardly as they lay on the floor. He hadn't had sex this uncomfortable since... actually since his last rendezvous with a PA ship. When Verly accepted any sexual advances, the PA officers did enjoy shoving him onto some hard surface.

Naite gave Verly's neck a quick nip. "Stay here," he ordered, and then he was up and digging around in one of the drawers.

The blood started circulating in Verly's leg again, and when he straightened it out, pins and needles coursed through the limb. "Strip. Off with the clothes," Naite demanded. Naite was naked and running a gakka-slicked hand over his hard and beautiful cock.

Suddenly Verly didn't care about the floor or the lack of circulation. He pushed his hips up into the air and unfastened his pants as fast as he could. Naite must have decided it wasn't fast enough because he came over and pulled at the bottom of one leg so the pants slid right off.

"Naite," Verly groaned. He spread his legs, expecting to feel Naite's talented hands reach down to his hole. Instead, Naite started stroking Verly's already hard cock.

"I want to feel you," Naite said, and Verly finally got with the agenda. Okay, he could do that. He started to push himself up, but Naite moved up and pressed his hands against Verly's shoulders, pushing him back down to the floor. "I could have lost you," Naite said with a desperate edge to his voice. Then Verly felt the slick warmth against the head of his cock. Naite was already slick, but he couldn't have done much prep because he was tight—almost painfully so.

Naite leaned back and rested his hands behind him on Verly's legs. It was an impossibly flexible move for a large man, and it meant Verly couldn't thrust. He could only grab Naite's knees and hold on as Naite lowered himself slowly onto Verly's overly sensitive cock.

Somewhere along the way, Verly started babbling. He could hear his own voice even if he couldn't figure out what words he was saying. "Please" had a featured place in there somewhere, as did "hurry up," and "you're killing me." Other words spilled out unedited and probably without making much sense.

Finally Naite had all his weight down, and Verly was buried deep. Without warning, Naite began to ride him with the same focused intensity as he did everything in life.

The next minutes were hot and sweaty and mindless. Verly writhed and struggled. He grabbed at Naite, only to have his hands slide off without finding purchase. He cried out, and then he finally got his knees bent enough that he could plant his heels and thrust up. Naite's face twisted into the worst ugly sex face Verly had ever seen, and then Naite came, warm splatters of come going everywhere. Verly's own thrusts grew wild and uncoordinated before he came deep inside Naite.

They were both panting and sweaty and looking rough, but neither moved for long minutes. Finally Naite sank down to the floor next to Verly.

Verly stared up at the wooden slatted ceiling and tried to reassemble his scattered brain cells. If he'd tried to describe any of that, it would have sounded spectacularly bad. Nothing they'd done should have worked. Right then they should both have been making awkward conversation and trying to escape each other's company. But somehow all the awkward bits fit together so well that it had been the best sex of Verly's life. He couldn't even move. If someone paid him to move or ordered him to move, he would still be lying boneless on the floor.

It was perfect. Naite's arm and leg were draped over him, and Verly traced circles against Naite's elbow. Everything else could wait. For one minute, Verly wanted to feel like everything was right in the world.

chapter
twenty-nine

TEMAR MOVED to the edge of the bed and sat heavily. "None of them?" he asked.

"They made their choice," Shan said.

Temar gave a sob. "You were the one arguing that we couldn't be so callous with them."

With a sigh, Shan sat on the bed next to him and took Temar's hand. For a second, he stroked the back of it before he threaded their fingers together. "When you left the ship, did you think you were leaving the rest of them to die?"

"I knew you would pick them up the second we were over the ridge. I thought being left to die would make them more willing to listen to us. If their commander believed they were dead, they could stay here safely without having their families threatened. I didn't think they'd kill themselves." Temar closed his eyes and fought back the tears. Yes, he'd scared the AFP into backing off—hopefully—but the price was too high.

"Temar, they didn't kill themselves," Shan said. He pulled Temar closer. "There were signs that some of them fought back. One man was on the stairs with a bullet in his back. The officers you took to the relay murdered them."

"What?" Temar jerked back so he could look at Shan's face. He had to be lying. No one could do that to their own people.

Shan's expression was troubled. "Natalie kept warning us about her people. I suspect we are very poor students who required something more tangible before we could believe the lesson."

"How many?" Temar asked. His voice came out as a whisper.

"Twelve," Shan said, not even trying to hide the truth of the horror. Twelve people murdered and now their bones and their ship were lost to the desert. Temar couldn't get his mind around the level of evil that required. Natalie talked about terrorist plots and attacking PA planets, but she hadn't said anything that would have led Temar to suspect that one or more of the officers would have walked around the inside of that shuttle shooting coworkers—shooting men they knew by name.

Temar leaped from the bed and barely made it to the toilet before he was throwing up. Acid burned his throat and nothing but liquid was coming up, but Temar's stomach kept twisting and heaving, trying to eject his feelings. Temar had been down this path before often enough to recognize the signs.

Eventually his stomach muscles were too sore and tired to work anymore, and the heaving stopped. Temar flopped back and sat against the wall and stared at the freckles of vomit on the toilet seat. Shan hit the recycle and then handed Temar a towel before sitting with his own back to the sink, their legs pressed together.

"What have I done?" Temar asked.

"I suspect you've frightened them badly." Shan rested his hand on Temar's knee. "There is no fear in love, but perfect love casts out fear."

"The Bible?" Temar asked.

Shan nodded. "Somewhere in Mark, I think, but then I never did live up to Div's memory of the scriptures. He said it had something to do with the church not being my true path. But the point is that those people live in fear, they killed each other out of fear because there's a profound lack of love in their world, and there's nothing you could have done to stop any of it."

"Except listen to you when you questioned the morality of the whole plan," Temar pointed out.

"If you had, would it have worked out as well?"

"Who knows?"

Shan leaned forward and caught his hand. It required effort, but Temar focused on Shan's eyes. "You have a gift, Temar, the same one Lilian has. I hate it because this is a hard talent to carry, but you understand people like no one else I've seen except Lilian."

Temar tried to laugh as he remembered his conversation with Lilian about how neither of them understood people at all but had to fall back on elaborate metaphors. Halfway up his throat, the laugh turned into a sob.

Shan scooted forward and wrapped his arms around Temar, pulling him close. Sometimes the feel of such strong arms would send Temar reeling away as dark memories pressed forward, but right now all he wanted was for Shan to hold him forever—for Shan to be strong enough to keep everything else at bay. "I wish I could carry this for you," Shan said, his voice breaking with emotion. "But I want you to think about it. How would my plan have really gone? Knowing these people, how would it have turned out if we had tried to reason with them in Christian charity?"

Temar closed his eyes. He knew the answer, but he didn't want to be right. He wanted to blame himself for twelve men dying. He wanted someone to come in and tell him he'd been all wrong and he would never have to make decisions like this again because he was clearly incompetent.

"What would have happened to us?" Shan asked softly.

"It took that much heat to get them to even consider changing the shape of their piece."

"What?"

Temar wiped his eyes. "They wouldn't have taken us seriously without that much pressure being applied. But those men who died… it was pointless."

"I pray they thought they were saving their fellow men pain and suffering, but I do have trouble assigning that motive when I was in that ship, and I saw how some of the men fought for their lives."

"We didn't hear anything. Naite and I didn't hear any of it," Temar said. "We would have done something if we'd known." Temar pushed against Shan's shoulder, desperate to look into Shan's eyes so he could see whether or not he believed that.

Shan sat back. "I know. I know your heart, Temar, and you wouldn't stand back while someone died. And I know my brother. He may not have cared all that much for what those idiots do to each other, but if he'd heard a weapon, he would have been afraid they were hurting Verly, and he would have been off that sled and in that ship before you could stop him." Shan stood and held his hand out for Temar. "Come on. I'm going to put you to bed and find you some soup."

Temar let Shan pull him up and lead him back to the bedroom. "We have to go out there tomorrow. Convince them that we understand sandrat movement well enough to predict it and they don't."

"Don't leave bodies or large quantities of blood lying around would be a good start," Shan said dryly.

"In a day or so, we should get in there on a whisper sled and drop a dead sheep, something to pull rats in close. Then we can warn them to stay inside. They'll try to figure out a migration pattern or something equally stupid that will keep them off-balance."

"Sure," Shan agreed. He helped Temar out of his shirt and guided him into bed.

"You know they'll read those early logs and see how many people died on the desert. They'll probably find the reports of sandcat packs."

"That will distract them with a few nightmares," Shan agreed. He'd promised soup, but he stripped off his own shirt and climbed in behind Temar, wrapping his arms around him.

"Those men... we can't let them die and then not use our advantage. Does that make me evil for thinking that way?"

"No," Shan said, "it means I've fallen in love with someone as smart as Lilian, which is terrifying, but not evil."

"We can't sell glass to these people."

"Okay."

"I wouldn't even take their water, only we need as much of it as we can get." Temar yawned. He was so tired.

"We do," Shan agreed, his voice soft.

"From what Natalie has said, they're desperate for raw materials, so we have to make them think that they'll lose more trying to mine here than they could possibly gain."

"Uh-huh."

Temar pressed his eyes closed and tried to imagine all the sources of heat.

"Shh," Shan whispered. "It's okay."

"I have to figure out—"

"Rich thinks that Verly might be pressing to make an honest man out of Naite," Shan said. His voice was soft and had a lilting quality he normally only had when he'd been at the pulpit. "It'd be nice to see a wedding on the farm, tables spread with food and the whole valley coming to see my brother dressed up and standing awkwardly in front of Div." Shan's hands soothed Temar. "Verly smiling. The slanted morning light spilling down the side of the valley and illuminating the dark veins and streaks of gray in all the brown rock. The crops swaying in the breeze and the pale outline of the second moon barely visible in the morning sky...."

Somewhere in all Shan's description, Temar slid off into sleep.

chapter
thirty

VERLY SAT at the side of the council room. There were too many seats pushed in here, and people were jockeying for a position. Since Shan wasn't a council member, he ended up standing next to Verly near the door.

"Our council meetings used to be a lot less interesting," Shan said.

Verly snorted. "No security checkpoints, protestors shouting from the back of the room, or threats of assassination. It's not that interesting."

"You always make the AFP sound so entertaining," Shan said with some humor, but he kept his eyes on Temar the whole time.

"Oh, that's the PA government meetings. I hear the AFP is even more fun. Mass arrests, secret police, poisonings… that sort of stuff."

Shan looked over as though trying to judge Verly's veracity. He shrugged. It was all true enough. If Natalie were here, she would probably confirm it. Well, assuming that someone other than him asked. She still wasn't his biggest fan.

"Where is Natalie?" Verly asked.

"Doing some repairs on the communication relay. I think she still worries about us leaving that place unguarded."

Verly snorted. After seeing the pure terror on the faces of the AFP guys who'd been trapped there for a week and a half while their government arranged for the water ransom, Verly was pretty sure no AFP ships were ever going to land. Convincing them that no one could travel the desert without knowing the sandrat migration pattern had been a stroke of genius. Even the PA was very careful and very paranoid about landing schedules now, so clearly the intelligence leaks went both ways.

In fact, when Temar had asked if members of the two governments could be working together in order to maintain an adversarial relationship that would justify enormous defense budgets,

Verly had been forced to admit that the idea made sense. He hated it…
loathed it… but it made sense.

He turned his attention to the council members. Ebi was arguing
with the tiny woman from White Sands who always poked her finger in
everyone's chest. Verly watched with amusement as Ebi tried and failed to
stand up to that bony finger. It left Ebi backing away around the edge of
the talking delegates, bumping into one after another until finally Naite
appeared. He put himself between the woman and Ebi and glared down at
her. She wasn't intimidated, though. She started poking him in the
stomach after he crossed his arms over his chest.

Verly couldn't hear the conversation over the general din, but he
nudged Shan and pointed in that direction.

Shan laughed. "Jecta. She's to Blue Hope what Lilian is here. That
woman's finger and Lilian's tongue have been in battles that would make
a general's hair turn gray."

Shan was nice enough to avoid pointing out that the people of Livre
were ethical enough to have that be a verbal battle instead of spilling
blood. Verly wondered if spilling blood was so taboo here because of the
small population or because of the way blood would attract carrion birds
and sandrats from miles away.

"I think this is why Naite hates being on the council," Verly said.

"Don't let him fool you. He complains about the council, but he
doesn't trust anyone else with the power. He'll be on this council until the
day God takes him, and this world is better for it."

On the other side of the room, Naite threw up his hands and turned
his back on Jecta. Clearly she was not finished because she followed him
as he walked over to the windows and glanced outside before he bellowed,
"Enough!"

The whole room grew silent, people staring at him.

"Enough people are here and some of us have fields that need
tending, so can we get this over with?" Naite asked.

Lilian chuckled. "I will miss you, even if you are a short-tempered
bull in a too small enclosure," she told him. She wasn't the landowner's
representative now. She'd made it very clear that if the others didn't elect
Temar, she would disown them all and spend her last days in White Hope.

Verly had never before seen a politician threaten people with the
possibility of moving away. Most times, the electorate was more than
happy to have their politicians as far from them as possible, and Verly had

never seen a politician fight to get someone else elected to their office. However, Verly was quickly learning that life in the PA had not prepared him for Livre. Despite having no official position, Lilian took the center seat, and no one had any challenge. Temar was at the table as well, along with Ebi, Kevin, Jecta, and Bari and several others he didn't know.

Other council members like Dee'eta and Aiden and Naite stood around the edges of the room, and he and Shan stood near the door. Neither of them were council members, but they were often asked for particular answers. Besides, Naite had made Verly come. He seemed to think that if he had to deal with too many politicians, there was a chance he would need someone to stop him from committing a murder.

"Temar," Lilian said, turning it over to him.

Temar smiled at the room, and Verly could see how someone might underestimate him. He looked so young, but he had a core of steel in there that would protect Livre. "The PA has sent a new offer for drought-resistant seeds. They will pay two tankers of water per settlement plus a shipment of equipment. I brought Verly to speak to the equipment."

Verly felt that same flash of panic he did every time he was in a room like this. He was better with ships or with animals than he was with public speaking, but he took a breath and started. "The communication equipment isn't designed for this sort of environment. It would work for a year or two, probably long enough to get everyone used to being able to call up another town, and then it would break down."

"And then they'd expect us to pay more for the privilege of talking," Bari said. "If I want to talk to someone, I can get up and go talk to them. Besides, I dislike the idea of encouraging people to speak to each other through a piece of metal and plastic. You can't see into a person's eyes that way."

Landing's priest spoke up, an older woman who moved slowly and always rested her hand on her stomach. Verly was still uncomfortable around religion, so he'd never gone to her service, and he didn't know her name, although he did know that Shan headed to town to hear her sermon every Sunday. "This perversion of religion these people suffer... I don't believe it would survive if the listeners could look into the eyes of these false prophets. I don't believe I would want more than one communication device in our town, and that would be to call for help, not to speak to one another."

"They have that sort of military emergency radio, but they haven't offered it," Verly said.

The priest turned to Temar, and he nodded. "We can describe what we want, emergency communication devices that can handle any weather or damage over long periods of time, but we will not ask for them by name. They don't need to know how much good advice Verly offers."

Ebi spoke up. "Blue Hope would be in favor of that." The others quickly added their agreement with Jecta asking for three additional units for when they had to launch rescue operations in the desert. Temar took notes on the requests.

One by one they worked through the PA offer, rejecting all but the water and a few raw materials. In their place, they added emergency equipment, heavy cutters, transports, replacement parts for their own damaged datapads, and on Verly's advice, a tripling of the water ration. High-quality genetic lines in crops were very valuable, and Verly would not have his new people cheated out of their proper fees. When he'd first landed on this world and seen the long sweeping plains of sand, this was not where he expected to end up.

"Next item on our shared agenda," Temar said. "The PA has allowed Verly to spend his credits to have materials shipped here. They've been rather unreasonable in their shipping charges, but Verly has asked that I not intervene on his behalf."

"Your people are sandcats," Ebi told Verly.

Verly shrugged. "They aren't my people, but I do agree with the sentiment, Councilman."

Temar smiled. "Verly will be paying for an apprenticeship in animal doctoring," Temar said, and Verly was slightly surprised at the smiles and small words of encouragement from the whole room. Naite crossed his arms and gave Verly that look that said, "I told you so." And he had. He kept insisting that people liked Verly—they liked him a whole lot more than they liked Naite. Maybe Verly was even starting to believe him. Verly smiled at all the congratulations.

"Verly wants to repay the kindness he's found here, and I've told him that he owes us nothing, but he insists," Temar said with some amusement, and Verly shook his head and sent hand gestures, which Temar firmly ignored.

"He's donating a tanker of water to The Valley's main reservoir and sending a tanker for the high-need program." Temar nodded at Ebi, probably because Blue Hope would get the lion's share of that water.

"It wasn't supposed to be public," Verly said as he glared at Temar. Unfortunately, the man was immune. He grinned back with undisguised amusement.

"Water is very public, and that much would be noticed," Temar explained. The rest of the room had gone quiet. Council members whispered and stared, but no one was speaking out, and Verly shifted uncomfortably.

"How much water were you able to buy?" Ebi finally asked.

"More than two tankers, and you don't need more information than that," Naite snapped. "I swear, you'd all climb a neighbor's house to stare in their windows."

"I asked Verly, not you," Ebi shot back.

"Well, I answered." Naite stepped forward and brought the full force of his glare to bear.

"It's not your water." Ebi put his hands on the table and looked ready to stand up and go toe-to-toe with Naite.

Verly stepped forward before that could happen. "It might as well be his water. If he doesn't want to share the details of the PA's deal with me, then maybe we should move on to other business." Strangely, the whole room sat up and took notice of that. Lilian was laughing softly, and Shan was laughing not-softly.

Verly turned around to find Naite was slowly turning red. "What?"

The priest answered, her voice lilting as she quoted something. "She is like the ships of the merchant. She brings her food from afar. She considers a field and buys it. With the fruit of her hands, she plants a vineyard. She dresses herself with strength and makes her arms strong."

Shan cleared his throat. "Verly is new enough that he doesn't understand our customs."

"What custom?" Verly asked.

The priest ignored him and gave Shan a sharp look. "You should get them to make this proper in front of God."

Shan held his hands up. "God needs to speak to their hearts because I am not a priest, and I am not getting into the middle of that conversation."

Naite started toward the door. "If we're not doing business, I'm not standing around here while you idiots make Verly uncomfortable." He grabbed Verly by the arm and started herding him toward the door.

"What did I say?" Verly asked. He was then shoved right into Shan's chest. Apparently Naite assumed Shan would move out of the way, only Shan never did what his brother wanted.

"Naite," Temar said.

"Move," Naite snarled at Shan.

"What did I say?" Verly demanded. He pulled away from Naite and looked around the room.

"It's a private matter," Naite said in that calm voice that meant he'd shoved all his emotions down. Clearly this wasn't a private matter because everyone else seemed to understand it well enough. They understood it and were amused.

"Temar?" Verly said, his voice a warning. He didn't like being left ignorant.

"It's a custom," Temar said, which was less than helpful. "Some people are married in the church. Others aren't that religious. If you stand in front of the council and announce that you are sharing resources with someone else, it's an announcement of marriage, and you can't take shared goods or leave each other without talking to the council about why and trying to work out the relationship."

Verly looked at Naite. He had just accidentally married him.

"No one is holding you to it. It was a stupid mistake because Ebi can't keep to his own business," Naite said, and now Verly knew what Naite was hiding. Since Verly had reached an agreement about his credits and back pay, Naite had made more than one comment about Verly moving on with his life, getting an apprenticeship or buying land. No matter how many times Verly had included Naite in the planning, Naite never assumed he would be part of Verly's life.

"I'm fine if everyone holds me to it," Verly said firmly. "I've told you in private, and I'll tell you in front of all the councils—what I have, you have. You are my home."

Naite stared at him. Verly suspected when they got home, Naite was going to pin him to the nearest bed and not let him up, which was fine with him.

Shan slapped Naite on the arm hard enough to break him out of his reverie. "Are you going to return the favor or leave the idiot waiting for an answer?"

"What? Of course I'll share," Naite snapped.

Behind them, cheering broke out.

Naite turned on them. "And it's still none of your business." This was the most interesting wedding Verly had ever attended.

The priest came around, catching Naite in a hug before he could retreat. "Congratulations, but I still want to see you at the church for a proper wedding." She then turned to hug Verly.

He wasn't used to people who touched much, but all the council members wanted to embrace or touch his arm. Verly stayed close to Naite as everyone moved past them. Apparently the meeting was over.

"Fine," Naite finally announced. "I'm married, and unlike the rest of you who seem to have time to do a lot of nothing, I have work to do. Temar, Shan, you have exactly three minutes to get on the hauler, or I'm heading back to the farm without you." With that, Naite made a break for the door, Verly's hand in his. Verly laughed at the shocked expressions on some people's faces. He noticed that neither Shan nor Temar appeared particularly surprised, not by the wedding or Naite's reaction to it.

Out in the dusty sunshine, Naite kept up his hurried pace toward their hauler. "I meant it," Verly said.

"You're an idiot. You can't even sell your own water now, not without my signature."

"That makes sense since it's our water."

Naite reached the hauler and whirled around. "I didn't do anything to earn that water. You worked for it, suffered for it."

"And I am choosing to share it because it makes me happy," Verly said, "and maybe because I'm fucked-up in the head enough that I am always afraid of being alone, and now the man I love can't leave me without having to go to the council and letting them try to mediate our differences."

Naite pulled Verly into his arms. "You moron," Naite said softly, but he held on so tightly that Verly suspected he might have a bruise or two tomorrow. That was fine. Naite might have a couple too because Verly was equally quick to hang on. "We're a sad pair. We'd better never raise children. We'd emotionally damage them." Naite made the words sound like endearments.

Verly laughed and leaned into his husband. Husband. He'd had a cousin who had planned for her wedding for two years. Verly was grateful that the people of Livre were more practical.

"So, are we leaving, or do you two plan to celebrate your new status in the hauler?" Shan asked.

Naite let go of Verly and glared. "At least I made a husband out of mine. I don't see you making any public commitments."

"I'm holding out for a church wedding," Shan said as he climbed into the hauler.

"When do we have time to plan one? A church wedding would require us to feed guests. Do you know how many guests would come?" Temar asked as he climbed in on the other side. Naite gave Verly a boost up over the side of the hauler and into the rear seat. That way no one had to move and push a seat forward for them to climb into the back.

"It would be good for the community," Shan argued. Verly held his hand down to pull Naite up.

"It would take forever. I've finally convinced families to settle on my farm, and now you want me to double their workload."

"Idiots are always happy to work harder to prepare for a wedding," Naite announced. Shan gave his brother a brilliant smile. "Not that I'm encouraging it because it's a stupid formality," Naite then added. "At least Verly was practical about our marriage."

Naite sounded gruff, but he curled his fingers around Verly's knee.

"He would have been practical months ago if he knew it was an option," Shan said dryly, and then he started the engine. It was late enough in the day that the winds were blowing hard, and Verly pulled his sand veil up. Between the wind and the hauler's engine, they wouldn't be able to do much talking until they reached The Valley. But that was fine. Talking wasn't Verly's first choice, and he knew Naite would probably be happier if some mysterious disease struck him mute—at least until he wanted to yell at some idiot.

Instead Verly held his hand out, palm up. Naite threaded his fingers with Verly's and leaned closer. Verly might not have known it when he came to Livre, but this was what he'd been searching for, and now that he'd found it, he wasn't going to let it go. He tightened his grip and wondered how much water it would cost to get wedding rings made.

Livre once offered Planetary Alliance miners and workers a small fortune if they helped terraform the mineral rich planet. People flocked to the world, but then a civil war cut the desert planet off from all resources. Half-terraformed and clinging to the edge of existence, Livre devolved into a world where death was accepted as part of life, water resources were scarce and constantly dwindling, and neighbors tried to help each other hold off the inevitable as the desert fought to take back the few terraformed spaces.

Temar Gazer claims to be the victim of water theft. His claims could be a simple misdirection intended to help him escape a term of labor after his criminal prank caused irreparable damage to a watering system. However as the only member of the council arguing against a short-term slavery sentence for Temar, Shan Polli can't escape the fear that something darker is happening. The more he investigates Temar's story, the more he finds that his world is not as free of politics or danger as he had assumed. Together, Shan and Temar must get to the bottom of the conspiracy before time runs out for the entire planet.

www.dsppublications.com

New ambassadors Temar Gazer and Shan Polli stopped one disaster on Livre, but the battle isn't over. Temar is still struggling to work through the abuse he suffered. Livre, too, stands at a crossroads: it could ally with the breakaway planets—risking strange and dangerous beliefs—or the older alliance, which offers human rights protections but seeks to control the planet's resources. With everyone keeping secrets, it's impossible to know who to trust. Shan and Temar do their best to navigate cultures they don't understand and avoid the dangers lurking around every corner. It's a delicate balance, but they manage… until a disaster takes Shan away from Temar.

It's up to Temar to rescue Shan and guide their planet through the crisis safely, and he isn't sure he's ready. Just because he and Shan have chosen each other doesn't mean their love is strong enough to survive when the stirring sands around them change.

www.dsppublications.com

LYN GALA started writing in the back of her science notebook in third grade and hasn't stopped since. Westerns starring men with shady pasts gave way to science fiction with questionable protagonists, which eventually became any story with a morally ambiguous character. Even the purest heroes have pain and loss and darkness in their hearts, and that's where she likes to find her stories. Her characters seek to better themselves and find the happy (or happier) ending.

When she isn't writing, Lyn Gala teaches history in a small town in New Mexico. Her favorite spot to write is a flat rock under a wide tree on the edge of the open desert where her dog can terrorize local wildlife. Writing in a wide range of genres, she often gravitates back to adventure and BDSM, stories about men in search of true love and a way to bring some criminal to justice… unless they happen to be the criminal.

E-mail: litgal1@gmail.com
Webpage: litgal.org/ficoriginal.htm

www.dsppublications.com

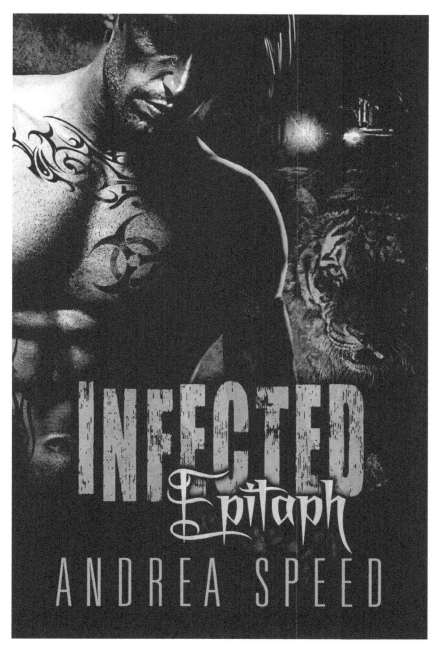

INFECTED
Epitaph

ANDREA SPEED

www.dsppublications.com

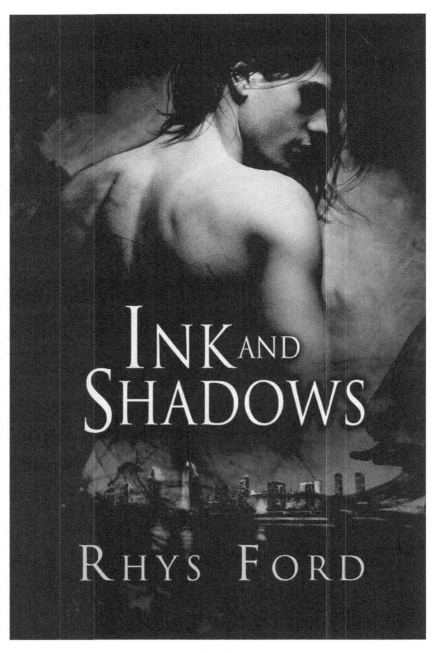

INK AND SHADOWS

RHYS FORD

www.dsppublications.com

the prince
and the
program

aldous
mercer

www.dsppublications.com

www.dsppublications.com

'TIL DARKNESS FALLS

Pearl Love

www.dsppublications.com

For more
great fiction
from

DSP PUBLICATIONS

visit us online.

WWW.DSPPUBLICATIONS.COM

Made in the USA
Las Vegas, NV
28 October 2024

10604498R00138